A middle-aged Sierra Leone native who came to the British Isles in March of 1989. A single parent of five children (three of which are young adults). Alusine went to three universities in the island nation: The University of North London (now – Metropolitan University) in Highbury and Islington and received his BSc (Hons) in environmental science. From Brunel University in Oxbridge, England, he received his master's degree in environmental science with legislation and management. From the University of Strathclyde Business School in Glasgow, Scotland, he received his master's degree in business administration.

He has worked as a manager at Poundstretcher Ltd., and various London borough councils: Haringey; Waltham Forest; Southwark; Dagenham & Redbridge.

His major interests are sports, environment and business, politics, and finance.

Hobbies include: social media debates

Interests include: physical well-being - health and fitness.

My five children: Kiza Deen (British actress), Zia, Akim, Zaki and Zara. They inspire me. And also my family members who have passed away including my late twin brother Alasine.

Alusine Akim Deen

ZOOM OR DOOM

AUSTIN MACAULEY PUBLISHERS
LONDON * CAMBRIDGE * NEW YORK * SHARJAH

Copyright © Alusine Akim Deen 2023

The right of Alusine Akim Deen to be identified as author of this work has been asserted by the author in accordance with sections 77 and 78 of the Copyright, Designs and Patents Act 1988.

All rights reserved. No part of this publication may be reproduced, stored in a retrieval system, or transmitted in any form or by any means, electronic, mechanical, photocopying, recording, or otherwise, without the prior permission of the publishers.

Any person who commits any unauthorised act in relation to this publication may be liable to criminal prosecution and civil claims for damages.

This is a work of fiction. Names, characters, businesses, places, events, locales, and incidents are either the products of the author's imagination or used in a fictitious manner. Any resemblance to actual persons, living or dead, or actual events is purely coincidental.

A CIP catalogue record for this title is available from the British Library.

ISBN 9781035800032 (Paperback)
ISBN 9781035800049 (ePub e-book)

www.austinmacauley.com

First Published 2023
Austin Macauley Publishers Ltd®
1 Canada Square
Canary Wharf
London
E14 5AA

It would have to be Austin Macauley Publishers who have given me a great chance to demonstrate my story-telling skills. I also hope there would be more of the same to come after this.

Story Initiation

Planet Zist's star, "The Grans", sits dangerously close, to only about ten thousand light years away from the super massive black hole at the centre of its Long Grains galaxy but that's the least of the yellow planet's (so-called due to the colouration of excessive amount of sulphur in its atmospheric) worries. The Grans was fast expanding, resulting in unbearable heat and dying in its last couple of hundred years of existence.

Zist inhabitants have witnessed other stars, not only those in their shared constellation but others outside it as well; inflate and explode, incinerating everything in and around their own respective solar systems. So there was this urgent need for Zistians themselves to find somewhere else safe to live.

Somewhere as far away as possible from not only their stellar surroundings, but the entire Long Grains galaxy.

Alas, all efforts to do so have failed for one reason or another as the other worlds were found to be either too far away and/or just too uninhabitable.

Having found no suitable choice, Zistians were planning to terraform one of the least inhospitable planets they had found in the neighbouring Andromeda galaxy, into making it something like home, when they struck gold; discovering an ideal location with similar temperature and habitat, like their own, in the Milky Way – a lump of rock called Earth – a.k.a. The Blue Planet. But this ideal world was five million light years away. Even though Zist's space craft can travel at light speeds, the distance can't be made in a life time.

All three galaxies: Long Grains, Andromeda and Milky Way are part of the 30-member local Local group Group.

Luckily, things changed for the better by happen chance with the discovery of a new fuel system called Zoll. One that can propel spacecraft at a million times faster than the speed of light. Which means travelling to Earth is now possible, taking only five years.

The miraculous Zoll hydrocarbon was accidentally formed when an asteroid, laden with water (A compound almost absent on Zist) coming from Earth's atmosphere, crashed into a dumping and incineration site on Zist. Where it reacted with some special and hazardous waste materials to form the basis of the novel fuel system. A second stage of this incredible fuel system – a far more powerful so-called Zoll 2 – was incidentally formed by an act of sabotage when a supposedly imbecile child (Who was actually a foreign spy) of the project's chief sponsor tried to destroy Zoll 1 by mixing it with other compounds and even peeing [spend-a-penny] in the compound after he was demoted. The resultant solution of Zoll 2 was found to possess vanishing capabilities, which can transform matter into an energy state. Rather like a sublimation process. This further enhanced the fuel's capability to create weightlessness and power objects to travel at just over half-a-billion times faster than light. Which means they can travel to Earth in just five days using Zoll 2 instead of five years on Zoll 1.

A transformation that didn't last for more than a single mission to planet Earth when Zoll 2 can't be replicated.

Several countries on Zist, with the help of their United Nations body, became embroiled in a (Cut-throat – almost literally) competition to pioneer a transportation system that could transfer all its citizens earth-bound, using Zoll. This is where rogue billionaire Marx Afaro Zytan became the most powerful player in this game theory of deals and counter-deals involving treachery, espionage and murder.

Marx was a bit of an oddball. He suffers from an extremely rare reverse nervous condition. Generally, in everyday life, he is in a nervous state. These are times when he would be feeling relaxed and in a good mood but could at the same time be seen shaking like a leaf. Strange for someone to be feeling super calm yet show visible signs of nervousness. Nonetheless, this paradoxical condition was normality for him. But no sooner he is anxious, scared, or angry, in a bad mood, he'd lose all signs of edginess and become at ease, steady like a rock.

Marx has a luminous Manx cat, and a blind rattle snake put on a leash, as pets.

Planet Zist, which is millions of years older than Earth and just as much far more developed and advanced, initially managed to transfer 80% of its people to the blue planet. They settled in subterranean undergroundscrapers 'undergroundscrappers' dotted all over our planet in places like the western

United States, the Saharan desert, the Australia outback, Siberian tundra, etc., without our knowledge, let alone our permission.

Next, they started slowly bubbling up from their underground colonies, resurfacing above ground and establishing themselves in worldly communities. And later, falsely claimed to behave been part of a lost civilisation that had predated the first-ever humanoid species on Earth. Hereby entitling themselves with pride of place legitimacy. Which wasn't so difficult for them to do since they very much resembled us.

Zist has seven races: black, white, brown, red, yellow, blue and green. Much the same like the Milky Way planet's, except for the last two, which they mutate from – by simple medication – to look more like us.

The aliens first travelled to Earth on their flying-ship, The Sublimation Glow [TSG], which piggyback on the Russian Soyuz space craft. These pioneers secretly joined the Russian FSB and Israeli Mossad intelligence services giving them access to setting up the stage for the later mass intergalactic migration of their kinfolk.

When transporting its people to Earth, the TSGs, with its superior technologies, blindfolded all of our space and land based surveillance systems so no one from our world was aware of this earth-shattering event. Unfortunately for them, one of their vehicles crashed in the South China Sea, igniting a tug-of-war between Washington's C.I.A. and Beijing's M.S.S. for rights to the scraps of the stricken vessel. Technologies and espionage engagements, quite literally out of this world, got involved in the mix. But it was the little-known Mongolian secret service, the General Intelligence Agency [G.I.A.], which initially had the upper hand in the poker games between the world's superpowers by gaining access to huge parts of the broken alien ship. Made so by the timely presence of the Altan Fisheries ltd belonging to Mongolian spymaster, Altan Snr, whose fleet was plying the South China Sea at the time of the crash. Rumour has it his fishermen did not only haul out huge parts of the alien ship from the waters but also captured one of its surviving pilots. Notably, five decades before the cosmic ship crash, Altan snr, had falsely presented himself to the Chinese intelligence as a **Double Agent**, out to snitch on his countrymen in Inner Mongolia [A province in mainland China],who were plotting to undermine Beijing's interests and return the region to Ulan Bator's sovereignty.

But actually, he was a **Double Agent-Plus**, one who feints betrayal of his nation by claiming false loyalty to his hosts. But he was actually still working on his native country's interest; feeding false data to Beijing, whilst spying on them and relaying the information back home to Ulan Bator.

After Altan Snr's pseudo-defection to china, he secretly started training his son Koke Altan Jnr and ultimately Koke's own son, Abaqa, on espionage activities – all on the G.I.A.'s instructions. It was the grandson Abaqa who then became the **3G** spy; third generation (Seeding from the Double Agent-Plus to a Third-Generation spook), and integrating to the new hosts with the title **A**djusted **D**ouble **A**gent **P**lus **T**hird-generation [**ADAPT**]. Abaqa's adjustments implied the complete renunciation of his ancestral linage and even a false refusal to learn any Mongolia language.

Altan Fisheries ltd. once registered in Monrovia, Liberia, (A former American colony, which alongside Panama, are the world's two biggest shipping flags of convenience) had moved to neighbouring Freetown, Sierra Leone to avoid Washington's scrutiny This is where C.I.A. free-agent Akim Mansaray, when seeking missing parts of the TSG, comes in to faceoff with the fishing company's manager who was residing in the west African city.

Hopping from one galaxy to another, this story takes humanity to life's extremes: from the virtues, of education, technology, pleasure, and love, to the vices, of death, deceit, theft, envy and a few more.

The dark-arts variants of espionage and diplomacy, which includes poison plots and sabotage, (Diplomacy has dark parts also) were some of the tools the protagonists deployed in attempts to forge an operational equilibrium between these supposedly extremes of spying and politics.

All this came to a head when the Zist people's desperate unstoppable force (Using the Zoll super fuel)to abandon their dying planet, collides with the unmovable obstacle (Distance and time) of five million light years between them and us here on planet Earth.

Readers could choose to decipher some of the questions raised in the story before getting the answers at the end.

Enjoy the fun

The author has written two fun books titled:
Educational Fiction Tales for the Young Reader .Volume 1
Educational Fiction Tales for the Young Reader Volume 2.

These two stories neither have any particular age ceiling nor a floor. The adjective 'young' in this context is not age specific. Rather, it's a generic term that encompasses all age groups "Young" here would generally mean the young at heart – which is the common denominator to all actual age groups.

There is also a third publication written by the author – My Book of Four Nursery Rhymes. Though this one's tile appears to classify the target reader, it can also be enjoyed by adults.

All books are available on Amazon.

All rights reserved. No part of this publication may be reproduced, stored in a retrieval system, or transmitted, in any form, or by any means (electronic, mechanical, photocopying, recording, or otherwise), without the prior permission of the publisher. Any person who does any unauthorised act in relation to this publication may be liable to criminal prosecution and civil claims for damages.

This is the rights of the author Alusine Akim Deen
56 Eleanor Close
London N15 4HX
07940174863

This book is offered for sale on the conditions that it shall not be lent, hired, resold, or otherwise circulated without the publisher expressing his consent.

1

Zist is an exoplanet from a giant solar system in the Long Grains galaxy. A collection of stars so named in reference to its shape like a cluster of rice.

The Long Grains sits just alongside planet Earth's own Milky Way galaxy in the same local Local group Group cluster made up of about 30 galaxies.

Earth observers, and probably others in our known universe, have no knowledge of the existence of the Long Grains , unlike Zist's, who were fully aware of the Milky Way's presence in this local Local group Group. And even to the extent of knowing about the existence of planet Earth in our solar system.

Which they were only regarding at the time, as one of countless others they've already discovered in their known universe. A universe far bigger than that observed from Earth.

Unlike any other planetary systems known to Earth's observers, Zist was an ecosystem teeming with natural life forms and artificial structures. Basically an advanced civilised organisation in a built environment inhabited by different settlements/nations, rather like the way we have it here on Earth.

Zist also has two powerful dominant nations: Bria and Pris, locked in a Thucydides trap. The latter; the rising power, trying to surpass the former; the declining one.

Long Grains galaxy's obscurity to any form of external observation is mainly attributable to its existence in a unidirectional viewscape. The galaxy is locked in a giant dark cloud formation opaque to everything else outside it. And as a result wrongly thought of as a stillbirth nebula void of any matter or energy. Yet those in its interior can make visible observations of others on the outside, as far as their telescopes can take them. This is one reason why Zistians can see Earth but we cannot see them.

All matter and energy forms, except for a negligible amount, will never penetrate the cloud formation. They simply bounce off its periphery reflecting its image of a titanic gas and dust structure.

The very little amount of energy that got through was absorbed by Zist's absolute reducing atmosphere. Which is predominantly made up of methane, ammonia and hydrogen but with no water and almost devoid of molecular oxygen. An excessive amount of sulphur is also found in the atmosphere, giving it its coloration and earning the nickname 'The Yellow Planet'.

What is rather contradictory is Zist, a comparatively far-advanced civilisation, is existing in primitive reducing atmospheric conditions, rather similar to what Earth's was hundreds of millions of years ago. Even though Zist is just as much the far older civilisation.

Generally-speaking, on most cases, the older the civilisation the more advanced it is expected to be, as it continually builds and changes its environment to meet its survival requirements. Just like we have it here on Earth. Though on the other hand, some civilisations do not change their environment, they simply adapt to it instead. Rather like we see in isolated communities living in places like the Amazon forest. These sorts won't necessarily be expected to be developing in sophistication with time. Therefore this story referencing Zist's atmosphere as 'Primitive' here can be a relative term. It could just be conditions ideal for their existence. For who is to say some time into the faraway future, Earth won't recede to its ancient reducing atmosphere with new living species and/or old ones adaptively radiating to the new environment. Maybe for that to happen, there would have to been a mass extinction of species and a likewise huge change in the global climate patterns with the onset of a new cycle of evolution starting off with a primitive reducing atmosphere.

Planet Zist's conditions defied the meaning of term primitive as an 'early evolutionary stages or unsophisticated'. It is a sophisticated organisation not in an early evolutionary stage of existence but still has primitive atmospheric conditions.

Back to Zist. The yellow planet – with its ancient-like atmosphere – has superior advanced technology systems enabling it to do far more observations than any Earthian observer ever had.

When Zist scientists first discovered dead and living life forms on other planets in their own solar system, long before their discovery of Earth, there was global fanfare and euphoria in their world. Some of its nations' media headlines covering the story read: "**We have neighbours**".

After living for millennia, thinking they might be alone in their galaxy and possibly the entire universe. Nonetheless, initially, the neighbours found were merely dead and living single and multi-cellular extra-terrestrial organisms, mostly of the blue-green slime sorts.

Few years later, there was bigger global jubilation when better developed creatures were found further away on distant planets circling neighbouring stars in their Long Grains galaxy. Which were astonishingly large vertebrate and non-vertebrate intelligent creatures displaying life characteristics such as movement, feeding, growth etc.

Some of these various animals were winged-ones like birds with feathers, fish-like, some with scales, others having wet-looks with leathery skin sorts similar to the cetacean class found on planet Earth like whales, dolphins, porpoises. Some ape-like ones like chimpanzees, orangutan. Nothing was found of any anatomical formation resembling a typical Zistian. Most of the media news then became messages like: **"We have found more neighbours; bigger and developed ones but yet none the same like us"**.

Few decades later, all hell broke loose when a galactic-shattering discovery was made. According to Pris Government sources, an abandoned ancient state-owned probe somehow magically made the closest contact ever with Earth by secretly getting attached to the planet's International Space Station (ISS). Zist scientists were said to have been lost as to how that could have happened within such a short period. They had only managed to invent objects that can attain light speeds barely a few hundred years before this miraculous event. So it was quite impossible to reach planet Earth that was five million years away travelling at the speed of light, and another five million years bringing the data back to Zist.

Not one observer could explain how it all happened so fast within their lifetime, which averages 110 years on Zist, to Earth's 59 years. Some soothsayers were saying it's the work of their ancestors. Others were not so sure. Some had even guessed; perhaps other civilisations millions of years older and far superior to Zist had mined this information from planet Earth only for the Zist probe to have hijacked it in space.

"We could have stolen it," some information outlets reported. **"Something is hugely a miss. Cosmological at that – the time factor,"** they added.

But that didn't stop the global euphoria and celebration.

Things really came to a head when the ISS images showed intelligent creatures – Earth inhabitants with far better apelike anatomies – looking more like the Zist people themselves, with straight-back posture. For the first time in their history, a Zistian has seen an extra-terrestrial being like itself. The findings were celebrated with the creation of their first worldwide holiday that lasted a whole week and badly affected the global economy. But who cares after such a life-changing discovery.

Every news outlet was full of it: "**Yes ! Yes! Yes! At long last we have come to discover neighbours similar to us living in faraway lands**." One of them reads. "**Shame about the astronomical distance, we can't reach them in a life time. Even at light speeds it will take five millions years to make that journey – one way that is.**" Another concludes.

"**Earth,**" the latest news headline continued, "**is where we belong next as our world nears its end.**"

This was something that had been bothering Zist habitants for a few centuries after discovering their star (Equivalence of Earth's Sun) has been increasing in size, resulting in unbearable heat, and dying in its last five hundred years of remaining existence before it will blew up. They had witnessed numerous stars burnt up in blazing radiation, not only in their Long Grain galaxy but also others in the local Local group Group neighbourhood and even beyond. Obliterating all life forms around it. Their research efforts to move to other solar systems in the Long Grains galaxy had all been futile for one reason or another.

For the want of a better environment, they had even started work on colonising some of these faraway lands, terraforming them to their standards. But fortunately, there was no further need for that after planet Earth, quite similar to Zist, was discovered in the very far away Milky Way galaxy. Some of the likenesses were really significant: Zist, for example, had seven races: white, black, brown, yellow, red, blue and green, rather like earth's, except for the last two.

The mystical Zist probe [story] relayed back further data spied on Earth's ISS, gaining more knowledge on the planet's geography, its literature, among other things. The blue planet's physical, chemical and biological structures were so much in resemblance to the yellow planet's own, it set off in earnest a desperate quest to relocate there. The sticking point was how to transfer all fifteen billion of its people earthbound. What was once a vital need, at a time when some had already given up to the doomed fate of their sun, to exit their world, had suddenly become a must-do event after Earth was discovered. The doomsayers changed course and started dreaming again.

Their relocation hopes was further enhanced after learning more from the ever-increasing images captured on the blue planet; showing it to be in a far much younger solar system. One expected to last for another ten billion years or so, in the also more stable Milky Way galaxy. This then call for international collaboration to speed up the transfer process.

Zist's United Nations organisation, roughly similar to Earth's U.N. body, began working on the escape mission mainly with its two most powerful nations of Bria and Pris. The Pris Government's own state project was called Mission Earth (ME). At first, Bria's Government named its own equivalence, Home Earth (HE) but later changed it to World Earth (WE), after feminist movements rejected it. All this was in reference to Zist's U.N. body having offered financial and moral support to help fund national projects, after realising they couldn't put together an international team cooperative enough to work on the same project. Too many bitter rivalries; between countries at national level between Pris's ME and Bria's WE, and also in the private sector with Pris's Galactic Universal Trading Syndicate (G.U.T.S) and Bria's Voyage Intergalactic Management (V.I.M.). Both firms were dominant in their domestic countries.

Every nation appeared to be working for itself even though an international cooperation was deemed to have better chances of success; pooling resources together. As a result, separate national programmes were then encouraged as an incentive for them to give their best. Something its U.N. saw as good for competition. With the renewed emphasis on domestic projects, the Pris Government held a meeting with a few selected officials from various public sector departments, marking the fresh start to the intergalactic escape mission on ME. But too many people attended and it became more like a small public conference.

Present on stage were the chief scientific adviser to the government, Dr Spaz Chibot, a late centenarian [On Zist, "late" in this context doesn't mean dead. It relates to age (Early, mid., late), e.g. early centenarian is someone in their early hundreds], his deputy, Dr Franz Annaz 65, political advisor to the Government, Mr Had-naz Tallaz 95 and a few other dignitaries. They were debating the latest report on Planet Earth when Dr Chibot, ever the conservative, took to the rostrum and publicly announced:

'Earth is of category one [C1]. Also known as a planetary civilisation. One which utilises its energy needs only from their planetary system. We are category three [C3], a.k.a. galactic civilisation. Far more advanced and utilises our energy needs beyond our solar system, well into other stars in our galaxy. How can we then see ourselves living on this extremely low energy Blue Planet?'

Chibot, of blue race, an ultra-conservative, is over 9 feet tall. Lanky, slightly hunchback with sloppy narrow shoulders and suffers from chronic back and leg problems. He had receding blue hair and wears thick-lens glasses which seem to magnify the size of his eyes on a horse like face and pinched nose. Chibot is always seen draped in ill-fitting oversized dark suits and white shirts, whatever the occasion or weather. A colleague once joked, 'Even in bed'. Hot summers, which was fast becoming the norm on Zist, the government adviser would only be seen wearing these suits. Out on picnics, out on the beach.

His clever and witty, alas also with flippancy tendencies, Deputy Dr Annaz, blue race [aqua marine-like to be precise], is 7 feet 2 inches. Slightly round faced, bright-eyes with long lashes, pointed nose, heart-shaped lips. She wears her turquoise-coloured hair in a flowing and wavy hair fashion and is extremely attractive. Naturally oozes sex appeal. She was wearing tight-fitting grey power trouser suit [Always flaunting her arse after winning "Rear of the year" award several times], and charcoal grey shoes. Almost a decade earlier, she was runner-up in the Zist Miss World beauty pageant. She was also reported to have at one time called up on stage a member of the captive audience at a beauty contest to physically try pulling out her eye lashes in order to prove they were real, after hearing rumours they were fake.

Sitting behind her boss, she stood up, responding: 'We have no choice. In fact, we are lucky to have found them [Earth] so similar to us physically and in many ways when we did. More so when we are running out of time. The similarities do not end there as humans; we have mostly the same flora and fauna species, even identical in most cases. With only slight variations in our chemical and physical composition. Nothing really that significant anyway.' Running her slender hand through her thick-volume hair, she continued:

'Not to mention the similar dress cultures as well. We owe it to our future selves to make this move as soon as possible,' she further commented, pouting her lips at Chibot.

He turned sideways, lowering his head down to his shoulders like a bison would, looking at her over the rim of his spectacles and laughed. 'It would be like taking a time-turner tens of thousands of years, if not hundreds of thousands, backwards in civilisation.'

'Then find a better location if you can. And that will be another hopeless challenge considering all our previous failures,' replied Annaz, rolling her eyes and looking away from him.

The stubborn chief scientific advisor responded: 'It sits against all odds we'll ever find ourselves comfortable out there. They are not even category 2 civilisation (a.k.a. a stellar one that utilises its own star's energies, a step better than C1, which only uses its planet's) where we could say, OK, let's manage and develop them to our standards.'

The Pris central Government representative who is its political adviser, Mr Had-Faz Tallaz, geared into the conversation looking straight at the audience as he spoke, avoiding eye contact with Chibot in particular, when he warned:

'It's not only G.U.T.S. and V.I.M. working on this project you know. Secret organisations are also involved in operations outside our knowledge and control. Rumour has it the V.I.M. group (From rival nation Bria) are already working on a category four [C4], a.k.a. a universal civilisation status. One which can harness energies from other galaxies,' he concluded with a smile.

To which Chibot quickly took off his glasses and replied rather rudely:

'Bullshit! A complete bull's turd. It's all a nasty heap of stinking dung to fend off attention from their declining years. They haven't got that damn ability I'd say,' as he went to sit down beckoning Dr Annaz to take over the rostrum.

Whenever his legs hurt, he would become impolite, and this was his way to help cope with the pain. He had to keep moving, sitting, then standing up again in short intervals, stretching those varicose legs. Something he does every so often to fend off a genetic disposition to deep vein thrombosis. Tallaz, his sidekick who always seem to be trying hard to please him, looked up at his face, nodded his approval and said:

'I don't believe anything that comes out of that joint.'

Annaz, raising her chin in the air, queried: 'I hear they [V.I.M.] have a P.M. inside G.U.T.S.?'

The PM is a code initial for the Post Man who delivers mails and parcels whilst spying. Using that initial is a good cover as those not in the know would think it means the prime minister. Addressing such state secret in what has suddenly turned into a public forum, though it was meant to be a closed-group meeting, was naïve at best but Annaz doesn't care.

'What does this have to do with us Government officials? It is for G.U.T.S. as a private firm to take care of its own security,' Chibot whispered to Tallaz who nodded without saying a word, though he was about to disagree and say it's to all our concerns as Prisians but he stopped short not wanting to contradict the old man, more so in a public domain.

The pain continued inching up Chibot's legs, he went quiet for a moment while the free-wheeling Dr Annaz, also never short of words, sometimes appearing to be rude, continued her opposition to her boss:

'I'd say we should take the risk over to the blue planet.'

This Pris Government team didn't know much about the added risks for life on Earth. They had no knowledge of the incident at G.U.T.S.'s premises that involved the death of two of the firm's scientists who died of oxygen poisoning when splitting water. That incident was kept under wraps as a very essential company secret, away from the Government and all outside the company.

'After all, Earthians, not unlike us, are humans themselves and we're very identical,' she also mentioned. There was a bit of muttering at the back end of the conference hall from where some attendees were finding it boring. Dr Annaz ignored it and continued:

'The remarkable thing for me is the skin-colour adaptions blending into different environments, much like we have it here.' She then adjusted the microphone a bit downwards towards her mouth.

'We could teach and transform them to being more like ourselves. It is not beyond us trying that,' she concluded.

Dr Chibot stood up, giving himself another opportunity to stretch those legs, groaned:

'Do you remember the last time we tried and failed so miserably to breed with some of those hairy creatures from that planet in one of our neighbouring solar systems?' As he shifted more of his weight from one leg to another.

'I can't even recall the name of that weird world. Boy! That was a disaster. How can it be any different now? Though having so many similarities looks promising, Earth people are very primitive to us. It would be a daunting challenge.'

He could hardly be heard at the end of his statement when he held a hand over his mouth to suppress a yawn.

Annaz looked up at the ceiling, rolling her eyes again signalling her frustration at his persistent nagging doubts, and then whispered under her breath;

'Talking of the dead old wood that needs replacement.'

There were further mumbling noises coming from those at the back. People complaining they can't hear him properly. He was just about to continue his moaning when Annaz barged in:

'Further investigations only found some rather superficial differences between us: our average male is 7' [feet] 2" [inches] tall, female 6'10". Whilst an average Earthian male is 5 feet 9 inches; female 5'4".'

It was almost like a war between these two for who's going to get a better word in, when Chibot intervened again, this time raising his voice for him to be audible enough.

'The shock of it all,' he moaned, 'was seeing photos of some of those hairy Earth people. Which we believe was a condition typical of our own ancestral heritage dating back thousands of years.'

It was at this stage Dr Annaz hurriedly closed the session, ending the Pris Government meeting on the voyage to planet Earth.

****

Trillian Freeze was relaxing at his G.U.T.S.'s office base on the sophisticated industrial complex in Pris (Nation predominantly of blue race) when he remembered he had a meeting to attend to.

Dr Freeze always like things plain and simple. He lives in a very modest house, drives a standard flying car, and also dress very casually. But it doesn't stop there; his taste in furniture, food etc. is of the simple variety. No surprise the same was for his office: whilst some top executives would have attractive interior decoration to go with their statuses, with for example, the likes of soft carpets [Foam as they call it on Zist], fine woodwork cabinet, etc., Trillian settled for a polished red-coloured concrete floor and ordinary bamboo-like soft wood chairs and desks. G.U.T.S's looming building is a futuristic five-storey folding construction which sits right at the entrance to the world exclusive Cosboz business estate in the country's southern polar regions. It's a folding structure, in the sense that extra two floors can be extended on top just by the press of a button, making it seven above ground. The building is a ground scraper covering a wide surface area and also goes down into underground sections. The entire space-age architecture resembled that of a sophisticated U.F.O.. Its exterior portrays an ageless silvery appearance, always gleaming as new even though it was built five decades ago made of thermodynamics material which seasonally adapt to hot and cold weather changes. This temperature reflective technology was borne more out of environmental concerns than for aesthetic reasons. Though it served both purposes magnificently: saving energy, minimising the usage of both heating and cooling systems in the colder and warmer periods respectively, also serving as a picturesque scenery and tourist attraction. This was quite resourceful in a world teetering on the edges of environmental destruction. Yet the Zist world's technologies were somewhat more representative on a regional rather than a global basis. The more advanced mostly confined to the richer areas, whilst the poorer parts are left in a state of a development shock. Much the same way as it is on planet Earth between wealthy and poorer regions.

Mr Freeze a.k.a. the Hatman, 110 years old, always seen wearing a hat, even when indoors at times, is turquoise-coloured mixed-race Zist nationalist. Nine feet six inches tall, born to an immigrant father from rival nation, Bria (Nation with predominantly green race) and a Prisian mother. He is the chairperson and founder of G.U.T.S ltd.

Trillian flung himself off the swivelling chair getting ready to attend a second meeting on the newly-discovered energy project scheduled for 12 noon that day. One he had summoned at their chief sponsor, Marx Zytan's office. The said project had been abandoned and shelved a decade ago at the first meeting due to economic reasons.

But now with further developments taking place, this second meeting was aimed at facilitating the necessary reassessment.

The usual attendees included: chief scientist, Prof. Nemad Scyzpr, [Surname pronounced Zee-pre] 85, blue, thick volume green hair, prominent cheek bones, hook nose, round eyes and lips. He is seven feet seven inches tall. The famed academic was wearing blue-rimmed granddad spectacles, slightly oversized white shirt and charcoal grey baggy trousers held up to the shoulders by matching braces. Also at the meeting was Zoorax Brazh, 70, white, expatriate , 9'10" tall, bespectacled deputy chief scientist. One never short of ideas. Former long-distance runner and male model. Broad shoulders, thin-faced with arched nose and round mouth. Rumour has it he was denied the chief scientist position due to racialist discrimination. Though that can hardly be true on a planet where racial awareness is only marginally mindful on a nationality basis, rather than the colour of the skin, which is just as insignificant as the colour of their eyes. Prysten Poiter was another attendee. 69, black, expatriate 9'10" tall bespectacled

Senior scientist. Also broad-shouldered, short dense hair. Round facial features – nose, mouth, eyes – on a round face. Twice voted the sexiest man on Zist and another one never short of ideas. Fellow attendee, Ms Bampor Ajina, 50, green, diminutive, thin, 5'8" tall a sophisticated dresser, elegant, good artistic appearance compromised by permanent sad-looking eyes. Can also be seen as a bit aloof. She was dressed in emerald skirt suit. Small head, small facial features and almost lipless mouth. She was lawyer and accountant to the project's chief sponsor, Marx Zytan. Another of the attendees was Freeze's own personal assistant Zapia Zill, 60, blue, 7'11" tall. Voluptuous, round fleshy face, flat sleep-like eyes, round nose. The "all-work-and-no-play" type. Never wears any makeup and dresses the most casual way possible.

All were seated waiting for Marx A. Zytan who was running late as usual, even for a meeting held in his own office and pushed back for 12 pm. Usually their morning meetings start no later than 11 am. The rogue billionaire; 95, green, thin, midget sort of a man at 5'10". Small facial features: lipless mouth, tiny slit like sorrowful eyes and a button nose. He wears a long artificial sleet dark hair covering a bald patch. Cleanly shaved except for a pencil-thin moustache and wearing his trademark strong-scented aftershave. He always carry a sword, situation permitting, and one almost as big as himself, attached to the right side of his waist. Also seen at most times with a small-sized glowing Manx cat usually held under his left armpit. The animal won't wear a leash.

He walked into the room almost 15 minutes late. Wearing a pink open neck. Shirt with an expensive-looking wristwatch peeing out of its cuffs, under a brown jacket, grey trousers and emerald shoes If he's not dressed in quite contrasting colours, he'll be all in black. Rushing in with the typical excuse.

'Sorry I'm late,' pretending to be panting as if he had been running to the office. 'Got snarled up with the air traffic controllers.'

Zytan fly-drives one of the latest and most expensive super-aero cars. He continued:

'And my 'ld lady wasn't feeling too well this morning. I had to tend her a bit.'

That old lady he was referring to was his Manx cat, not Branitz, a partner of ten years with whom he has two young kids.

Zytan claimed to have first met the cat as a kitten when she walked into his house and sat on his favourite armchair. She looked very poorly with ribs and bones poking through her skin, and I nursed her to health, he had once claimed.

Once or twice in the night time, he almost mistakenly killed it by sitting on the tiny kitten. To avoid any such further accidents, he injected the animal with the luminous gene of the jellyfish to make it more visible in darkness. At least that was the story he has been telling to society.

Marx Zytan was an odd ball sort of a Zistian human who suffers from a reverse-nervous condition. Normally he'll be seen as anxious and shaking even though he's feeling relaxed and in a good mood. On the other hand, he would become calm, at ease, steady like a rock when feeling anxious and in a bad mood.

Sitting his diminutive figure in the huge upholstered suede office chair it appeared as if his feet are hanging loosely above the floor, except for the front parts. Almost dwarf like in a world where the average human height is seven feet tall. Marx's smallish frame aligned with very youthful looks gives a deceptive appearance of a college student, especially times when he would shaved off his moustache, until you take a closer look beyond the juvenile camouflage. Behind it sits a violent man, fiendish at times. Once described as the scariest of the scary cats out there, which was quite interesting for someone mostly seen with his feline friend.

He just sat there in his characteristic stoney-faced mood at the meeting, stroking the animal.

'I'm all that she has for a tail.' He once proudly purred of the cat after it was refused entry to a business executive conference. 'I give her her balance and she gives me mine.'

'Those two spots at the back of her head looks remarkable,' Trillian said, reaching out to pat the cat, as they were settling down to start the meeting.

Marx quickly responded, pulling the animal away from him and chided:

'Please don't touch. It's forbidden to do so. Those two large dots represent the eyes behind our backs looking out for what's going on behind us; our "natural disruptive-colouration" defence mechanism. I have the artificial variation tattooed at the back of my head hidden behind my hair.'

Nemad whispered in Poiter's ear: 'Something that could have been coached to him by his speech writer, I guess.'

Of which Poiter replied: 'I thought so too. So unlike him to use those expressions.'

Seeing the two scientists conferring in whispers, Marx felt offended and reclined further into his chair and again purred:

'We have more in common that you'd think: [according to a seer] the same birth day, not the same year of course. We have so many enemies and don't care. And we're also both left-handed.'

At the previous meeting, the first on the novel energy project titled "Planet Earth-H2O" held ten years ago, G.U.T.S.'s founder, Mr Freeze, a failed astrophysicist, had promised: 'We'd get Dr Zytan sponsoring a secret mission to capture this water element from Earth, turn into a gas form, and import it into Zist. They say it's highly dangerous but invaluable as a raw material to making the Zoll fuel.'

Zoll was the newly-discovered hydrocarbon that had been scientifically proven to propel objects up to a million times faster than the speed of light. By far surpassing their previous monumental achievement of moving matter at light speed.

The new fuel's capability was just too good an opportunity for G.U.T.S. in their quest for interstellar, or even intergalactic travels.

Despite this scientific miracle, not everyone was convinced on the Zoll project.

Zytan who always had an eye for profit, had responded:

'The transportation costs carrying the water cargo, even in a gaseous state, from one galaxy to another, would be too astronomical and not economically viable. And it would also take a total of ten bloody years to get there bail it out and bring back here using this Zoll fuel.'

Trillian had also countered: 'But the vast amounts of the Zoll energy, we will get would make up for the costs.'

Still not convinced, Marx Zytan was reported to have stated: 'For me, time is money. I can't do it, sorry.'

With the main sponsor pulling out, the project was set aside, though not abandoned.

But all that was a decade ago. More developments on Zoll had occurred since that first meeting, prompting the need for this second one which some staff members had dubbed Zoll 2.

'Let's now weigh up the fresh costs and benefits, yeah?' Trillian explained, while pacing up and down the room in his usual gait.

'We already know at the first hydrocarbon stage, just call it Zoll 1 for simplicity sake, the fuel can propel our spacecraft at speeds faster than light one million times, that's miraculous isn't?' He adjusted his hat on his head with his left hand.

'Yet quite astonishingly, that factor was still not good enough to convince some of us here on the project. Now things have changed for the better, or should I say the best. Since that last failed meeting, never before has it been so frequent at the forefront of my mind to get this project done. And the new results which I'm about to explain, now also dubbed Zoll 2, is the timely shot in the arm. The latest finding was that Zoll 2 can structurally alter flying vessels from a physical matter into an energy state. Thereby gaining the advantages of weightlessness and moving objects many times faster than Zoll 1's incredible speeds. It all seems like science fiction but every detail is factual,' he stated.

Obviously, buoyant in a good mood bringing back his pet project to life. He then paused for a moment walking halfway towards the PowerPoint presentation, which was conducted on superimposed electronic cells on the wall which acts like a projector, turned around looking at the others and continued:

'Meaning the effective weights of our space ships, even when laden with crew and cargo, would amount to zero and be able to travel at just over half-a-billion times faster than light. It's ingenious, isn't?' as he burst out in little snuffles.

The accident-prone Trillian Freeze walks with a slight limp; a result of repeated falls off horses in his early teenage years.

'No mass, no friction.'

Still not getting much response from the others, some of whom were only smiling, again he adjusted the hat on his head and carried on:

'Such advancement has changed the whole figuration dynamics of the project itself, making it far more profitable than at first thought possible. The combination of a new powerful fuel source with weightlessness has given us the capability to travel extremely fast. What would have been a ten-year return trip to Earth (using Zoll 1 fuel) is now only ten days (with Zoll 2).'

Someone then asked if what he was saying is that with Zoll 2 their flying ships will ridiculously travel at almost five hundred and fifty million times the speed of light, –breaking Zoll 1's incredible record of a million times light speed. He quickly replied:

'Yes, of course. Quite incredible isn't it with the Zoll transformation we are now sitting on. You can see the reason behind me giving it another go, finally getting our project off the ground for the second time around and getting back to considering the business venture. I don't do things by halves.' He was basically just repeating himself. Little wonder his colleagues got bored. And that's one of the most annoying things about Trillian. He always want to be seen in some sort of control: doing stuffs like calling, at times unnecessary, meetings, giving, more or less worthless, presentations.

'This man could talk the hind legs off a donkey,' once said of him by a female staff member.

His mobile gas phone (Which recharges itself by extracting carbon monoxide from the air; an element that is scarce and costly on Zist) started ringing. He took one quick look, stopped the ringing without answering the call, and placed it back into his pocket to continue the meeting:

'We can just get their water [Main ingredient] convert it to Zoll and sell them the wastes which our science people say is a fuel and medicine in Earth's industries. It's a huge form of international trade, I mean intergalactic trade. First of its kind.'

He was so satisfied, the broad smile on his face showed it all. If you want Trillain Freeze to be happy, get him to deliver business or science concepts to an audience.

'So then everyone is a winner,' mogul Zytan interrupted, who was then just beginning to like the revised concept, now that the business end had taken an incremental dimension.

The permanent frown on Marx Zytan's face got a little frownier, which is his own way of smiling when things are going his way. Then Trillian's mobile phone started going off again. This time he turned it onto silence mode and dropped it into his pocket and went back to his seat. Nothing distracts his attention when discussing business interests, not even a call from his grandma, his most favourite person.

Prof. Nemad Scyzpr's response seemed to have dampened the short-lived euphoria, after saying:

'I heard from our Government's spy probe grapevine planet Earth is experiencing persistent global heating problems. And are currently converting from hydrocarbon usage to alternative energy sources; like solar radiation, wind power etc., the so-called "Renewables". So they might not be interested in our Zoll waste by-products.'

Trillian, not too happy about this, snarled back: 'Earth is locked up in an ice age, so they'd need to warm up their world a bit.'

Nemad quickly responded: 'But that was about 12,000 years ago. You must be mixing up their historical records with the latest info. We have on them. They are at present in a new interglacial high. I hear their world is melting.'

'But I thought they are still living in a damn freezer. I hate to think it would now be difficult for them to invest in our hydrocarbon scheme, since, as you say, they are now heating up all over the place,' moaned Trillian, sounding a bit disappointed.

As if to make some atonement, the chief scientist conferred: 'But we can still send them back into the ice age.'

Marx was abrupt:

'You what? How is that possible?'

'Well at least some parts of their world,' Nemad replied, looking at his fingers toying with a pencil jabbing dots aimlessly on a blotter.

'Their northern hemisphere, particularly in the west where most of the rich nations exist, is where we should target for the new freeze.'

Before his colleagues could ask how that could happen, Nemad started explaining his thoughts:

'We melt most of their ice sheets, especially in the North Atlantic,' as he unfurled a laminated map of Earth flat out on the table. Others sitting a bit away got up and met at his end of the huge conference table.

'For the love of science,'

Marx cut in sarcastically.

'You have a world suffering from heating, and that would mean their ice melting, which they claim is a result of their use of fossil fuels. Which again they are planning to stop using. Now our (He was about to say mad scientist but stopped short of saying it) maaaaan, is saying we have to further melt their ice cover so we can sell them more hydrocarbons for them to burn. If you lot would excuse me, I think that is a complete and utter crackpot idea that doesn't make an iota of sense.' There was a bit of muttering around the table, doubting the professor's concept.

Trillian was slightly nodding his head in support but he suddenly stopped and tipped his hat partially covering his face and pretended as if he was taking notes soon after Nemad looked towards him, as if to say, you know Marx has no academic knowledge. Don't you trust me? Such behaviour was something he had never seen before from their science man.

The chief scientist made a grunting noise, clearing his throat and commanding more attention from the others. An uneasy silence followed.

Once they had obeyed his order, he continued dishing out his master plan:

'As I analysed moments ago, the ice sheets we'd attack are mostly in the north; the Arctic Circle parts of northern America, Greenland, northern Europe, and Siberia.'

Still unconvinced but listening, the others remained muted. He paused for a few seconds, surveying the room to assess their attitude towards his efforts.

'The melted ice,' as he continued.

'Would increase the sea levels in the northern Atlantic Ocean and dilutes the Northern conveyor belt, which is part of their global termohaline circulation that brings warm waters from the equatorial regions to the tropics.'

He paused again, searching around the conference table and somewhat seemed to be enjoying his control over the quietened lot.

Unlike Trillian, Nemad stayed in his seat when giving the presentation. He then continued his explanation, ignoring and cutting off Marx who was about to make another comment.

'Severing off that warm conveyor would plunge those northern regions, where you have the main policy makers, into a mini ice hemisphere. Even for the times when the conveyor is stronger than expected as it sometimes happen when excessive evaporation increase its salinity (That is its degree of saltiness which makes it heavier and works better transferring warm waters north), the extra waters from our melting would dilute that also and stop the conveyor in its track.'

Ignoring some of the quizzing looks on some of their faces, most of which were not about the feasibility of his plans but rather their lack of understanding its complexity.

He then carried on, speaking more slowly, taking his time and prolonging some of his colleagues' agony in listening to some stuff that is completely alien to any business plan they've had in the past, and they have had quite a lot.

Trillian, though well known for his love of money was beginning to feel tired and unwell, and showed little interest. Despite his famed physical strength, framed into that giant-like body mass at almost ten feet tall, he is a chronically sick man with ailing heart conditions.

As his phone went off again, this time buzzing, he simply switched it off all together. Thinking it's an unwanted distraction that could hinder his chances of convincing Zytan taking on the project. Characterising a psychological Fear Of Missing Out [F.O.M.O.] disorder.

He lives by his phones; he is never more than a moment away from his communications items like phones, iPad [which they call slates]. He has to have at least one by his side at all times. Rumours have it, a couple of deals were missed when several business interests couldn't reach him on his gas phone when he was having a bath. He then swore to never let that incident repeat itself. To make sure he never missed out on any important contacts ever again, he programmed his phones to running his life: buzz when he has to eat, since he never eats between meals, buzz when he has to exercise, buzz for almost everything he does.

All throughout this second meeting, Trillian's attention had been focused more on Zytan and how to convince him parting with his cash this time around.

He slowly got up to his feet once again, raising his hand ordering attention. Abruptly taking over from Prof. Nemad without permission. He rolled up his sleeves and took to the powerpoint presentation he had set up to conclude the meeting with, even though they've already agreed to now carry on with the project.

His final presentation was a complete waste of time, and of little or no use to his colleagues. It's more about giving himself another opportunity to satisfy that power-hungry ego. He likes to be seen in charge. He then manoeuvred his huge body frame almost blocking the projector screen. Every now and then, he would twist the hat around the back of his head, covering a lump sticking out from his thinning hair.

He had just seen Prof. Nemad used his brains to commandeer all of them and had felt envious. Now is his turn to show authority, having not being satisfied with his earlier performance, he thought.

He would usually set up an incidental music played in a low tone in the background. Low enough not to disturb the meeting but also audible for everyone sitting at the table to hear. The music is an old concerto piece his mother would play when putting him to sleep. It all started for the five year old toddler after he fell down two flights of stairs landing on his head. The child suffered concussion but woke up, with a lump the size of a golf ball at the back of his head, one that never went away, seen smiling a week later to his mother miming along the Zist famous maestro, tenor, Tabbla Muziz, singing La Corrido on radio. No sooner she had turned off the radio to speak to his son, he started crying. Instinctively, switching it back on to the delight of the child who immediately started smiling again. Since that day onwards, his mum would put him to sleep to the sounds of La Corrido which she had bought on a compact disc.

Up to this day about 11 decades later, Trillian would employ the same trick; playing, at times humming, the tune for both comfort and strength.

He had been so engaged trying to convince Nemad of his ideas, switching off his phone and missing the buzzing for him to take his daily medication for a heart condition. He switched it back on immediately after the meeting and heard the phone buzzing again; this time as a reminder for him to collect parcels from the post office and also to buy some medicines. All which he did as he headed home.

On his way, with his thoughts still focused on Nemad's pessimism, he felt weakened at the knees, even though he was sitting in his car driving home.

He had left the meeting in a good mood, satisfied at least this second project is far more viable and could realise his lifelong ambition to become a billionaire. He had always admired Zytan, whom he had known since their secondary school days. Even at times think, if Marx Zytan, always at the bottom end of the class can become so rich, a billionaire at that, so should he who was far better in school.

He was still behind the wheels thinking of the day's events until he got to the A1 Meltpot junction where he suddenly had a heart attack. Halfway after crossing the red lights, he tried to pull over away from the heavy flowing traffic to the side of the road but the increasing pain arrested his effort. He snorted out loudly to help relieve the agony and reached for his gas phone that was buzzing again, giving a second reminder that he had missed taking his medicines half-an-hour ago. But the phone fell off his trembling hand onto the foot well on the passenger side. He then stretched himself trying to retrieve it but the pain in his chest nailed the left side of his body to the driver's seat rendering him immobile. Not looking where he was going and still in tormenting pain, he mistakenly turned the car into the opposite direction facing the oncoming traffic. Ramming head first onto a delivery van and died instantly in the crash.

That was the life of Trillian Freeze: a man who had lived so much by the command of his phone; not wanting to miss out on business deals, not wanting to miss taking his medication, not wanting to be late or miss out on anything in his life, has been killed ignoring his phone not wanting to miss out on a potential deal and later trying to retrieve it not wanting to miss out on life.

Due to religious reasons, he was buried the next day just before noon time.

Now that project Planet Earth-H2O (with Zoll 2) has been revamped in that successful second meeting, details of how Zoll 1 was firstly discovered was made available to all the team members. According to the scientific finding, water [H2O], a compound almost absent on Zist, was found inside an asteroid that had travelled all the way from Earth and smashed into one of G.U.T.S.'s special scientific waste containers, waiting for incineration, near their biggest landfill site. The crash burnt holes through the solid waste containers and caused a huge explosion. The H2O locked into the rock was actually super-cooled water droplets, at -80 degrees centigrade but still in a liquid state despite the sub-zero temperatures. It had reacted with mixed hazardous and special chemical wastes to form a substance that was continuously bubbling with sizzling noises.

In a joyful abandon blinded by childish curiosity, G.U.T.S. scientists placed samples of the highly reactive waste-water creamy effervescent mix in a petri dish for further tests, unknowingly contaminating it further with a remnant solution from the previous day's experiment. The already poisoned creamy mix reacted with the residual contaminant solution to accidentally form a highly-energised gel substance, which they named Zoll, after an ancient mountain in eastern Pris. Zoll is a colourless jelly-like substance that gives out a foul smell like burnt rubber. It's over a trillion times more powerful than any known combustion fuel in the universe. Laboratory tests proved this novel energy source has the capacity to propel spacecraft accelerating at a million times faster than light speed.

Every aspect of this incident at G.U.T.S. was a closely guided secrets worn [sworn] on loyalty to the company's brand. Not even the Pris national Government was made aware of it.

But there was this indispensable need to get more of Zoll's vital ingredient; H2O, which is negligible in their own atmosphere. Scientists mined some from celestial objects like comets but alas, tests after tests all failed to get the ideal compound. The harvested water was found to be more of the deuterium variety, too heavy to produce Zoll. The type of water needed was an identical one found in that crashed asteroid that came all the way from planet Earth..

One time during the failed experiments at the company's laboratory, Prysten cried out:

'Look, there are crystals in here as well,' sounding all excited as he prised open other parts of the rock, dismantling it.

'Let's see what it is made of.'

They found it to be more of that elusive water. This time in a solid form.

But having the key ingredient is one thing, repeating the trick to get Zoll is another, since it was purely discovered by accident at the dump site with all those assorted chemical waste – it was a daunting task. They do not only have to have similar or identical amounts of special and hazardous waste materials like those left by the incinerator but also the right chemical state of those wastes when the asteroid crash happened. Not to mention using that incidental mixture with the contaminants left overnight in that unwashed petri dish. The whole incident is a complete freak of nature and man, designed by accident.

Nonetheless, Prof. Nemad correctly guessed every measure of the dosage, state and time duration, to almost perfection, of the incidents and their contents, giving them the perfect mix. Eureka! More of the novel Zoll energy stuff was recreated.

This was a powerful trade secret. No one outside the firm knew what was going on. Every bit of information hushed up in secrecy secured within the company walls. At least that was part of G.U.T.S.'s strategic plans.

Meanwhile, the Prisian central Government and other countries on Zist, like Bria, continued with their own independent scientific research programmes into ways of reaching planet Earth. Reportedly none of them knew of the Zoll discovery. Generally, Zist scientists had already attained propelling objects at the speed of light but that would have taken them five million years to reach Earth.

G.U.T.S., with the unique advantage of having the novel Zoll 1fuel system, can afford that journey within a lifetime – in merely five years on a one way trip [Ten years return].

Bria's own powerful exploration company, Voyage Intergalactic Management [V.I.M], formerly known as Voyage Amalgamate Intergalactic [V.A.I.], had its name changed from V.A.I. to V.I.M after G.U.T.S. started mocking their V.A.I. initials as V.A.I.N. "Voyage Amalgamate Intergalactic Nowhere" and not leading to anywhere. "The Vainglorious".

2

Back at G.U.T.S., a whole decade had passed after Zoll 1 was accidentally discovered. Since then new developments had also taken place at the company, there was restructuring with some of the old guards gone, most of whom were vehemently opposed to Trillian's plans with additional staff and promotions made. One of the new workers, a young fellow named Maila Zytan was indirectly brought in by his adopted father Billionaire financier Marx Zytan. The young man, green, 39, 6 feet 3 inches tall, small facial features that earned him the nickname "The Bird". He had green curly hair. Maila wasn't qualified for the position of a lab research scientist but got the job anyway due to Marx's influence. It wasn't too long before he was found out to be totally inept. He was so clumsy at work his colleagues nicknamed him "The bird with butterly feathers". Yet they didn't sack him in fear of Marx's wrath. The threat of losing his financial support was too much of a risk. Instead the new employee was demoted to being a lab technical assistant. Something he didn't take too kindly to. He felt angry and humiliated. Seeking revenge, he secretly started sabotaging some of the chemicals in the research pipeline in the hope of making them pay for his disgrace. Even the newly-discovered Zoll 1 wasn't spared. He wrecked it, mixing it with various other compounds and even peeing into it for good measure. Sealing and replacing it back in the cupboard. But he wasn't to know he could be destroying his father, Mr Zytan's ambitious deal. A man whom he admired so much for helping him time and time again after fostering him as a child, taking him from the criminal underworld and getting him a job at world-famous G.U.T.S. With all this guilt riddling his mind, he asked to be transferred to their metal work business where he was better fitted using his trainee welding skills.

It was only a week or so later when senior scientist, Pystrn Poiter, went into the walk-in cupboard to retrieve another compound mixture sitting on the shelf when he found out Zoll's container appeared like a half-bottle, from the top, with the cork stopper still in place, down to the middle part, was in suspended animation hanging over the shelf. The bottom half that was meant to be sitting on the shelf, missing. The missing bottom half of the bottle had contained the liquid but was now also absent. Looking as if the top-half of the bottle was hovering, without any movement, a few centimetres above the shelf.

Poiter just stood there staring, thinking, the bottle's bottom half had disappeared it seems. Giving the impression the gel, which can hardly be seen because it is very, very transparent, was still in its jelly form standing by itself in the shape of the bottle.

From thinking he started whispering to himself:

'This can't be happening. My eyes could be deceiving me.'

Gently grabbing the visible top part of the bottle, then pussy footing out of the cupboard room in footfalls he can't even hear himself, and carefully placing the bottle on a table top as if it was made of egg shells. There was this thud of a sound as the invisible bottom half of the bottle came into contact with the table top, announcing to him the bottle is still in its whole shape though he can only see the top half. Getting so much excited, he yelled out for his fellow scientists. Some came dashing in from the adjacent rooms.

Pointing their attention to the Zoll bottle, with an almost nailless forefinger (Worn away out of habitual nail-biting), without saying a word.

'Is it broken?' asked Zoorax Brazh, alias the Quiet Brains.

'And where is the bottom half?' another colleague added.

Slightly raising his voice, still in excitement, he tweeted:

'Search me, I have no clue. I walked into the cupboard room and found the bottom part missing.'

Dropping his voice again he continued: 'Well, appearing to be missing really.'

Brazh quipped: 'Well to the naked eyes perhaps. Let's get an electron microscope and prove it.'

Professor Nemad rushed back from the men's resting room where he had been easing his constant peeing habits, and asked:

'What is all the shouting and excitement about?'

'We have accidentally discovered a vanishing gel.'

Poiter explaining as he took off his spectacles polishing them with his handkerchief and putting them back on, as if to say he cannot believe what he is seeing and had to take a better look.

'It did a disappearing act on us. I have read science fiction telling stories similar to this; changing artificial matter into energy forms. Some of which were reversed again from energy state to the physical after several hours, though the reversal process can be hastened in an ionised atmosphere.'

Poiter said, and further went on to explain what he had witnessed.

Chief scientist Nemad quickly grabbed a hand glove, just wrapped it around his right hand without wearing it, and grabbed at the invisible base of the bottle.

He then screeched:

'Karammmmmmbaaaaaaa. The bottom half is still there, hiding in plain sight but we can't see it up to the level from where the gel ends. I think the gel has made that part invisible.'

They quickly started using all sorts of equipment to inspect the glass container but still can't see what they can feel. It finally dawned on them that Zoll is not only an energy source a million times faster than light [Zoll 1] but is also a vanishing compound [Zoll 2].

After having a few discussions, they concluded (Though without any solid proof), that the Zoll gel had not only transformed itself into a gaseous state but also that part of the glass bottle it had occupied. The sublimation process they also guess was due to the excessive heat in the cupboard powered by the old generators.

(Nevertheless, they allowed their emotional excitement to have overridden a duly and thorough observation that was needed before reaching that hasty conclusion; for whilst there was a disappearing appearance, the whole bottle was still there. So there wasn't any sublimation process, the invisible glass was still in a solid state.)

It was on the basis of the newly-found invisible properties that Trillian Freeze summoned that second hearing into the project [Zoll 2]. Saying, 'beyond any doubt, the new finding would more than make up for the project's worth'.

And he was successful in launching the second campaign in that second meeting.

Whilst in Bria, word was around that Pris's G.U.T.S. were making faster progression on the Project Earth – H2O race. This, quietly attesting to the fact that Prisian development is far ahead of their rivals than at first thought. In desperation, the Bria government then decided to heavily subsidise their biggest private aeronautics company, Voyage International Management [V.I.M.], who already had a sleeping spy mole working through the ranks at their rival's.

'I think it's high time we activated our 3G spies in Pris,' said Mr Saztah Ajina, V.I.M.'s managing director. Saztah, 65, green, 7'2", slightly horse faced with almond-shaped eyes, pointed nose, prominent cheekbones, big brown wavy hair, tall athletic built, expansive shoulders, broad back and slim waist that earned him the nickname "lion-shaped".

'As I understand it, our double-agent-plus has borne the 3G fruit already'.

Kai Londo, brown, expatriate, 65, the chief scientist, ex-national body building champion. Who would look better placed in an exercise gym than a lab: Ten feet five. Large head, big smiley face with huge funnel-like nostrils, slightly thick lips and big round eyes. Well-spoken, well-educated. Surprisingly in a soft voice, he responded:

'Don't forget about the "principle of the unripe time". Is he mature enough, trained and ready to act yet?'

Zapir the accountant, 80, yellow, short cropped blue hair, pint-sized, small symmetrical facial features and quite handsome. Was lost as to what was being debated at the time so he asked:

'What is this double-agent-plus and 3G spy business all about?'

He was somewhat trusted at the firm, having followed his lauded Dad's footsteps, serving 40 years and still counting with strong loyalty to the company. Yet he is not part of the inner core and not trusted with their top-secrets. General information he may have chance bumping into every now and then, fine but nothing beyond the casual; sadly that seemed to be lost on him as he would continue thrusting his nose where it is not wanted. Any stuff outside money matters is almost alien to him but that won't stop him seeking information.

Ontus Ajina, the chief security officer, 7 feet 6 inches tall, 85, green. A five-inch horizontal scar, part of which is lost in his wrinkles, run across his forehead. Eagle-like face, bushy eyebrows, huge eyes, sharp thin nose, sharp thin mouth, and slightly pointed ears. He got up on his feet, walking towards the huge bay window. Halfway across the room, he turned around to face their figures man and said:

'So you've never heard of a "double-agent-plus or a 3-G spook" before?'

The accountant, with a quiz look on his face, replied he has heard about double agent spies but never about double-agent-plus or 3G spies.

'Who are they, if I may ask?'

Ontus, replied:

'OK, my old friend, let me explain.'

He then unwrapped a smokeless cigar he had just released from a pack, struck it repeatedly against its container to compact the electronic tobacco, hold it halfway to his mouth, paused, and said:

'Double-agent-plus, otherwise known as "triple agents", though some intelligence analysts still call them "double-agents-negative", are spies who go into their mission to convince their host she/he is there to betray his/her organisation, just like double agents do. But only this time the double-agent image is pretentious as they would continue to secretly work for their land of origin: feeding misinformation to the hosts and working against them in any clandestine way possible.' Zapir then queried:

'Then afterwards what is the benefit other than misleading with information they might even find of little or no meaningful use?'

'What's wrong with you today, chief accountant? You keep on asking amateurish questions. Our man would then become a source for a 3-G spy at G.U.T.S, no one would be the wiser?'

Zapir, quite known for asking frivolous questions, probably one of the reasons why, generally, he is kept out of vital secrets, continued his comments:

'Double-agent-plus, 3-G spies, jargon after jargon, which could all have little or no significant meaning in the end.'

Ontus turned sideways facing Kai as if asking for his supporter at least to help put a stop to the inquisitive nature of his book-ledger man. Showing a bit of impatience, he responded:

'And before you ask another silly question, let me explain what that entails. Sometimes I wonder how you got this job. Stick to the audits, I'd say.'

Saztah who at times is very protective of their chief accountant, cut into the conversation: 'Look gentlemen, please, let's keep this respectful. This is of national importance and no time for petty squabbling.'

The chief security officer took a long pull of his cigar, blow up the minty-perfumed smoke towards the roof whilst giving Zapir a wry smile.

'Look here 'ld man.'

'I'm not your old man. You're at least five years older than me. So don't you forget that.'

'Not old man as in chronological age but rather in nature. You know, physicality, manners attitude…'

'Oh shut up and get on with it, Ontus. You can be so annoying at times.'

'Where was I anyway? You keep on interrupting with silly questions.

Saztah cut in saying: 'You were explaining to him what is double-agent plus and 3G spooks.'

'Yeah that's it. I have already explained what a DA+ is. A 3G spy is rooted from a DA+, mainly for suitability reasons. In the eyes of the hosts, some DAs might not be trusted, so they have to make no contact with their source organisation. But then, let us assume the double agent [DA] is a 'he'. He raises his child, mind you, not for that child to become a spy, since DA's own espionage scent may still be fresh on the hosts' minds and could still being watched and monitored. But that scent mark could have faded or even extinct – altogether in the eyes of the host – by the time his grandchild would be born. Who then becomes the third-generation spy – somewhat like the one we are about to secretly unleash in Pris. So during all those years of lying low, the grandparent and his child (Second-generation) would have gone off the radar in their eyes, yet they were all along sleeping cells laying the foundation for this third-generation agent – the actual spy.

'This new spy would have to adjust/adapt to having dual citizenship. With us here at V.I.M. his/her code would be DA+3G, with a full title known as "Adjusted (or Adapted) Double Agent Plus Third-Generation", or **ADAPT** for short. I hope this explanation helps and you don't tell anyone that would leak our secrets to G.U.T.S.'

Dummy, as he cursed in his mind.

Mr Saztah suddenly asked:

'Oh, how about that Zapia lady now at G.U.T.S who used to work for that defunct science organisation?'

Without answering his question, Ontus stared at Saztah, then looked across at Mr Zapir and back to Saztah again (Gesturing secrecy), who seemed to nod slightly understanding the situation. Whilst they don't mind Zapir knowing about the mole at G.U.T.S., they don't want him to know about their plan on Zapia.

****

In the eyes of Zapia, Trillian's P.A., chief scientist Nemad, is a strange and awkward bloke, regarding the history between them..

At G.U.T.S's head office, she had on four different occasions rejected his sexual advances, all in a space of two weeks. But he seemed to be oblivious to it all, and even stranger for someone rumoured to be have completely lost interest on love relationships after the death of his wife.

Then one day Zapia saw him walking towards the kitchen in his trademark poker face expression.

Here looking all innocent again, fooling society, she kept thinking.

She paused, straightened her mini shirt that was riding up her thighs and hastened towards him down the corridor. She made a gentle but firm grip at his wrist, dragging him behind her into the printing room as he followed sheepishly.

'Hey! What are you playing at and what do you think you're doing?'

He demanded but still allowed himself being towed.

'Look here.'

She sneered, stilling holding on to his right hand.

'Twice last month you made inappropriate contacts with my body; at first, you deliberately thrusted your crotch against me, then the second time, brushed against my rear in this same printing room when you also called me Sugary Fiz.

If you are to continue with that sort of behaviour, I will report the matter to Mr Freeze. I also hope you are aware of what he thinks of you anyway, he may like you but also think you're quirky.'

She then threw away his hand but still staring at him. He used his other hand to hold up the sore wrist in the air, nursing it.

Initially, he seemed lost for words with a puzzled look on his face before getting himself to say:

'I don't know what you're talking about. I never once brushed against you, or whatever you mean by that.

And I also don't take kindly to false accusations. I have been away for a couple of weeks and could hardly recollect my time off work. I could also report you for assault…'

Before he could finish his sentence, she leaned further towards him, fanning her fresh minty breath in his face and growl-barked:

'Now you're losing your mind saying you've been away when you've been here at work all the time.

This is your last warning, buddy.'

All her thoughts were that this cute little fella is playing mind games with her, as she turned around and started walking away dancing her hips for his attention. But he was only looking at his sore wrist.

Even though she had pretended to be angry, she simply wasn't, and even enjoyed getting so close to this handsome, intelligent but non-entity of a fella, she thought.

She had known him for over a decade and was a college friend of his late wife, and that is how they first met. Nemad had also been one of her bosses at their previous employment where they really got on well together until he politely declined her offer of a date, straining the relationship a bit, after the death of his wife.

Now she just can't understand his recent behaviour with all those sexual attacks; why not just make it real, she kept thinking. After all, it was he who turned down my offer. All this funny business of touching here, brushing there, and the name calling is all childish.

'I think I made a mistake confronting him.'

Whispering under her breath.

It was only after Nemad had reported Zapia to Trillain, who had a quiet word of advice with her, that made her starting to really hate him, thinking he had used and abused her. She then forwarded her own complaint to the human resources department but with no success.

This humiliation, combined with the loss of a long-promised pay rise and promotion as a reprimand for her behaviour, was all too much to bear.

She regret not letting Max Zytan, their chief investor, knew about this before lodging a formal complaint.

Max and Nemad don't really get on well.

With all the stress that followed this incident, her appearance changed for the worse; once somehow fashionable dress sense, gone, the enviable hairstyles, now dishevelled and at times really outright messy. For her own security, she was sectioned to a psychiatry hospital. It was whilst she had been locked there against her will that her mental state deteriorated.

****

Marx Zytan (Surname means swordfish), from what he had told of his family, hailed from a tradition of swordsmen/women going back for centuries. He always carries the weapon attached to his trousers belt – at times alongside with his cat. A couple of occasions Zytan's private jet was unavailable, the tycoon had adamantly refused travelling to some business meetings when a few commercial airlines refused him boarding with his pet and weapon. Some of the airline staff nicknamed him "The Fat Cat with the Manx Cat".

He lives in a sandstone manor house hidden deep in the Anatraza forest on an isle surrounded by a lead-poisoned lake. It's a four-storey mansion.

The house appeared bigger on the inside. Hanging on the high-ceiling just behind the front door is a huge sword that scares the wit out of visitors. Most of whom would never return. One Zist historian, who had studied Earth's fabled history (From data snooped on the ISS), said it would feel like the "Hanging sword of Damocles" in Zytan's house. The strong smell of incense hangs heavy in the corridor area and gets stronger further into the sitting room. The whole residence setup looks like a museum of dark arts. On the adjacent walls to the left from the main entrance were two medium-sized crossed Japanese-like Katanas swords. The weapon seems to be hung all over the place. An eerie-looking skull with cracks that appeared like a frown on its face sits on a shelf just above his bed; never before had a skull been observed as showing a facial expression. Another equally eerie-looking wall-hung rug depicting a spread-eagled human-like figure was alongside the bed. Rumours have it is the frowned human skull and skin from a sworn enemy still expressing hatred for him even in death. And he gets spiritual strength seeing it most of the time.

Max denied this; first saying it was that of a chimpanzee, later changing his story saying it was an early human species, though he won't allow it to be scientifically proven. One time his favourite sword, the fabled Zytana, inherited from his grandfather with similar folklore to King Arthur's Excalibur, went missing. He got really desperate and offered two million wands [₩2m, wands is the national currency in Pris] for its return. It was reported to be the oldest, largest and sharpest among his family collection but one that is also said to be cloaked-up in what they take as fact an ancestral curse. Marx has never seen the weapon since it was stolen from his house. Thieves had broken in, burgled several artefact, jewellery, cash etc. but strangely enough they broke in again three days later and returned every item except the mysterious Zytana sword; Marx had wept like a baby for his beloved weapon. (The second time ever he had wept over the age of four. The first was when he got bitten by a stray dog aged ten). Rumour has it he intimidated his estranged wife, Hatzas, into marrying him after she got scared and had her hypnotised with the sacred sword. He is not legally married to his current partner Branitz, red, 69, 5 feet 9 inches tall, short stocky-built, with mop-like hair, fleshy faced, fat nose, swollen [Not hooded] eyes, one that hardly see her pupils. Everything is fat about her but she is extremely polite and hardworking. Even Marx can't convince her to give up her hospital nursing job and several charity works. They had two teenage children who are at boarding school. How these two seemingly different individuals got together is anyone's guess. Well they also say opposites attract.

Zytan had gone home from that meeting, turned on the television set which is just a huge single electronic cell on the sitting room wall, with a remote control that wasn't working properly. He managed kicking off his expensive seaweed shoes, put his feet up but too tired to take off his jacket and just collapsed into his favourite armchair, cheerful on the day's events after finally concluding the deal. The house felt lonely without Branitz, who was as usual, busy at work. Some people say she throws herself at her work to get away from him.

He went through the channels, finds nothing interesting. There was the usual news on the latest political events, sports, the weather and the likes. He tried to switch off the telly but the remote wasn't working properly with dying batteries. Cursing under his breath for forgetting to get his housekeeper to change the batteries, he got up walking towards the TV monitor. Thinking how forgetful he was, and grateful for having a partner, who seems to even at times remind him to do simple things like having a bath or even to eat. Had it not been for her, he thought, I'd have probably been penniless or even dead by now.

Struggling to find out the touch screen buttons on the wall to switch it off manually, something he hadn't ever done in his entire adult life, he kept thinking life without Branitz would be hell. Then right in front up him on TV was the "Breaking News: Famous space exploration, plant manager, Mr Trillian Freeze, owner of Glacial Universal Trading Syndicate, the world renowned (G.U.T.S) has died in a car accident".

Marx's still crouched down staring at the screen he could neither understand what was being reported, nor was he sure he heard his colleague's name alright. Badly wanting the sound turned up but not having the remote control, he started poking a finger at it, mistakenly switching it off and on until he got the right volume button. Watching the news and realising what was being said he felt his face heavy as lead in shock whilst moving backwards to his favourite armchair again, not wanting to miss anything. Eyes still wired to the TV, he tripped over a footstool and fell backward shitting his head on the coffee table and passing out. The last images on his mind before he got knocked out were that of the deceased Trillian Freeze all over the news. No one could come to Zytan's aid.

The household staff, busy in other parts of the huge mansion, would only come into the sitting room area to either do domestic chores or answer calls from their employers. With his partner at work, he just lay there half-unconscious still in his jacket, not being able to shout out for help even when he tried, he was thinking, Branitz, Branitz.

3

After Zapia was released from mental hospital, she reapplied for her old job but was turned down. Not only on medical grounds but also on Nemad's insistence he'd never work with her ever again. Making allegations against him directly to the head of Human Resources [HR], intentionally by passing her line-manager, was unhelpful. Though the case was rejected, he still carries no forgiveness for what he saw as the intolerable pain she had put him through for six whole months. Before this entire incident, these two got on pretty well. In fact, it was he who personally head-hunted Zapia from his own former employers, bringing her with him to G.U.T.S. So the turn of events resulting in them now being seen as enemies, is something even the company's experienced Human Resources manager, who also happened to be a professional psychologist, couldn't fathom either. Especially on the alleged sexual assaults. These two have worked together for ten years, the last five at G.U.T.S, and nothing like these incidents had ever happened before between them. So why now?

To what she regarded as a way of coping with the stress of having no job she started struggling with substance abuse.

After the H.R. Rejection the embittered P.A. took her case to an Employment Tribunal, citing unfair dismissal. This time around armed with CCTV evidence of her encounters with Prof. Nemad in different parts of the office. These tapes weren't available to her at her first case hearing.

At that internal investigation, the chief scientist had produced emails and text messages as evidence of what he had described as constant harassment from her. And that was then quite good enough for him to be acquitted. But now the external investigation had demanded CCTV evidence not exhibited at the previous trial, which proved as right her complaints against him.

Nemad denied it all, come hell or high water, and was very determined to further clear his name. He swore to his life and that of his only devoted and beloved 11-year-old child, Baisa, greenish mixed-race [Blue Dad, Nemad and yellow mom, Chanzan].

As a single-parent, he lives by his daughter and does almost everything by her. Regardless of his work's demands and commitments, he would take a day or two off to personally mind the child whenever she is ill and away from school.

Losing at the case hearing and being suspended from work destroyed his selfbelief and dignity. For the first time ever, he started neglecting the little girl, stopped cooking her meals and would only buy unhealthy fast food, stopped helping with her homework. Parts of their daily lives had changed for the worse but yet she wouldn't complain about it to any one, not even to him. But for her school's timely intervention, the neglect will have continued unreported. She idolised her dad and would do everything she could to protect him. Somewhat more in fear of losing him, after learning of a classmate who was taken into care from her single-parented mother for child neglect. Unlike her school friend, she badly wanted to stay with her old man at all costs.

Finally, Nemad was suspended and taken into hospital. Ironically, at the same mental clinic that treated Zapia.

****

Marx (In the presence of his lawyer Ms Bampor, who doubles as his accountant) had deposited ₩ 1 billion towards the project, and a further billion for a new bank account to be set up in his proposed new identity on planet Earth. After the first project stalled, he had refused to withdraw his funds, citing, only losers and cowards retreat in the face of adversity. He was content enough to see it through as sunken costs that cannot be withdrawn. Marx learned from the last stock market crash to hold shares position in the face of economic downturns. 'The only way is up,' he would say. Which has always been his mantra. He doesn't see it any different now even though the amount of money involved is huge, in billions.

Marx suddenly woke up from a snooze in the balcony of his rented holiday penthouse overlooking the Mustard Yellow sea [Zist seawater is a thin yellow gel almost as fluid as water is on planet Earth], trying to catch up on lost sleep. Even forgotten he was on holiday. With the sun in his face, he stretched those tiny arms, yawned majestically and settled down to planning again. He thought about having a couple of Omole (Zist's equivalent of Whiskey) shots on ice but that strong alcoholic drink wasn't available, so he chose Mampama white wine instead.

He had been up most of the night wondering how to navigate the constant calls from his creditors. These are the type of business interests I have to keep happy to continue this life of luxury, he thought, even if I have to rob one to pay the other.

It has also just dawned on him most of his main colleagues are in some sort of a bother, either dead or sacked or/and sick in hospital; Trillian had died in a car crash; Prof. Scyzpr still mentally incapacitated, Zapia, the same and now sacked. Maila basically a non-entity. Leaving himself only with Bampor to contend with in running the daily business operations at G.U.T.S. Without the group's pooled talents, he began to wonder how long he could cope with so many missing vital parts of Trillian's determination, Nemad's inventiveness, Zapia's brilliant management skills. He started wondering for the first time if he hadn't made a mistake not withdrawing his money when the project was written off in the first meeting as economically unviable.

He quickly phoned finance manager, Ms Fannie Zypisth, 39, brown, tall, thin, part-time model, glamorous looks, not-so-round, not-so-long face. Firm medium lips, almond-shaped eyes, excellent teeth and smile, asking her which way his other investment options were going?

'Norf extremely well, I'm afroid. [Not extremely well, I'm afraid]'

She managed to muffle out holding the phone in one hand and dipping a fork into a plate of cheese-stuffed chicken salad with the other hand.

'Look here Fanny, it's bloody rude to having food in your mouth as you speak.'

She hastily apologised saying sorry but Marx continued the abuse:

'Show us some class at least eh! According to your references you went to a finishing school, didn't you? Was it a flipping one? Why don't you just put the damn fuck [Saying fuck instead of fork] away and talk business with me for a minute, eh?'

She sensed the anger and impatience in his voice, and apologised again:

'Oh, I'm so sorry, sir. It's late evening and I had been very busy working throughout my lunch break and after hours as well.'

He didn't say anything, just waiting for her to reply to his question.

Marx hadn't realised they are on different time zones at that moment.

Damn it, she hissed in her thoughts, as she bared her fangs out for a fight.

This is not my working hour. I just got home feeling tired and my job doesn't pay me for overtime. Having already spent an extra two hours at the office.

His uncontrollable rudeness ignited her anger; the foul language, talking her down like that, pronouncing her Fanny in a vulgar way, was all just too much disrespectful.

She remembered forgiving him a few times before for similar behaviours.

He suddenly ranted again: 'I want bloody answers right now.' Taking his frustrations on the poor secretary.

Whilst he was cursing down the phone, she quickly put her meal away, went outside her house, passed on the phone to her left ear, chin up in the air, chest puffed, and right hand on her hips and started fighting back:

'It's all bad news, sir, kaput-pants.'

Really giving it to him in a stern voice taking revenge for what she regarded as his usual rude and impatient self.

'Stock…markeeeets…are…crashhhhing all over the place. Businesses… going…badddd. Most of your holding stocks areeee…down at the moment.

Nothing has changed with the low lending rates environment either, making interest on your savings account…kaput. Also don't forget that one…billion Wand is still missssssing.'

Deliberately spacing apart and dragging some words in her sentences making them sound more playful and childish.

(Marx has an abnormal habit of transferring funds to unusual places. Mainly because he keeps on hiding money away from creditors, most of whom he had taken the cash from in the first place for his numerous Ponzi schemes.)

Normally on similar previous dire situations like this she would express consolation towards him, with hopeful words at times but not at this moment.

Sensing she is a bit revengeful he decided to not only punish her but to also prove who is boss by asking her to repeat all what she had just said, as he stood up passing the phone from one ear to the other.

Which she did, only this time spacing apart some of words farther than she did before. He was disappointed she did but felt helpless doing anything about.

With the new staff members and the trusted colleagues not available except for the inept Maila, and Bampor, he felt disabled.

Fannie Zypisth knew he just wouldn't sack her nor make any sort of trouble for her as she had enough information on his numerous illicit deals that could put him away behind bars for a long period of time. Or even cost him his life, depending on whom she betrayed him to.

He just stood up in shock. The personal towel (Always travel with his own draperies and even toiletries) wrapped around his narrow waist dropped down to the floor bearing his nakedness.

He had his right hand pressing the phone against his ear very hard, as if that would help him hear better, and his left hand supporting his weight that was feeling heavier against the railing, he started feeling faint.

His attention completely focused listening to his company secretary giving him not only harrowing stories but adding insult to injury disrespecting him as well.

Two young ladies at the opposite balcony were giggling at him but he was not to notice, completely blind to their behaviour.

It was only after a male hotel guest from the other side of the building saw what was going on and yelled:

'Cover up, man.

Not all of us are interested in seeing your tackle.'

It was at that moment he realised he was naked.

He quickly sat down, not even picking up the towel to cover his nudity.

He then tried to tell off the insubordinate Fannie Zypisth and but could not even understand what he had just said to her. He then paused for her to reply so he would at least recall what he had said. Only for her to asked in a sarcastic tone.

'Excuse meee, sir, I didn't hear you?'

He replied: 'Never mind,' and hung up the phone feeling all defeated with droopy ears.

That was the moment Ms Zypisth knew her boss is powerless.

For Marx Zytan at most times would have the last word in.

He was never the billionaire he made himself appear to be.

It was rather more about how he wanted others seeing him, than as to whom he actually was.

Most of the ₩2b he invested into this venture were raised through debts from the shadowy underworld's loan sharks.

Banks would not trust him anymore after several loan defaults.

The rest of the money had come from a Ponzi scheme taking cash from investors, living on some and passing on new cash to old customers.

These funds are held in bank accounts operating under different aliases.

The next moment he jumped on his private jet with pet on tow and whisked back to Pris. He got home just over seven hours later and immediately called Bampor, asking her to come over to his place. His partner, Branitz, was out, working as usual. He badly wanted the comfort of her presence which he feels protect him as well but Bampor will do for now, he thought. Nothing sexual, just that friendly companionship, that's all. Marx thrives on feminine comforts, and not just from his live-in partner and Bampor but from any female willing to offer it. He would pay considerable amounts of money to having prostitutes just sitting down and having chats with him, no sexual contacts at all.

Whilst waiting for Bampor he began some self-comfort thoughts: there is my two billion wands invested in the Zoll project, though half has not been accounted for lately. That's not too bad eh? That half could be sitting somewhere. I hope to find it.

Though being suspicious of Bampor's involvement in the missing one billion fund, he just couldn't bring himself to openly question her about it.

She got to his residence around 8:30 am that Monday morning. Moaning to herself it is a bit too early, even for a weekday. But when Marx growled it was urgent she had no choice.

She was wearing different shades of tight-fitting clothes in matching green; a pine green crop top baring her mid torso, tight fern green mini skirt, army green cap and tea green shoes.

'My favourite colour,' she hissed at him. 'I saw you looking at me from head to toe, probably thinking what's with all the green.'

She pulled a chair opposite him, placed her lime green handbag on the coffee table, breathing heavily as she sometimes does being an asthmatic patient, and sniffed: 'You're still wearing that awful aftershave aren't you? It's just too strong, Marx.'

'I told you it's that invisible wall that keeps some of my enemies at bay,' he replied.

'And probably keeps friends at bay too, not that you have any anyway. Sorry,' she quipped. 'Next time I'll buy you some "toilet water" (A diluted form of perfume).'

What she doesn't know is that his blind serpent identifies him by that strong smell. Once or twice he ran out of his "snake piss" aftershave only for the creature to get seriously ill. Even when Marx bought a similar scent, it only made things worse. So he stocked up gallons of the aftershave and doesn't give a piss about what anyone else says.

Before she could say anything further he quickly raved: 'I think that missing fund is an inside job and I have Nemad on my mind,' he said without so much conviction to his voice.

'Who, Nemad? Leave it out Marx. That guy wouldn't steal a cent even if his or his precious little daughter's life depend on it. He is as honest as the word itself.

This is the same guy who took his late grandfather's entire property portfolio worth millions to the local police station after the old man on his death bed, had not only sent him the keys to his house and but also the combination to his safe but forgetting to tell him there is no will. Nemad was the only surviving relative.

All he thinks of is his daughter and scientific research stuff.'

Marx replied, looking away from her, 'OK, that's your opinion. But we still have to pay him a visit.'

****

It was only when Nemad got home from the hospital that he starting really doubting his own mental state.

First, he thought Zapia was telling lies about him sexually abusing her, because he thought he didn't. He then realise CCTV evidence at the office proved he did.

He started thinking, all this time I had wrongly concluded she was making false claims against me until her evidence proved otherwise. Maybe I'm really having mental health issues.

As he picked up the phone to call her, he heard his own CCTV camera buzzing from its dying batteries. He dropped the handset, leaving the call for later, and replaced the batteries. He was just about to reset the video cassette recorder and delete the old recordings to make room for more when all of a sudden it sprung to life; the tape playing itself without his effort.

He thrust a finger forward to switch it off but accidentally pressed the slow rewind button. He then thought, it's like the machine has a mind of its own. He stopped it halfway and instinctively plays the tape. There in front of him were the dates he was meant to be at work but found himself just slumped at home in his sofa. When Baisa was away on school holidays with her maternal grandparents.

'Wow! Talking of divine intervention,' he whispered to himself.

The recording seemed like a double of himself unfolding right before his own eyes, a doppelganger effect, lying on the sofa for five days without moving for the entire working week, yet I was also reported to have been at the office.

'Hold on how can this happen?' audibly questioning himself.

My home security camera tape contrasting that of my office. Each showing me at two different locations, at home and the office, at the same time.

The Prof. kept on running and rerunning the events in his mind; these were the same days I was supposed to have lost my memory and stayed off work but yet shown on the office CCTV involved in the incidents with Zapia.

He replayed the tape three times, making sure that was him alright before ejecting it and carefully placing it inside his safe.

He then reached for the cupboard, made himself some strong coffee and continued with his thoughts. While some people would take psychoactive drugs like nicotine, marijuana, alcohol etc. for relaxation and comfort, he'd go for strong ones like the caffeine variety.

Once Nemad started thinking of something, he'll think it to the absolute end, which means to his satisfaction. And he doesn't just let things go easily. I told the tribunal my daughter was away and came home feeling unwell and for the next five days was sleeping on my sofa, he was still in thoughts. I came back to work refusing to tell anyone, since I don't want them to think anything weird about my mental state and jeopardising the custody of my child. That was the situation before I ever smacked her for the first time after losing that case. Then I asked myself if I wasn't at the office for a week, incidentally at the times I was alleged to have attacked Zapia, then who was on the office CCTV committing those crimes? He concluded the thinking, well, for now.

He went to the fridge took out a beer flipped it open before realising he hadn't even finished the coffee yet which had gone almost cold. Advancing towards his favourite armchair ready to call his old employers when Marx and Bampor rung to say they are on their way coming to see him.

He quickly shut the safe door that had been left ajar. Keeping the tape secret, at least for the time being, having no trust for anyone.

About 20 minutes later, they knocked on his door, and he let them in.

On their way coming to see him, Marx had speculated Nemad has got some idea of the missing money. 'Involved in some way,' he reckoned to Bampor, who was clearly not convinced.

Sensing his aide's disagreement, he started narrating his own theory:

'Nemad took part in embezzling the funds. Which is no surprise to me since he spends a fortune on all sorts of things: collection of expensive artefacts like paintings and classic cars, his generous charity donations and unreasonable expenditures on that precious little daughter of his. Unreasonable in the sense that spending on the child also means spending on whosoever is accompanying her like friends and their families to social events and even exotic holidays whenever Nemad would be busy at work.

'And I'm talking here about first-class flights and accommodation with all expenses paid for by Nemad.'

'Where is your evidence for accusing the professor?' she queried, frowning at him.

He replied: 'You interrupted me! I was getting there. Where was I again?'

She snorted out loudly and said:

'You talking about his wild expenses on his child.'

He responded: 'Ah yes. Not that I'm saying he stole the money but rather he has some knowledge of the missing fund's whereabouts.'

'What's the difference?' she demanded.

He didn't respond. Taken aback not knowing how the answer that question. There was an awkward moment of brief silence as they drove towards the chief scientist's house.

He turned towards her and said, 'Nemad spends for more than he earns,' breaking the pause.

She simply shrugged her shoulders and chuckled, as if to say, so what?

Turning back to facing the road, he continued his detective story:

'Nemad [Marx would hardly address him as professor], in a deliberate ploy to avert attention from his thieving, started sexual attacks on Zapia in the hope…'

Bampor gasped out loudly, stopping him in his tracks, and then hissed:

'That's a bit harsh and unfair calling someone like Professor Scyzpr a thief and a liar. He has always been your whipping boy, hasn't he?

I'm sorry, Marx, but I think you're just too folded up into yourself as a victim to see anything else outside your wild imaginations. You're only speculating, remember?'

He paused in response for a second or two, forcing himself to disagree with her and restarted his story:

'He was attacking Zapia hoping she will report him and he would at least be suspended. Giving him time and opportunity once outside the office to siphon my money away.

'But unfortunately for him, Zapia didn't forward any complaint, so he reported her to Trillian, whom we all know had a soft spot for him. Photographic evidence proved her to be right against him.'

Bampor who had just moments been looking straight through the windscreen as they drove and listening to Marx speak, turned sideways looking through the passenger side window, away from him as if something else was attracting her attention. She then fished out a chewing gum from her purse, unwrapped and tossed it into her mouth and turned towards looking out of the car window again.

He noticed this and went quiet for a bit, still feeling hurt by Fannie Zypisth's apparent in subordination earlier.

Maybe I'm losing power and influence, he thought.

Still having no response, he glanced at her again and cleared his throat, calling her attention.

She responded, turning towards facing him for a second but still not saying anything, and went back to staring at the road ahead just keeping a straight face.

With that little authoritative victory, Marx yet again continued his monologue story as she was keeping herself busy chewing the gum.

He screeched the car to a sudden stop at the red traffic lights, he was about to drive through. But for their seat belts holding them back the forces of inertia will have sent them through the windscreen.

Bampor lost her patience with him. She snorted again. Louder this time as she pinched the gum out of her mouth, threw it outside the car window and sneered:

'You could have killed us with your unwarranted obsession with Prof. Nemad stealing your money. I know you don't like him but probably Trillian, not Nemad, knows more about the missing funds than anyone else does. He is probably still alive, holed up somewhere else far from here enjoying the heist. I say this in regard to…'

Abruptly cutting off her sentence, Marx reacted in a way that shocked her. He pulled over to the hard-shoulder side of the road designated for emergency stops only, with the engine still running ignoring the fact that he was violating traffic regulations.

'You can't stop here. You're breaking the law.'

He quickly pulled back onto the main road almost colliding with an oncoming vehicle.

He then slowed down the vehicle, not saying a word, until he turned into a nearby filling station. Parking away from the pumps.

'Are you saying Trillian is not dead and could have my money?' in a voice that scarcely sounded like his own.

Replying to his question with one of her own:

'Didn't you notice there wasn't a proper burial and only four people attended the service that was all done less than 24 hours of the crash?

It was all just too sudden for my liking.'

'Yeah, so what?' Marx replied. 'That was for religious reasons and the state of the badly disfigured body.'

'What religious reasons?' Looking Marx straight in the face.

'When did you ever learn about Trillian being a religious person?' She countered.

'And if he was in any way, why wasn't there a ceremony of some sort to go with any such practice?'

Marx now realising how untrustworthy Trillian can at times be. Not least of all his previous failed business concepts with the financial deposits which were at most times written off as "Sunk costs" (Money that cannot be refunded as they were already spent pursing the business).

He just sat there staring at her, searching her eyes but all he can see is that TV image of the car crash.

He restarted the ignition and they continued the rest of the journey in silence going to see Nemad.

They rang his front door bell, instantly followed by a rather impatient and heavy rap on the door. The front path to Nemad's house was beautifully done; lined-up with ceramic buds, vases and honed stone pots. Most of which have inscriptions of different parts of the universe. His favourite planet, excluding Zist, of course, Earth, was emboldened on a side patio towards the main door entrance.

As they waited, they could hear several clangs and clank sounds as the professor was taking some time to unlock the door.

'Boy, Nemad is a bit fussy on security, isn't he? With all the modern-day digital locking systems this guy is still using mechanical bolts and locks. Jeeze, Maybe we need the men in white suits to get him again.'

Marx making faces as he spoke.

Bampor defending the professor, commented: 'You just can't be too careful living on these hilly exclusive parts of the Prisia suburbs. Electronic locks are vulnerable to burglars with computing skills.'

Marx chuckled and quipped:

'He should move to the cheaper lower grounds then.'

'He needs the hilly heights for the benefit of his telescopes,' Bampor countered.

No sooner the door opened, Marx remarked: 'You don't normally…'

The professor interrupted, saying: '…get the door. Yes, I know. My staff have a day off,' as he stepped aside to let them in.

It is a huge five-bedroom house laid over three floors. Parts of the two floors above the first are not directly overhead. They seemed to be attachments to one side of the main building, allowing direct sunlight swamping to parts of all three floors. All the rooms have high-ceilinged structure and giant bay windows flooding daylight into the living spaces. A huge black-framed washed timber furniture adorned the right side of the lobby. Opposite on the left was a tall, slim glass-fronted hand-painted cabinet showcasing his daughter's chess championship trophies, Pyrex glassware, art treasures and the like. Further into the sitting room area the fixed high ceiling gave way to a stargazing roof built of transparent plastic sheets with a retractable ceiling. The entire structure give stunning views of the skies on a clear night. Couple of floors upstairs in other sections of the house, not directly above the ground reception are a library, a man cave, prayer room [Nemad is very religious] and an observatory housing a huge telescope, with attachments to a couple of desktop computers, pointed towards the heavens.

'Please take a seat,' waving them towards the oak flooring sitting room decorated with an empty marble-lined wood-burner. The adjacent dining room area with its porcelain floor tiles is part of an almost open-planned design. It has its own glass sideboard, displaying more china and other artefact. An ancient wood-burning stove and a dining table and chairs fill up the rest of the space.

'Nice place you've got here, prof. I like it that it's so spacious with so much light,' Bampor chirped as she was looking around.

'Thanks and if I have the resources I'd get a bigger place,' Nemad replied, as Marx regarded his aide who ignored him.

Nemad had noticed Marx's indifference right away and knew this is not a social visit. Both his visitors declined the snacks and drinks offered to them, Marx lying they've just had a meal and a few drinks at the wayside fuel station. Bampor had no choice but to follow suit.

But strangely enough, Marx detached his sword and placed it on the floor next to where he chose to sit, in a dining chair. Initially, Bampor was about to sit in an armchair but changed course and took a chair next to Marx at the dining table.

The professor clasped his hands together started rubbing them against each other and giving his guests a wry smile. A brief moment of strange silence ensued before Nemad spoke again.

It is sort of a customary Zistian lore to signal all is not well by rejecting your host's hospitalities.

He then asked how was their journey. It was Bampor who replied with a single word, 'Fine'.

Nemad paused again, for a couple of seconds, staring at both of them with a forced smile, as if to say, OK my friends what is the problem, and then managed to bring himself to say:

'What purpose brought your untimely mission here. One without proper notification if I may ask?' Unable to hide the slight impatience and annoyance in his voice tone.

He avoided joining his visitors and sat in an armchair adjacent to the dining table with his back almost turned towards them. He was now returning the hostile body language and the situation was getting more awkward by the moment. Bampor broke the ice chatting about new equipment in the manufacturing pipeline.

Whilst the development analysis seemed somehow interesting, Marx had hardly paid any attention to it. He was too focused on wanting to question the chief scientist whom he had once before thought of as an agent spying for V.I.M. He saw all this talk about bringing new products on line and the like as a distraction wasting precious time.

After failing repeatedly to hack through G.U.T.S.'s data on Zoll, V.I.M. had sent a mole to burrow through instead.

The spy did a fine job getting the formula and relaying it to V.I.M.'s "Post Man" [PM] working in Pris, who then pass it on to the HQ in Bria. Yet V.I.M. officials were not satisfied with the results of the tests they had; the fuel wasn't working effectively.

'We need to have a small sample of Zoll itself to see where we are getting things wrong,' says Kai Londo, their chief scientist.

Their mole was at G.U.T.S. for only a fortnight. Not long enough time. But who was that mole?

One would hardly notice he had a cyborg left hand. The natural one was amputated as punishment by a criminal underground unit he was working for after blundering on one of their significant operations He left the underground world in fear of losing his good right hand. He then resurfaced above board into open established organisations when V.I.M. later hired him for his ruthless and fearless reputation. The company promised to fit him with a better artificial hand; one that only two other persons on the entire planet Zist have. The mole was eager to get one and started working hard towards earning it.

That botched work with his last employers occurred when the target he was meant to infuse with a delayed-action comatose drug, wailed in pain in public, drawing unwanted attention to the incident when the needle pricked his hand. The mole was apprehended by some bystanders and evidence was found on him linking to his bosses who punished him as a result.

At V.I.M., they also used him as a guinea pig trialling the newly-invented "Digestive condom" which some call the internal armour. He was made to swallow the indestructible suit that fits from outside the mouth, covering the lips, through the mouth, down to his stomach. A separate forked inner tube is also inserted from the nostrils down to the lungs to aid breathing. The mole could drink or eat anything whether poisonous or whatever and none of it will come into contact with any part of his internal organs. All contents are captured in a plastic/lead sac [Lead ones can contain some radioactive poisons] which would be emptied later by either inducing vomiting or through an external pouch attached to abdomen. The suit is not reusable. Any top intelligence officer would notice someone wearing that inner condom by the user's unusual speech patterns, and/or not using the toilet and just having an inflating stomach. Reason why the user would rarely eat or drink much, most times beers are avoided. They could drink you under the table with hard liquor .

As a guinea pig, the mole had excelled and was promoted with the promise of the new cyborg hand after the Zoll operation.

V.I.M. were still working their way to getting their hands on Zoll. They started planning to either send in another mole, which is too risky, or hijack one of their rival's employees who could possibly give them a better insight into the new fuel system if not a fuel sample itself.

After Zapia's attempts at getting her job back had all failed, she then applied at V.I.M.. These two firms compete so much they would only employ each other's workers, if such applicants was prepared to betray his/her former employers. G.U.T.S. and V.I.M. were the only two firms on the entire planet Zist that employ C3 civilisation technologies, others are no better than C2. A global disparity somewhat similar to Earth's first, second and third-world countries status.

And it's the race to becoming the first C4 which was further driving the competition between these two multi-national giants.

Zapia got the job over all the other 20 applicants, who were mostly better qualified, and she knew this. The job advertisement appeared on her local paper which was quite unusual. For employments with big multinational firms will only appear on the broadsheets; the kind of newspaper important and educated people tend to read. One time abroad on holiday she was approached by a V.I.M. representative who encouraged her to apply with the firm. They were well aware of her acrimonious split from G.U.T.S. which made her valuable in their eyes.

She was marginally above average intelligence. But her work ethnics and organisational skills were second to none, making up for any academic shortfalls in comparison with other staff members. At Glacial Universal, she was only filling the void for Trillian's P.A., who was on maternity leave, when the firm took her on a fulltime basis. Similarly at V.I.M., the bosses were so impressed with her work schedules they gave her a permanent position with the firm after only two weeks into the job. Zapia was stunned with the speed at which she got the new job promotion. It's was all too easy, she thought, before concluding she had been lucky to have got away from Nemad and his ilk when she did. But little did she know that Marx Zytan was still after her head.

Back at Nemad's residence Marx and Bampor joined Nemad in the armchairs, if only to start easing off the hostile atmosphere after initialling choosing to sit at the dining table. Bampor got off asking the prof. how his health was, his daughter and chatting also about Zapia's decampment to the enemy.

Nemad was thinking at the time, you two didn't come all the way to my house to ask after my affairs, just spill the beans, I have other things to do today. Marx Zytan noticing the impatient expression on Nemad's face started getting down to business.

'That money paid via Trillian's contact should be traced,' he warned. The business woman's contact details seems opaque to me with no specific identification of who is in control of the enterprise.

Nemad didn't say anything about missing funds or Trillian. He has heard rumours about Marx believing Zapia'a story of the events over his, and had become tired to the bone of all this mistrust. He hastily got up from his armchair, saying something inaudible under his breath about time to clear the air or something as he opened the safe to retrieve the video tape. Which he then slotted into the machine without returning to his seat, choosing instead to sit on the floor next to the TV monitor, as if he was guarding his evidence. The tapes: showing the days he stayed at home, away from the office, the day when the Marx's fund was paid and also the days Zapia had accused him of sexual assaults. Showing him waking up on the sofa one morning, standing up and then slumping back onto it, and staying there for five consecutive days without getting up.

'Don't give me all that trash,' Marx rapped. His signature nervousness changing to relaxation as he was becoming angry.

He then uncrossed his legs and stood up as if he was about to attack the scientist.

'This is an electronically-doctored tape,' he snarled.

Pointing his little bony finger at the TV and widening his eyes at the professor.

'You were in that meeting when the payment was made?'

'No, I wasn't,' his host countered.

'I knew all along I neither attended that meeting nor sexually attacked Zapia. Both incidents occurred in the same week I was lost, unaware of my own whereabouts.'

Zytan sat down again, this time on the edge of the seat, hands clasped together and elbows resting on his knees.

'Well you just said it yourself, you were lost, unaware of your own whereabouts. Meaning you could have sleepwalked into the office and did what you did.'

Bampor had known Nemad for several years and believed in what he is trying to prove.

Zytan had been harbouring suspicion of Bampor herself about the missing money but could not bring himself about to say it. Why is she so certain Nemad knew nothing about it except of course if she knew more than she had said so far, he thought.

Using the professor was his way of indirectly quizzing Bampor, hoping she might just let something out when trying to defend the science man.

He couldn't take her to task rather for the same reasons he couldn't punish Fannie Zypisth for being insubordinate; they knew too much about his shady business dealings and secrets that could land him into serious trouble. So his thoughts were he has to be a bit patient and play it safe when dealing with them.

The tense situation started dying down once he began showing some politeness. All three then briefly discussed what they've just seen on the tapes and agreed they had to get Zapia talking.

'We have to get her at all costs, even if it involved kidnapping. It's my guess she could be part of a scam with Trillian to defraud us,' Bampor said, whilst looking at Marx for a response.

She had never liked Trillain; after a very brief casual dating, sleeping together and he dumping her unceremoniously. And Marx knew this.

He just chuckled and said:

'Oh I'm starving and need some food.'

Before quickly realising he had only less than an hour earlier, turned down Nemad's offer of food and drink.

Looking embarrassed, trying to save face, he said:

'All this missing-money talk has made a bit hungry again. Let's go out for a meal and cool off the heat.'

They went to the Orange Horizon restaurant at the Ocean Heights hotel where they were ushered to window-table views of the flowing city life below The entire restaurant floor was beautifully awash in natural light. Some of the costly menu's dishes demand a waiting time for at least 15 minutes but Marx felt uncomfortable sharing all that time in a private meal with Nemad. So he said:

'I can't stay out too long.

I'm only having puffed-up pastries, probably stuffed with cheese and vegetables or something. And no strong alcohol for me.'

Bampor followed suit and Nemad read the situation and opted for the same, which they all washed down with cool mampama white wine.

Not knowing that there are more serious issues at hand like the V.I.M.'s Post Man spying on their work.

Before they had left his house for the restaurant, Nemad was reluctant going out with them after the attitude both had showed him at his place. But Nemad is a "People Pleaser" and would do most things asked of him if he can.

It's no secret he and Marx don't really like each other. Marx Zytan has never forgotten an incident that started on a long-haul night flight coming home to Prisia, capital of Pris, from an international business conference. when Nemad's daughter, Baisa, woke up to use the toilet and saw Marx's glowing Manx cat walking down the dim-lit aisle coming towards her. She was frightened stiff, running back to her dad saying she thought the animal was St Elmo's fire (St Elmo's fire is a luminous electrical discharge sometimes seen on a ship or aircraft during a storm). The very prickly and inconsiderate Marx was so angry with the little girl's comment, he exchanged bitter words with her father who was only defending the poor child.

'She had only just woken up from sleep in the middle of the night and had never seen a luminous cat before. Most people will be frightened in the situation,' Nemad was reported to have told Marx who was having none of it and had argued back, saying:

'My cat gives me light during the darkest moments in life. Insulting her is like dimming those lights. And that is unacceptable.'

A few other staff members who were passengers on the same flight said they were also scared of the glowing animal.

Generally, Marx Zytan doesn't seem to get on well with society. In fact, he never seemed to like anyone except his cat which he adores more than his own children. The situation with his partner, Branitz, is more about him using her for comfort than for anything else. As for Bampor, no one knows for sure why he was so protective of her, even more so than he does for Maila.

Rumours among some staff members reckoned Ms Bampor had something on him which she could be using to her own advantage.

Zytan had bought her a luxury flat in a modern apartment block overlooking the Central Garden Square in the exclusive Date Palm River Front. The luxury estate is in a private gated community boasting of a driveway, sweeping lawns, and canal tow path were residents do fitness activities like exercising, pet walking, riding bicycles.etc.

At one time in a staff meeting, almost everyone was supporting the need to having extended family members put onto the company's health insurance policies, as opposed to two other alternatives, of having a new ultra-modern canteen, or a new fleet of cars. Bampor, who had no family as far as she knew, and mostly works from home, voted to having the third option of new vehicles even though the current ones were less than two years old.

Marx Zytan was arguing for having the second option of a new canteen which he sees as far less expensive and will benefit all members, instead of incurring extra costs running an already bloated healthcare facility or unnecessarily purchasing new vehicles.

Out of a total of 120 votes; only two voted for new cars. The majority voted for the health option with the second alternative of the canteen coming in at a distant second.

Marx was reported to have cancelled the vote, behind the scenes, and stealthily introduced the car scheme in a gradual process. Which management disguised as discount purchases. All to please Bampor. It was easy to see why some people were saying she had something on him.

'Maybe he's fucking her.'

One disgruntled worker was overheard saying in the canteen after a multitude of complaints against her were dismissed by the human resources department on the orders of Zytan himself. The purchasing manager chuckled and then quipped:

'Then that must be one hell of a fuck given the sacrifices he has made for her. Personally I think there is more to it than the eyes can see. Some also say because she is smart, which could be the reason. But honest to God, I don't see it.'

A HR manager walking down the corridor overheard the conversation, she popped her head through the doorway and quipped:

'Some people have all the luck eh? She has two jobs in one; covering both his legal and bookkeeping businesses. Which is quite strange given these two professions are quite distinct from each other.'

She then inched a bit further through the doorway, almost into the room.

'One basically deal with figures, whilst the other with literal reason and logic. It's almost unheard of a professional accountant who also happens to be a professional lawyer.'

The catering manager added: 'Yeah. And if you'd have noticed more or less all staff members call him Dr Zytan with the sole exception of her, with whom he is on first name terms.'

A title he bought under dodgy circumstances just before he got listed at the national treasury office as a business consultant. Even his partner and children refer to him as Dr Zytan. His youngest was once reported to have called him daddy in public and he told her off. The child hasn't recovered from that shock ever since. She's terribly scared of him. Probably reason when both of his children are not in boarding school during half-term breaks or holidays, they always go away to their maternal grandparents.

4

There was rumour the Pris Government was beside itself with anger when they found out about G.U.T.S.'s secrecy on Zoll. Rival nation, Bria had leaked the information in the hope that the publicity would disrupt G.U.T.S's programme. The V.I.M. mole had left and returned home to Ob, the capital city of Bria, before the second stage of Zoll, the vanishing capability, was also accidentally discovered.

Bria bosses were beginning to realise Zapia's usefulness was overestimated, she neither had any useful information on Zoll nor other trade secrets for that matter. They didn't seem to be winning the battle with their rivals: first, the mole didn't get much, and now Zapia's uselessness.

Ironically, V.I.M. leaking the Zoll secrecy had unintentionally helped to unite the Pris Government and G.U.T.S.

At the first joint convention between these two organisations, chief scientific advisor to the State, Dr Chibot, in his trade mark dark suit, remarked to G.U.T.S. officials:

'All is forgotten now. No more secrets. We all work together for the worldly benefit of the nation and our planet as a whole. The only limitation is our imagination, not the budget, which has no boundary.'

'You're well on-point. I can't agree more.'

Tweeted Dr Annaz, the very influential deputy chief scientific advisor (d.c.s.a.). Smartly dressed in overcast-grey power trouser suit worn over a dark-white grey shirt with gravel-grey shoes to match.

'We know we are all merely existing on borrowed time. A time here on Zist that is fast drawing to a close.'

Chibot was going to say something but she won't let him. She then went on to say: 'Let's make it a duty to ourselves working together. Never more so cooperative than now. Simply because our future lives matters the most,' she concluded.

Dr Prysten Poiter, G.U.T.S.'s senior scientist, then thought, full of overblown rhetoric, clichés, and the lot. It's a bit misleading saying the budget has no limits, only our imagination has. It's the other way around round, sir. How many times we hear government joint operations with private entities run short of funds – many times. He was in fossil-grey suite with matching ash-grey tie and steel-grey shoes.

The love of grey was one of the things he had in common with Dr Annaz. Some say it was the love for that colour that attracted them to each other when they were dating.

Once she started talking, there is no stopping her:

'We need to save ourselves. They at Bria would also benefit but only after we have moved all our residents to Earth first. Brians would then follow us, rather as second-class passengers,' she said. Some in the audience couldn't help but burst out in rude laughter.'

Dr Rannas Annaz is well known for her somewhat undiplomatic behaviour at times. Critics put it down to rudeness, or uncivility even. But also highly intelligent with so many different parts to her personality; from kindness to ruthlessness.

The Government and G.U.T.S. working together in the new joint national programme was rather a good idea. They complement each other strategically: the company's scientists are known to be far better knowledgable, whilst the central government had the deeper pocket to fund such a huge project, so naturally the idea to combine these two vital resources was borne.

During his own time to speak, Dr Poiter remarked:

'We have to zoom out of here or we're all doomed. It's a choice we have to make, zoom or doom.'

There was cheers of approval from some of the others when he then continued:

'Ah, which reminds me. What about renaming the programme from Project Earth – H2O (or Home Earth) to **Zoom or Doom**. It's more about moving home than just fetching water.'

There were more cheers and laughter from both teams as they agreed to the name change. Annaz wasn't one of those cheering.

After the joint group had started experimenting with Zoll on the newly-named Zoom or Doom project, they met again in a mini convention in reduced numbers, held at a Government department in an old grey building. The room appeared to be cramped up with old office cabinet; an environment far below G.U.T.S.'s usual high standards. The situation wasn't helped with weak lighting and poor air conditioning systems in the middle of a very hot summer, made worse by their runaway annual increases in the global temperatures. Despite the sizzling heat, Dr Chibot was in his trademark dark-coloured clothing complete with a tie. Just about the only dressed as such.

Poiter and other men were in open neck shirts without ties nor jackets.

Dr Annaz, the main speaker, was cladded in an unusual manner rather unbefitting for the occasion: her loose lengthy wavy hair locks all over the place, and wearing oversized high-waisted straight black and grey trousers. White shirt underneath dark grey jacket with turned-up sailor collars and excessive makeup. Completely looking out of place and demonstratively sitting at odds with her relatively high office. All done with wilful neglect. Gone were her usual power suits and smart dressing.

On Zist, it is a customary snub to underdress on an occasion. Signalling contempt or dislike for the event. Knowing her ex-boyfriend, Dr Poiter, would be wearing grey colours she was going to wear bright ones to differentiate herself but she just can't stand wearing any other colour in a formal dress. So she still had grey but in a very outlandish way.

After a very brief introduction and hasty pleasantries, she started off with such noticeable enthusiasm:

'This is the moment to alert you all we now have a mini lab named "The Sublimation Glow [TSG]" built on super-galactic technologies. Actually it alternates functions between a static laboratory and a flying ship. If you'd allow me to further explain some of its brief capabilities, I'd be happy to.' She flung her head backwards sweeping the long hair from obscuring her face and continued:

'The huge space boat or should I just simply say the TSG, has an outer shell made of carbon nanotubes that can heal itself if hit by space debris or even radiation. In fact, that's only a secondary defence mechanism. These cosmic vandals won't even get that close as the ship itself produces an artificial magnetic shield around its fuselage protecting itself from any physical contact out there. Its ingenious. OK, OK, enough of the out-of-this-galaxy technology.'

She then took a sip of water, avoid looking Poiter's way and continued her presentation:

'A simple application of G.U.T.S.'s Zoll, well, our Zoll, now that it belongs to us all as a group, sprayed onto the TSG, would transform it from a physical space vessel into a light-energy force. The fuel structurally change the space craft from matter to energy. Somewhat like solid ice becoming a gas without the in-between liquid stage, hence the sublimation title. Isn't it wonderful and appreciable now that we are getting our due reward for all our years of hard graft working on the need to exit not just our solar system but the Long Grains galaxy as a whole?'

On hearing someone sighed in admiration, she felt elated; paused, took another sip from a glass, beaming with pride:

'Quite incredibly our three-man crew manning the craft won't be seen also, as long as they remain inside the vessel. For your information, the TSG is now attached to Earth's ISS. This is without their knowledge of course. As you all know, before this project commenced, we had already attained light speeds at the basic level of 186,000 miles per second, which has now been enhanced exponentially with the application of Zoll to new levels of millions of miles faster than light itself.'

Poiter cut in with a correction, saying:

'You mean a million times faster than light speed, not millions times faster?'

She quickly replied, leering deeply at him:

'My oh my. What is this, a physics lesson?'

She then wryed her nose at him and continued with the presentation.

'Bah! I have no time for minutiae.'

This time pushing the glass of water away instead of the usual sips as if her ex-lover had poisoned it with his interruption. With a slight drop to her voice, she went on to say:

'What we have just found out is that the Milky Way's solar radiation from all their stars is quite different to ours in the Long Grains. How different you may ask; basically their light passes through our objects as if it's not there and therefore cannot see it. Meaning they can't see us in anywhere in their galaxy. Making the need for Zoll 2 redundant.'

(From one moment of praising the usefulness of Zoll 2, to suddenly another moment rendering it as unnecessary – all in more or less the same breath.)

Feeling satisfied she had had a dig at G.U.T.S, she took one sip of water from the drinking glass and continued:

'At first I was overawed at the project's prospects, learning about this novel invisibility factor but later realised there is much more to the story. Zoll 2 is not so magical and necessary anymore.

Thus far I also don't feel the full impact of our combined efforts has worked its way through as yet.'

With her saying all this, there was twitching and uneasiness amongst some of G.U.T.S.'s representatives, who saw it as a put down by her belittling the usefulness of Zoll's invisibility. 'Jealousy perhaps,' whispered Ms Bampor to Marx.

Poiter stood up to make a comment to stop her possibly brushing him off:

'Our natural invisibility in Earth's atmosphere lasts for only 24 hours.

Once we go pass their blue line into their ionosphere our atoms start to ionise and within a single earth day we become visible again, as their radiation start reflecting off us instead of going through. That 24 hours coincidentally is what makes a day on planet Earth. Whilst that of Zoll lasts for 72 hours, making the fuel system very much useful for that extra time resource it would afford us,' he concluded. To some positive noises of admiration at his brilliant observation.

Annaz shifted her standing posture thrusting her right leg forward leaving the left leg behind carrying more of her body weight, feeling a bit uneasy. She had always admired Poiter's intelligence. If only he would have behaved more gentlemanly and faithful, what a man, she thought. But then again she is a fighter and good at hiding sentiments that would show her up to be weak.

She replied tersely:

'Sir, the result is the same. One day, three days, all invisibility will be gone soon enough. So why waste our limited resources fighting nature. I don't do superficial stuff. We simply don't need Zoll 2. All we need to do is temporarily dumb their monitoring systems and do what we have to do.'

The government had given the main presentation responsibility to Dr Annaz without consulting G.U.T.S., who were expecting Chibot doing the job.

Annaz is well known for her ultra-liberal views, openness and "take-no-prisoners" abrasive attitude.

'Since we are so similar with them our crew would have little or no problems humanising into Earthians. Well, not humanising really, for we are humans too. But you know what I mean – just a minor superficial adaptation. One that would involve taking only a few hours for our lungs to accustom itself into digesting oxygen unaided.'

She was deliberating fronting her comparatively better knowledge of biology over Poiter's own on physics.

He then asked:

'How do we know this for sure, recalling how two of my colleagues suffocated and died after inhaling their oxygen?'

She was quick to reply as always:

'Our crew on board the vessel had already used special filters breathing tiny doses of Earth's oxygen for about three hours, before their bodies became acclimatised to it. So it's obvious we can get used to breathing the gas.'

Mr Tallaz, the political advisor to the Pris Government, whispered into a colleague's ear: 'I think these two squaring up are using this platform for a personal vendetta. It had to be stopped.'

Nemad turned around quickly looking towards the new site manager Mr Strazna Tallin, Trillian Freeze's replacement. They had all along been wrongly thinking the government's own space project was way far behind G.U.T.S's, but how wrong they were.

The G.U.T.S.'s chief scientist has never been fond of Annaz, and once described her as very self-opinionated, rude, stuffy, petty and pretty alien to new ideas/technologies when they had worked together on previous joint projects. And now to be having her assuming control in this stuffy atmosphere was nerve racking for him.

He had on a couple of occasions before felt thoroughly done over by her behaviour in what he sees as her lack of protocol and respect.

And here we go again, he thought, but still managed to regain control of himself and continued to listen.

Dr Annaz feeling on the up was quick to notice Prof. Nemad's uneasiness and she liked it. Then carried on to say:

'Initially, the forwarding TSG crew will set up identities for a billion of us, the first batch, complete with residential homes and bank accounts on Earth. Then subsequently doing the same for the next sets of billion until we all got there.'

'A billion just on the first batch?' Tallin queried, in a voice deliberating clutching at his pearls (Expressing himself to be more shocked than he actually was).

She threw her chin at him and replied:

'Yes, a billion, why not? It's only seven-and-half eight billion of them and 15 billion of us. How many trips can we afford to take us all there if you're thinking of smaller batches?'

'My doubt is more about how many of us they can accommodate rather than the amounts of people we can transfer at any one time.'

'Look here.' She quickly cut in a smartening and impatient voice as if in a hurry. 'I hear all of their population can stand on one tiny island in the Caribbean sea. In fact, their entire populace can live comfortably in Texas State in the United States. Which is not even the largest country in their world.'

Poiter stood up and said:

'It just so happened their own scientists say not more than 9 to 10 billion of people is Earth's maximum capacity. It's not just about land areas. What about stuff like resources limitation, pollution causing ill-health and all that?'

Before she could respond, Dr Chibot intervened:

'This is neither a debate nor a time to display any geography knowledge if I may call it that. It's also not about the viability of planet Earth as to whether they can accommodate us or not. There are no alternatives. No second string really as we have no choice and they have no choice either. They just have to take us in.'

She was then asked to continue but appeared to becoming emotional with teary eyes, unable to handle this deep-seated feeling she still carries for her ex-lover. Coming face-to-face with him again and hearing his voice for the first time, at these meetings, since their high-profile love split only six months ago was getting too much for her. There was this sudden pang of desire for wanting him back. They had met at medical school and dated for four years but she has still not forgiven him for breaking her heart.

Chibot was quick to notice this and took over the presentation:

'Our capsule would hitch a ride onto planet Earth in the slipstream of one of their space mission vessels, Soyuz as it is called, benefitting from the towing effect. All the necessary arrangements and adjustments have been made to conditions travelling in their atmosphere. But since we can't be 100% sure nothing can go wrong, hitching a ride on the Soyuz's blind spot is our safety-first option, as we utilise their ship's power and protection as both an energy saver and heat shield respectively. Saving us a lot of our concerns on our craft's suitability in an atmosphere we've never experienced before.

It must also be noted they only look forwards not backwards - their vessels have no rear-view mirrors. Not even electronic ones like ours.'

Surprised at not having any of Annaz's habitual interruption, he half-turned sideways towards her, checking if she's alright before resuming his speech – she sat quietly for a bit, nursing her still broken heart.

'Even if they had mirrors, our space boats are so configured to their ship; it would seem as if both vehicles are one and the same.

But there is a problem we are working on at the moment: how to land without them seeing our men. We're considering detachment from Soyuz at some stage and land separately somewhere in the open. And for security reasons our crew are armed with smart guns firing magic bullets.'

'Magic what? Annaz enquired, seemingly coming back to life.

'Magic bullets,' he replied.

'For a moment there, I thought you said magic pellets,' she said.

'Well, bullets, pellets are all projectiles, just different configurations and effects. And as I was saying, these magic bullets are projectiles which can hit their targets with an eye-of-a-needle-precision shot. You can even be the universe's poorest shot but still hit your target using this ammunition technology,' Chibot concluded.

Mr Tallaz asked him:

'This invisible bullet, how does it work?'

'No, they are not invisible,' he hastily replied, turning towards his colleague. 'The invisible bullet works by firing energy rays. Magic bullets are different and very visible. And before you'd ask another question…'

Poiter whispered to Nemad:

'These government people are something else. I find them very rude and patronising.' Nemad replied: 'You can say that again.'

Dr Chibot continued, '…let me explain how magic bullets work. Before being fired the rifle's camera captures an image of the target and relays that to the bullet. That image is what directs it onto the target. It simply doesn't miss. Every movement by the target is followed by its image already locked into the bullet's sensors as it follows it around. In fact, one could deliberately turn the gun away from the target, after the image had been stored in the bullet, and still can't miss. (Dr Chibot missed out explaining this condition; there are certain angle limitations as to how far away the bullet can be turned away from the target and still manage to hit home). With the more expensive version, all you do is speak to your gun describing the target.'

After listening attentively, Tallin asked:

'How can we communicate with them and what if they demand our crew give them our location?'

'Oh Straz.'

He replied without mentioning his title though they were not on first name terms.

'What's wrong with some of G.U.T.S's people this morning? Don't you think we've covered those basic angles already? Come on man. OK, fine, let them come and have our location, and we can happily swap it for theirs.' He rudely laughed.

'Look, whilst they were attached to the I.S.S.,' Chibot continued.

'Our crew learned two languages they've been eavesdropping on. They deciphered one (Russian language) as common to all members though with different accents; a second (English) mainly spoken between others who sound and have similar facial resemblance and accents.'

The meeting was getting fraught with patronising insults and innuendos, Chibot then decided to conclude the day's events and asked if anyone would like to make any small contribution or any question to ask. The silent response he got was so still you can hear the clock ticking in the adjacent room.

Then Zoorax Brazh, was just scribbling down some notes and flipping his pen between his fingers when he suddenly raised his head and broke the silence saying:

'Why are we still using the TSG title anyway? I think it's a bit misleading.

Though the vessel appear to disappear it is still in a physical state. There was no sublimation process at all; the sudden vanishing euphoria blinded us all at the time into reaching that wrongful and hasty sublimation conclusion. Hard to change the initials at this far stage of progress I guess. Maybe we can just refer to it as Trans Stellar Galactic instead of the Trans Sublimation Glow. We'd be transporting ourselves first through our stellar and then our galactic spheres before reaching Earth – T.S.G.'

He then went back to continue the jottings on a pad.

Prof. Nemad sitting just behind, patted his deputy on the back, and said, 'Ah, I like that. Why not?' Brazh continued toying with the pen in between his fingers and smiled at him.

Most of them had burst out laughing out loud applauding Zoorax Brazh's talk, with the exception of Dr Annaz, who whispered to a female colleague:

'That's irrelevant anyway. All this talk about TSG and its magical disappearance is quite unnecessary. The success of the project is no longer riding on the invisibility aspects of Zoll. That's over and done with.'

The female colleague chuckled and replied: 'If I can recall alright we are as yet certain that their light doesn't reflect off our objects; it's not been proven out rightly. Meaning Zoll 2 can still be vital to the project, for now at least. On the matter of name change, I also think he's right to suggest changing the title since there is no sublimation process at all.'

Annaz grimaced at her, feeling disappointed not having the support she would have liked. She pulled her chair closer to the table as if she was trying to move away from the colleague.

Apparently, the government team's contempt for G.U.T.S. officials was punishment against the private firm for keeping the Zoll discovery away from the joint enterprise.

After this humiliating convention, Marx Zytan was more determined than ever to getting his hands on Zapia.

****

The plan to kidnap Zapia was not an easy task. She not only works for an arch rival but is also residing deep inside enemy territory. Marx wanted to contact her at all costs. If anyone would know where that missing money is or in what direction it had gone, then it would be Zapia. Nothing goes through the G.U.T.S establishment without her knowledge, he kept thinking.

Sitting alone at his office desk, bored and tired thinking about the money, he reached out for the Omole alcoholic drink in his bottom drawer. He then reclined further into the huge leathered chair, which almost swallowed his midget frame. (Anyone standing a couple of metres from the back of the chair would be forgiven for thinking it is vacant). He pulled his head backwards and swilled generously from the bottle, without using a glass, before slamming it on the foam carpet making a soft thud sound beside his feet.

'Get me Lucian on the phone.'

He ordered out to the new secretary who had only just replaced Zapia.

Lucian Starday was a semi-retired chief inspector of the police federation. He is 100, brown race, 5 feet 10 inches, round fleshy face, big eyes puffy cheeks and thick lips. Stocky built with excess belly fat which seems to be the first thing you'd notice of him, hanging loose over his trousers belt. He always has something in his mouth by way of food or a chewing gum. Some people say that stops him salivating, no one knows for sure. But what most people do know is Lucian's well-known bad habit of spewing spittle when he speaks. More so in anger. Even in meetings he'd be secretly sucking away on some sort of a treat like a toffee or even biscuit absorbing that loose saliva and saving his face. He has only one good eye. The other was gorged out by a teenager in a street fight he was trying to stop in his first few weeks as a cop. From that moment onwards, then sergeant Starday would avoid violent incidents as best as he could. He used to tie-up the dirty loose ends of Marx's shady deals; securing it from the prying eyes of the law. Even in retirement, he still enjoyed enough influence and control to continue remotely pulling the strings at his former Serious Investigation Notices (SIN) department.

At one time to even be able to access and delete police information that would have place one of his illicit contacts behind bars for a long time. The prosecuting attorney swore to his mother's life the evidence reported as missing by the criminal investigation team was still lodged on the court records until he tried printing copies when the whole system crashed and documents deleted. Losing out on materials vital to the case that was then aborted as a mistrial.

'Hi Star, how's the going with you skipper?' Marx barked out loudly.

Calling him Star increases your chances of getting something out of him. Any other name, even his real full ones would only get you so far.

'Doing fine I'd say. Thanks.'

'You still having to sponsor that mixed martial arts tournament?' Starday slurred, sounding like a toad choking on its snail dinner.

He's most likely to be chewing on something.

Marx could hardly hear him properly from a voice scarred by drug-fuelled smoking and heavy drinking, made worse by always having to have something in his mouth.

All he heard was the words "doing fine" and "tournament".

'You have to speak up; I can barely hear you. What's wrong with your voice?' Marx suddenly regretted asking that question.

Previously, Lucian Starday would always say pressure of the police job was taking a toll on his vocal cords but now that he's retired for the past five years he would only skip the embarrassing question. Having just realised his mistake Zytan quickly changed the subject, getting straight down to business:

'I want you to do a job on our ex-secretary. We'll meet next Saturday for 6 pm down at the Tunnel bar, Slope beach…' But before he could give further details, Star quickly spat out what was in his mouth and started off with apologies in a voice which had suddenly become quite clear enough:

'I'm now off that scene, Marx. No longer in the liquidation [Their code word for murder] space, sorry.'

Marx who had been relaxed in his customary nervous state started getting calmer in anger, then asked:

'Wait, wait, wait. Who said anything about killing?'

'Don't feel offended, Mr Zytan, the last thing I want now in my part-time work is to have blood on my hands.'

Marx was getting angrier and so more relaxed:

'Look here! Behave yourself. Had it been anyone else I would have hung up on you. My, oh my! Retirement must have drained your once steely balls empty of energy.'

He then took a couple of seconds not saying anything, restraining his annoyance, and also not wanting to be seen as pushing back too much on the ex-police chief; he needs his help now and always does. He then took two more stiff swills of that Omole drink halfway down the bottle.

'It helped agitate the nerves,' he whispered audibly under his breath.

'What was that?' Starday asked anxiously.

He knows Marx can still do him some considerable damage even though he is semi-retired from the force. I have to keep him sweet, just like I do the others, you know, nice them up at times, he thought.

There are two main issues about Starday that marked him out from some of his former colleagues who were themselves somehow embedded in the criminal underworld. Whilst personal weaknesses like greed for money, love lust or even political ideologies would lure some to work in underhand activities, for him it's more about being seen as important and earning respect. He hated homicide detective work and tries staying away from that as best as possible, focusing instead on financial crimes. All it took was a couple of times bungling on murder scene investigations for him to be transferred. The psychological effects of losing that eye was telling. What saved his police career was his second-to-none investigation skills. He was really good at it. So good in fact after his retirement the federation got him to set up a private consultancy auxiliary to the force, which he still operated and continued giving him access to police files.

'Are you still there?' He asked again as Marx was about to hang up on him. But he won't do that, not only for Starday's brain power but also aware the ex-copper now knows he is up to no good with Zapia. After cautioning himself, he narrated the story of the missing funds and Zapia's defection and said he only wanted to ask her a few questions, that's all.

'Phew! That's fine,' as he blew out his cheeks. 'No worries!' He then crossed his right hand across his chest indicating relief.

'You should have said so earlier, you had me worrying there, Marx. Look here, no qualms. I'll meet you at the Slope beach front bar at 7 pm next Wednesday, OK?' He was so much happy murder wasn't involved he suggested the time and date to meet, if only to show enthusiasm.

'Yes, OK. See you then,' Marx replied, and they both hung up.

Marx Zytan then drained the last drop of the Omole liquor into his mouth and promised himself to help see Prof. Nemad Scyzpr on his upcoming appeal. More so now that Zapia is almost in the bag. I may not really like the guy but helping him clear his name would also mean narrowing the investigation to just one person.

(Slope beach got its name from its physical appearance: it seems to be on a gentle gradient downwards to where the sea gets lost into the horizon. Defying science and making a mockery of the geographical term: sea level. Tourists flock there to see the landscape wonder. But once you started moving towards the horizon, there is no slope but if you look back towards where you started from, there is one behind you. It's a topographical illusion science still hasn't explained. Some say it's to do with the sloping landscape, others disagree. Slope beach will always be a slope beach).

****

After Marx and Bampor had seen Nemad's video evidence at his residence they supported his second appeal at the Employment Tribunal based on that fresh evidence.

The five-person panel couldn't reach a verdict – a split conclusion; three supporting the chief scientist and two against. To reconcile the divide, a forensic search was recommended to prove if there was actually an imposter as Prof. Nemad is claiming, or it was just him committing the crimes all along. Alas, there was further bad news for the science man: finger prints belonging to him was found at all the places shown on the office CCTVs the days he claimed to have been drugged and sleeping on his home sofa. The final part of the hearing was set for the following week.

Nemad was resting at his home having a phone conversation with his daughter who temporarily resides with her maternal grandparents.

'Bye for now,' he tells her.

'OK, papa. See you later and please be strong.'

Her words emboldened him. He had briefed her about his office problems before anyone else will, and she was supportive. A man about to resign to his apparently doomed fate has suddenly sprung back to life with just the simple sentence: 'OK papa. See you later and please be strong'. I have to be strong at least for her, he promised himself.

Moments before the phone call, he had heard rumours of the fingerprint finds matching his and had already given up as a result.

In a bit of a joyous mood, for the first time in his life he went to the local shop and bought a bottle of Mampama white wine. He hardly drinks alcohol and would only do so occasional when out with friends or at some parties. He got home and was about to crack open the bottle when he heard his front door bell ring.

Damn, who could this be by this time of the night, he wondered, as he pulled back the window curtains and peeped into the inky darkness of the night and saw Prysten Poiter's flying car hovering on his drive way. It was only 9 pm but for Nemad that was a late time for visiting.

What does he want? Why wouldn't he let me know he was coming? Sympathies is for the office and I need to be in a quiet place right now and reflect on my misfortune, he kept thinking as the bell rang again this time for a longer period than before, after a bit of delay.

As soon as he opened the door, Poiter walked past him into the house as if he wasn't standing there, left with a quizzing look on his face.

'We have to talk,' Dr Poiter said, still ignoring the quizzing look on Nemad's face.

Before he could say anything, his visitor continued: 'I have reasons to believe someone impersonated you at the office and I don't care what other people think.'

'What are you on about?' he managed to ask. Knowing too well his colleague is not one for silly or idle talk, and very well respected for his polished manners.

Though not so polished tonight coming to my house without notification, he thought.

As if he had read the professor's mind, Poiter said: 'I called your phone couple of times, it was switched off apparently.'

Nemad with shoulders dropped and looking poorly, replied: 'Yes, I turned it off after chatting with Baisa.'

'We have to start looking at the possibilities someone acted as you at the office during that period when you were supposedly off sick. When you told us you were off sick,' Prysten Poiter said as he was slacking his neck tie.

Nemad with a surprise look on his face asked him: 'You don't believe I was off sick then?'

'No! It's not that I don't believe you,' Poiter said, as he walked further into the corridor in a house he's very familiar with. 'Your video evidence appears to support your claim. I am only speaking from the law point of view and have to be open-minded.

Though I must say the probable impostor was behaving quite oddly you know; characteristics out of tune with your good old self. Well at least as I know it,' the senior scientist said with a smile.

'And I have some little clues.'

Nemad was quite sure he wasn't the one who did all those sexual assaults and stuff, so he chose to listen.

Closing the door behind him he quipped:

'And I hope you're not trying a pull a prank on me for the one I did on your birthday?' With a weak smile on his face.

'No, damn not, no such thing. This is not the time!'

'Now that you've mentioned the 'P' word, some people think you committed those crimes as a prank that went wrong. Look, prof., I'm here to help you out.'

No sooner he had said that, Nemad felt a bit more relaxed and offered a drink which his visitor declined and said:

'We have serious issues at hand to sort out. The drink will wait for later.'

Dr Prysten Poiter had a degree from one of Pris's leading law schools but later went on to a science career he had always dreamed of as a boy. He didn't know his father well, a well-known legal practitioner who passed away when the lad was only four years old. As a sign of respect and honour, he initially followed the old man's career after he was told his late dad used to say the young Prysten would grow up to become a top barrister.

'Please take a seat while I turn off the tap. I was running a bath before you came by. I'll be back in a short mo [moment].'

Whilst in his bathroom, Nemad started thinking how helpful his colleague has always been to other staff members. He recalled one time he was giving him a lift home when his car got caught in a yellow box at the traffic lights of a busy road junction. The city traffic authority sent him penalty fines which his colleague told he would defend against. Just as promised, Poiter replied as a defence witness, detailing the event when two other vehicles went through red lights from the left side of the road, forcing Nemad to stop in the yellow box even though the lights ahead of him were green. He asked for the prosecution to charge the offending drivers with traffic contravention and also being the proximate cause of Nemad's breach. The traffic body simply dropped the charges against Nemad.

On another occasion, Poiter was driving Trillian's pregnant sister home when her water broke in his car. It would have taken them at least ten minutes in that rush hour traffic getting to the hospital. He just changed course putting the car into reverse and backing up through a one-way road to the clinic in less than two minutes. CCTV images captured the incident and sent him a penalty charge. The senior scientist argued it was no offense to reverse on a single-traffic carriageway. That charge was also dropped.

Now he is here to help me, I better grab the chance, Nemad thought. From the bathroom he went to the kitchen where he grabbed some honey seeds and creamy leaves cakes, available only on Zist, some of which he offered to his guest.

Prysten Poiter then briefed him on his suspicions of the office intruder:

'The guy even asked us for Marx's and Bampor's phone numbers claiming he had misplaced his phone. Another time he couldn't recall the date of that Zoll discovery incident. This is so much unlike you.'

Most people at G.U.T.S. knew quite well about Prof. Nemad's legendary memory. At the tender age of two, toddler Nemad memorised his parent's home and office land lines and mobile phone numbers up to this day, even though the landlines lasted for only three months when they moved into another county. He learned the full periodic table of elements and the multiplication tables [2 to 15] aged only four. So there is not a chance in hell the prof would ask the questions the imposter did.

'What chances have I got given that the verdict will be out in a few days, a bit too late, isn't it?' He then took a bite of the cake.

'And from what I've heard so far they are going to find me wanting yet again.'

Poiter got up from his chair and lowered his head towards Nemad like a parent does when castigating a child, and said:

'When he accidental cut himself with that broken beaker, he insisted on changing the whole carpet that had his blood stain in it, even though it was thoroughly cleaned with chemicals. Was he trying to hide something?'

Nemad staring into the wall as if he was blind, replied:

'That sucker even had my fingerprints forged. Reason why I could be convicted again next week.'

Poiter picked up his phone , keys and a couple of biscuits from the plate on the stool next to the chair where he was sitting, stood up and said:

'So long Pal. See you at the sitting where I'll defend you to the helter.'

After he had left, Nemad came to the window staring at his car flying away with the rear red lights dimming into the distance. Left all alone again, he started thinking: What a man! What a friend! What a colleague! They don't come that many. He then went in for a shower instead of having that long soaking in the bath he had been yearning for long before Poiter's visit.

His thoughts were: I now have the soaking confidence I needed; first it was talking to my daughter, then to my good friend and colleague.

He was lying in bed trying to take his mind off the impending case, thinking of Poiter's inventiveness, not only on legal matters but scientific ones as well:

Though his colleague was not the first to say planets are not round as we see them but he was the first to give a particular reason for them being seen as such, explaining they are mostly oblong in shape but we see them as circular because of the spinning effect. Whereby as a planetary body rotates, its edges seem to appear in every angle at the same time, making the objects visibly round in shape, rather like the blades of a fan in motion.

Poiter's other observation is that the universe is not expanding as we think it is, rather it appears to do so with the constant appearance of light reaching us. He gave an example of an observer walking in a big open field with a torch in hand, in complete darkness. As he moves forward, he'd discover more ground coming under the focus of his torchlight. Saying the more light reaches us from ever-increasing distant stars, the more we see of the fixed universe appearing to be getting bigger. Which is similar to the dark field already having a fixed size. Poiter had made public this observation on social media a year before it appeared in a national newspaper by someone else. He doesn't know if the person copied him or not.

Nemad then thought, for every Zapia in this world of ours there is also a Porter, before he fell asleep soundly. Something he hasn't done for a long time.

****

Marx unexpectedly saw Starday standing with his back turned towards him at the entrance to the Sun Fries bar and restaurant. This was just four days before they were supposed to meet at the Tunnel bar on Slope beach, to discuss the possible kidnapping of Zapia. The Sun Fries bar, where every meal is cooked by solar energy, sits on the 12th floor of the newly-constructed Blue Earth building, Blue Riverside, in the more exclusive side of Rasnul in greater Prisia.

Always cladding himself in different shades of brown: the hats and trench coats tend to give away his profession as a detective. It seems like a cultural custom on Zist for most its citizen to be seen dressing in matching colours.

Marx sneakily tiptoed towards Starday's back, like a thief in the night, and wrapped his hands over his eyes.

'Who is this?' the ex-cop woofed anxiously as he grabbed and peeled off the small hands covering his face.

He then turned around. 'Ah, it's you, Marx. I thought it was one of my nephews pulling a surprise prank on me.'

Zytan responded mockingly: 'Never mind your nephew. What are you doing here? I thought now that you're semi-retired this sort of place would not be to your liking – if I can put it that way?'

The ex-copper found it deeply offensive, he paused, just stared at Marx and was about to walk away when Zytan gently grabbed at his arm offering apologies saying he was only trying to lighten the mood.

'I may be short of a few bob or two, Marx, but I can still pull my way around any of these so-called exclusive joints.

If you'd excuse me I am here on an official basis to meet a client of mine,' he said, while he wrestled his arm free.

Marx became more apologetic:

'Come on, Star, can't you take a joke. Where is all that sense of humour you're so well known for.

Look. Sit down and let's have something to eat, eh?'

Being called 'Star', and the food offer softened him up a bit.

He replied: 'OK, just a short meal and nothing more.'

Both men went quiet for a moment as they settle down at a nearby table. Marx ordered cured hippo steak coated with goose fat for tenderness, stone-cooked slowly with cassava chips. Whilst Lucian was forking delicacies of shark-penis soup and a tongue-of-whale, both seasoned with volcanic ash salt served with hot cheese made from giraffe milk.

When Marx said:

'Pulling a kidnap in Bria is risky, I'd rather you use your influence at the Bria metropolitan police to forge a case against Zapia so she will be arrested and deported back to Pris.'

Starday, with the metaphorical steam spewing out of his ears, dropped the cutlery on the table in a loud clang as if they were burning hot. Drawing the attention of some other diners. The agitation ruffled and displaced his toupee making it look a bird's nest perching on his head.

'Are you out of your mind?' He yelled, visibly angry. He has a nasty habit of involuntarily spitting bits of saliva whenever he is speaking in anger.

'We're talking here not only about a completely different country but a deadly rival at that.' With both hands folded into fists resting on the table, he continued the ranting.

'There are more chances of a New York Mafia boss getting a retired Russian police chief to help set up a false arrest warrant for a deportation order on former American turncoat intelligence officer John Snowdon.'

Marx listening attentively will every now and then wipe off the spits flying in his face. All that wasting of saliva had left a sudden dryness in Starday's throat. Badly wanting to moisten his vocal chords he took a sip from the white Poyo wine. Though it smelt like stale piss, what with all the anger and all that, he forced it down anyway. Leaving a bad aftertaste in his mouth 'That's way, way beyond me,' he bellowed. As he slammed his fists on the table, rattling the empty glasses, still staring Marx in the eye.

'Even our security services wouldn't task me to do such an impossible job,' he concluded.

'Hey! hey! What's all this hysteria, Lucian? I thought you'd stop but you kept on going.

Don't tell me you can't draw on your past experience and contacts working with Intermob (The underworld's equivalent of Interpol)?' Marx asked.

Starday ignored him and seemed to have given up on the food when he ripped the towel off his chest that was serving like baby's bib.

But he still remain seated waiting for some reaction from Zytan as if he was scared to just get up and leave. He was in a way asking for permission to do so. Marx's inaction scared him a bit, so he dropped down his voice sounding more conciliatory:

'Look man, I know you're an ambitious bloke, probably reason why you're so rich but this is way beyond my arm's length. Not even at the height of my working days. Sorry.'

A waitress who had brought them more drinks saw the drama and said:

'Here are your drinks, sir. Can I be of further help.'

She had a smug smile on her face that embarrassed Starday. Both men thought she was making fun of their public spat and didn't reply. It was Marx who simply waved her away.

She left holding her hand to her face covering her mouth.

One thing Marx Zytan knows about Starday is he is not so much interested in money or fame. Make him feel wanted and important is all that he yearn for.

'OK, Starday, no worries.' Deliberately not calling him Star this time.

'I can see if someone else bigger over there can help. Only need to pull a few strings from the big fishes, that's all.'

The ex-police chief straightened up, pulling himself upright in the chair. One thing he wouldn't tolerate is disrespect and Marx knows this.

You have to give it to the rouge billionaire for trying to outsmart an outsmarting former detective. Though failing the trials, Marx Zytan, having gone through some training as a potential spy had endowed him in the art of debate. Part of which is referred to as "Oiling" in some of planet Earth's top educational institutions like Oxbridge.

You can see the blood pressure rushing into the former police chief's face, expressing a sullen mood. Without further ado, he started explaining his old knowledge of the Bria operatives and how different they were from Prisian's. Marx was listening attentively but pretending not doing so. The ex-copper would go deeper and deeper trying to get some more reaction for his efforts but to no avail. He then became agitated as Marx was looking away, saying something about the swans on the river.

'These two will date for life. Even if one partner dies the other would hesitate finding a new mate. They are better than us in that regard.'

Starday didn't reply to that effect, so wanting for more of Marx's recognition, he started revealing some more police secrets on Bria.

Marx Zytan now beginning to get what he was aiming for, getting the cop to talk and hopeful he would later act on his behalf, asking one or two odd questions while still looking away from Starday as if he had little or no interest.

By allowing himself to become more irritated and annoyed on such a petty issue, Starday was also letting himself being used by Marx. Despite knowing this basic trick as an ex-cop, his nature of wanting to be taken seriously at all times is now his own undoing. It's like a chronic alcoholic dying of liver disease but won't stop drinking.

After chatting for a while, Starday realising he's not getting anywhere, finally agreed on the original "Search and Grab Squad" the S.A.G.S plot, as he called it. To kidnap Zapia if he couldn't secure a deportation order.

They also agreed to still go ahead with the following week's meeting at the Tunnel bar, Slope beach – 'For far more important issues,' Marx had said.

The ex-police chief thought he had won by sticking to the kidnapping. Zytan thought he won, by getting the kidnapping plot he had always wanted and only using the near-impossible Bria police issue as a smoke screen to pull that side of the trick. The whole trick was getting Starday revealing to him vital information secrets, some of which the ex-cop had told him in the past he had no knowledge of. Marx exhaled air heartily from his lungs, feeling proud of himself.

Starday suddenly realised he had just been conned. He cursed in his thoughts and promised himself to settle scores with Marx for using him. And it was for that reason he still wanted to go ahead meeting with him at the Tunnel bar in a few days' time.

'We still meeting for next week, are we?' he checked.

'Yes, of course, we are,' answered Marx. Who then thought, why would we still be meeting again after today's nasty event?

I answered to him, 'Yes we are.' Only to make an effort to end our meeting amicably after our argument. Anyway, I'd come with new plans if need be Mr ex-police chief, Marx Zytan kept thinking.

So they ended the bitter encounter with each man having in his thoughts plans to outdo the other in their next meeting. They didn't have to say it out loud, it was all buried in their minds.

5

Since emigrating to Bria and working for V.I.M., Zapia's lifestyle has changed remarkably. Once a creature of habit; a slave to time and precision, was now living an irregular lifestyle, mostly controlled by others. Once before, Trillian reckoned he would time his own daily schedules around Zapia's habits. 'I try to synchronise my routine with hers,' he was once reported to have said. The most significant change in her new life was the end of a singleton relationship status, and in with a new companion. One who in every way is snooping on her without her knowledge. They shop, eat, drink, sleep and live together in an exclusive gated community where armed guards patrol the premises.

'Jeeze, Don (Full name Donno),when you told us she lives in a secured property I didn't know it was this secure.'

'This could be one hell of a job,' moaned Hifray, who was one of the three-man snatch team sent on the mission, as they took cover behind some trees while scanning the part of the compound wall they'll have to scale over.

They have been sent over by Starday's shadowy contact in Bria, a Mr Boy Daymier; an infamous criminal mastermind.

Hifray's mate Donno replied:

'Secured but not that secured. We could still burst it.'

Hifray was still not convinced:

'Now you're talking in riddles as usual. It's either secured or not. No halfway measure,' as they crawled to the rear side of the fence away from the road's views.

Donno, the squad leader, tossed the grapnel rope high over his shoulder to the top of the wall. The grappling hook got hold on his first attempt.

'Well done, mate. All in one go.'

Said Baz, the third member of the group.

Hifray didn't respond. All three got on top of the fence.

Donno was about to lead and jump down into the yard when they came under heavy machine gunfire:

Rattaaa rataaaaaa. Bullets flying around them raatttaaaaaa raaattaaa.

They jumped down, aborting the raid to seek cover behind the trees again as more bullets rain in, showering them with bits of grass and dust.

'I should have never trusted you in the first place,' whinged Hifray, whilst leering angrily at Donno.

'This is the third time in as many weeks you're getting us into trouble with your recklessness.'

Donno didn't response as he kept surveying the fence with his field glasses.

Hifray not having any response from Donno upped his anger:

'You should have made better plans. I'll be the first to report you to Boy Daymier. This is the last time you'll ever lead me on a suicide mission.' That was enough to trigger a response from Donno. Turning his head backwards looking at his companion, he said:

'Look here, mate, I don't give a cockroach's greasy arse about your opinions. We are here on a job and having a little setback should not in any way scupper our plans. Alright? You either stick with me or you can just leave right now. The choice is yours.'

Hifray was now furious at what he sees as Donno's arrogance and once again not admitting his mistakes.

'A little setback, you call it? Damn, you're something else. You couldn't lead cub scouts in a playground parade. We almost got killed.'

Baz, the quieter man among the lot, was getting fed up with the argument.

'Stop all the squabbling you two. We're…'

He couldn't finish his sentence; shocked to bits seeing the entrance gate to the building swung wide open with two armed guards gingerly coming out searching for them.

'It seems as if they thought they had us hit in that salvo of bullet shots and now they are out to grab the spoils.'

Said Donno, as he took aim, opened fire with his submachine assault rifle (With silencer attached) knocking them to the ground The male guard caught in the head, the female in her chest, both killed instantly.

'Now we go in,' he said.

As they rushed towards the gates.

Hifray wanted to protest but there was no time for that, he just followed his companions.

He had neither forgiven nor forgotten the way Donno got the team leader job after Hifray's cousin, Maz Muthith a.k.a. the dazzler (Nickname for his love of flashy jewellery), who was then the leader, died in a raid by the anti-narcotics agency. Hifray still believes Donno is a mole who works for the authorities, and it was he who guided the drugs squad's efforts that day. How come Don was the only one away from home that fateful morning, he would at times ask of his other mates, who would choose not to respond. Also how come he is living above the wages we get: the car, the holidays, all of which he claimed was coming from his girlfriend; a retired senior police officer's daughter of all people?

A few minutes later, they made another attempt. This time foolishly crawling through the opened gates. No sooner they were spreading out to the particular house they've been told Zapia lived, heavier gun shots rained in on them from the front wall's parapet. Concrete plaster and dust flying around blurring their vision. They can't see their targets and began firing blindly around which further gave away their positions to the guards.

'I'll get you for this someday. And it's a promise.' Hifray consoled himself of Donno, as they came under more fire.

A couple more sentries with heavy weapons emerged from the front and side walls and had the kidnapping gang clawed in a pincer grip. Donno and Baz were peppered with bullets, killed on the spot, while the badly-wounded Hifray was captured alive.

Normally, the security guards at this wealthy estate would use magic bullets on their smart weapons, to help maintain peace and quiet as only those involved in the shootout would be aware of it. But on this occasion, the shooting incident occurred at the sentry point, a bit far away from the residences. That was the reason why conventional gunfire – though some with silencers – was used. Not a single resident was aware of all the troubles.

Before sending his men in, Boy Daymier wasn't aware there was a new resident in the gated community which had increased the security regime five folds. A young lady from a very wealthy family had fallen for a humble entertainer she had met in a public show, guy from a far different cultural background, whom she holed up in one of the luxurious houses. She would visit him every now and then whilst still living with her very protective parents.

(An equivalence of this episode on planet Earth would read like a young rich Arab princess falling for a Latin American [flamenco etc] dancer she had met at the Rio carnival in Brazil)

She had joined him dancing in the streets, and the rest as they say, is history. A couple of times her father offered to pay him off, and when he refused, on her insistence, he was planning to kill him. Her papa couldn't go through with it after she vowed to commit suicide so she would continue love with him in the afterlife if he was murdered. The old man got scared. He not only spared his life but also rented him the expensive pad, as long as they don't get married, and both lovers agreed to the deal.

Having failed to get Zapia, Marx Zytan turned his attention to a much bigger problem; to work ways around mitigating the failure to reproduce Zoll 2.

At G.U.T.S., every effort was made to repeat the trick. They summoned all the scientists who had been part of the experimenting process since Zoll was firstly discovered and found nothing amiss but they still failed to get the result.

Word quickly spread out about the scientific alchemy, reported as only a one-off magic wonder.

One baffled public official, some of whom in preparation for the earth-bound move were becoming more familiarised with the planet's literature, remarked: 'This appears to be a one-trick pony alright as much as it is also single-legged.'

Some of these commentators weren't aware the project had been slightly altered to a public-private partnership, renamed, ***Zoom or Doom*** and were calling for the second abortion of H2O-Earth, referring it by its former title. Most were sceptics Marx had always regarded as enemies who wanted to see him fail. They hated his dominant influence over most of the other stakeholders. An influence that was waning until the recent Zoll discoveries gave it enviable shots in the arm. But now that the most influential second stage of the project can't be repeated, he began to panic about his investments and feeling vulnerable to the circling vultures.

With all the uncertainties floating around, word reached the Government team on the Zoll 2 reproduction failure. Though the informant told them G.U.T.S.'s officials were planning to make that announcement at the forthcoming second convention (One classified as national emergency), Chibot and Annaz were angry at what they both regarded as yet another secret being held from the joint operation.

'We gave them that side of the partnership to do with the Zoll engineering while we tidy up the finance ends, but sadly they've fluffed it and not even bother reporting the matter to the joint group,' Chibot complained. 'I can't wait to see their faces in the next meeting.'

Prof. Nemad refused attending.

"I can't stand anymore of that Annaz woman," he was reported to have said and didn't show up. Dr Annaz was dressed in a white blouse, charcoal grey tight-fitting blazer and matching pencil skirt. She was a bit taller that day in killer heels. When the acid-tongued government personnel noticed Nemad was absent, she began throwing bards at his current troubles, yapping out loud enough for all attending to hear:

'Ah! So the professor is not here today?' Holding her head in her hands as if in shock.

'What a shame. You have to feel sorry for the poor fella having to go through a third tribunal hearing.'

No one responded. To make sure the captive audience knew it was the prof. who has been accused of wrong doing, she proceeded to say:

'Hope this time his defence sticks and he gets an acquittal.'

Prysten Poiter was very annoyed at her behaviour; firstly, he fished out a pencil from his jacket pocket and started using it as a chin-scratcher, in frustration of not knowing where to start.

He then cleared his throat loudly, indicating disapproval and drawing attention to himself, before saying:

'It's obvious there is some misunderstanding and I'd stake my name on Prof. Nemad undoubtedly winning the case…'

She jumped in before he could complete the sentence and said:

'Well, we don't know that. We…' But he also jumped back in not letting her continue abusing Nemad in public.

Raising his voice a bit : 'Professor Nemad is someone I've known for over a decade. He's honest and faithful to…'

Only for her to pile in obstructing him again as they both jostled for control of the air waves.

She then got so irate, unconsciously pulling her hair out:

'You can't talk over me sir. How sad such words coming from you of all people. I won't in the slightest expect you to know anything about faithfulness or should I say unfaithfulness.

With all the problems going on at your end you get the impression the government needs to have more of a hands-on approach to this joint project if it were to succeed.'

Poiter can't even get a word in. He was drowning in her onslaught.

'Trust,' as she continued the verbal attacks, 'is of the essence and it could be very much an issue here.'

There were loud sharp intakes of breath from the audience with almost every word she uttered in the ongoing bedlam.

Bad enough for Dr Chibot to gently, but loudly, slammed the table top with his fist and said with emphasis:

'Unfortunately, we haven't got the right Quorum attending today.'

Glancing at his wristwatch.

'It is time we call it off. According to article 6 of the company's charter, such a meeting should become invalid. More so when an important issue is at hand – a national emergency at that.'

This was just a legal escape technicality to postpone or delay conventions on which matters are found to be problematic – when things are not going right basically. So it was referred to another sitting, one in which Prof. Nemad was convinced to attend, and so he did.

At the rescheduled event, you can sense the pulse-racing tension hanging in the air. Once you've got inside the building you feel immersed in this unpredictable situation. Previous Pris public/private partnerships between G.U.T.S. and some government departments had at times become fraught with rivalries and conflicted interests, mostly in which the private firm had accused its public partners of neglect. A strained relationship that had worsened over the years, raising tensions in almost every collaboration they've managed. Dr Annaz's recent behaviour, partly stemmed from her grievances against Dr Poiter, hadn't helped.

Some of G.U.T.S's stakeholders, who weren't consulted on the public/private partnership, felt not only betrayed by that but also angry having heard about Annaz's antics.

They had become determined and very supportive of Prof. Nemad. It was they who convinced him to appear this time and wowed to attend also. Which they did in good numbers. A large attendance made possible with the convention being held on a much bigger premises, giving access to more people and open to all the stakeholders.

On the G.U.T.S's side: Marx Zytan, all dressed in black and smeared in his strong signature aftershave, was accompanied by his loyal furry friend. He had dusted down his latest biggest sword, the only one with a polished pure silver handle, for the occasion, which he had tied to his waist. Prof Nemad showed up in casuals; open neck sky-blue shirt with matching braces and no ties. Wearing black trousers and black ankle boots, Dr Poiter was in smart casuals, sitting next to the professor, would every now and then be seen scanning the conference hall as people kept pouring in. Both men wore poker-faced expression throughout the day. Ms Bampor, like her boss, was in black too, ditching her favourite green for a change.

The whole environment played out like a battle preparedness scenery between two warring sides rather than a collaborative meeting between partners.

On the Government side, only Dr Annaz wore black. She was looking very much combative than ever before. Her colleagues were dressed in the usual official attires. Most of whom were making conciliatory efforts approaching G.U.T.S. staff; exchanging pleasantries, having informal chats, before the formal meeting was to begin. Apparently, all in an effort to distil the poisonous atmosphere created by their deputy chief scientific adviser at the last meeting.

The built-up tension started dying down once Dr Chibot took full control this time around, and gave a resounding speech. The 180-year-old should have long been retired but no suitable replacement was at hand, and having the controversial Dr Annaz at the helm didn't seem to appeal to anyone.

A unanimous decision was reached to continue on with the project even though the second stage of Zoll was no longer available.

'We have to continue marching on regardless, and be realistic lowering our sights to practicalities and forget about that magical vanishing nonsense. I never once believed in it anyway.'

He then puffed up his cheeks and audibly blew out air from his mouth as if he was trying to get rid of the vanishing Zoll talk.

'We all know it's a universally acknowledged fact our planet will soon be dead, so we have to move out soonest,' he concluded.

Only for Mr Tallaz, the political advisor to the Pris Government, to come in saying:

'But without the invisibility cover, Earthians will see our spacecraft and probably try to attack it.'

You can see the effort Chibot was making to suppress laughter; bowing his head down, hiding his facial expression with tears misting his eyes. He really found it funny.

He gathered himself and managed to say:

'They, on Earth, attack us?'

'Please don't make me laugh. There should be more to you than asking such a silly question. Sorry, I don't mean to be rude but these people are way, way, way behind us in all matters of life. They just won't be able to.'

(It's like someone on Earth today expressing concerns about Neanderthals of some 40,000 years ago attacking an American aircraft carrier. On this, one can readily sympathise with Chibot).

He took out an handkerchief then mopping his eyes.

'I even understand they are going through a corona viral pandemic; a similar, if not identical, medical issue our ancestors suffered about four thousand years ago. And before you'd ask, we've found ways around that problem; each and every one of us will be taking three different types of medication before we got there.'

He then went on to detail the Government's plans that were previously put together without so much as consulting with G.U.T.S.

Poiter, Nemad and the rest of their colleagues just sat there throughout most of the conference, listening as if they were nothing more than observers, as the Government team were picking praise for all the work done so far.

'Last week we sent our operational plans to G.U.T.S. [with some arm twisting done since Marx's fund is unaccounted for and the State Government is bearing nearly all the costs] which they have approved. It's the same plan as detailed in the last meeting. The only differences now are two fresh issues:

[1] Now that we've forced ourselves to abandon Zoll's vanishing act, we would have to dummy all of planet Earth's satellites and land-based observation systems into seeing everything else as normal except for our ships and crew which they won't see at all.

[2] With one or two trips we'd transfer fifteen billion Zistrians earth-side (There was a loud sighing chorus from the audience at the huge figure). Yes, all

15 billion of us. Far more than the 15 trips with a billion people a piece Dr Annaz was trying to say the last time.'

He then turned backwards to face Dr Annaz who had suddenly called his attention, whispering something to him in protest against his reference to her on the number of flights and passengers needed. She thought it made her look incompetent. He simply waved her away and turned towards facing the microphone again:

'We'll build mega-subterranean cities in self-contained, super-ventilated underground scrapers all over planet Earth, to house us all. As it will happen: three billion Zistians to the Sahara desert; another three billion to the Australian outback, one billion the Gobi desert, three-and-half billion the Russian steppes, one billion each in north America and south America, two-and-half-billion in Antarctica. All living underground,' Dr Chibot added.

Nemad was going to say something before Chibot rudely pretended as if he hadn't noticed his efforts, and continued:

'Our planet is just a couple of thousand kilometres bigger than Earth – so we are similar in sizes. Though with vast population differences, ours doubling theirs. Which means they are not resourceful enough, wasting valuable spaces.

And further to what Dr Annaz mentioned at the last meeting…'

She can be seen twitching in her seat when her name was mentioned again.

'All of humanity on Earth can fit into that American city. What was the name again,?' Turning around towards Annaz.

Annaz and Tallaz both answered in chorus: 'Texas; it's a State not a city.'

'That's it,' replied Chibot. 'And not only Texis…'

'Texaas,' Annaz corrected him, this time putting emphasis on the pronunciation causing him to pause.

'OK I got it. They can all fit into that state. And it's not even the largest in the American union. Also not to mention the entire country is not the largest on Earth,' he said.

It was easy to see why Poiter and Nemad were having reservations about the blue planet's resource capability to more than double its population basically overnight, accommodating all of the yellow planet's inhabitants.

Something which Poiter himself had raised previously.

'I need to conclude this briefing. Details of the entire project will be sent to you all. One thing for sure, we won't be using anything like their tunnel boring machines – boring by mechanics, boring by nature. My, oh My, technology our ancestors were using couple of thousand years ago. An identical copy of the ones they now use on Earth is in our national history museum. Even our laser technique drilling tunnels and stuff is now becoming obsolete in our world.'

As he started folding some of the scripts, he had been reading from and placing them away into a folder. (He hates reading from electronic devises, unlike Dr Annaz who reads from notes literally appearing on any hard surface she would choose by simply placing a square inch electronic cell on . Even at times reading from words data suspending in the air coming from the cell. Out of this world technology).

'OK, enough mocking of our potential hosts. Let's show them some respect and gratitude. Please don't ask how we'd dispose of the spoils and all that, which is no worry. None of their monitoring systems will be able to see what we do anyway. We can either choose to empty it into their oceans or dump it in deep space. We'll do whatever we like, and at will.'

As if to show some measure of intelligence, Maila asked:

'It would be good to know what we are going to do with all that soil dug up from underneath?'

'He probably didn't hear me. We will dump it all in deep space.' He chuckled and turned sideways facing Tallaz, who chuckled too. As he always does to appease him. The political adviser had long become the science man's puppet, and they both knew it. Even forcing himself laughing at his jokes at times when no one else does.

'You never know the earth spoils might accrete and form an asteroid or mini-planet even,' quipped Tallaz who meant it as a joke but Chibot was impressed enough to swipe another look at him.

This time with a little frown on his face as if to express surprise at the Government political adviser's clever educational guess.

****

Marx got home from the second Zoom or Doom convention a bit satisfied the project is still on, having been wondering if the failure to reproduce Zoll's second stage would have aborted the entire programme.

He then thought, oh it's gym time in the next few minutes. He snatched a juice drink from the fridge, poured himself a tumbler full, pulled a chair by the dining table and started reading the briefs from the meeting. No need to go through all this stuff, I'll leave it with Bampor, he thought.

He then grabbed the car keys and was about to head off to the gymnasium when his adopted son Maila walked up to him:

'Dad, we have to talk.'

Not wanting to be bothered with any idle chatter, he replied:

'That will have to wait, son. I'm off to do some physical exercises. Say over roast dinner on Sunday perhaps, then we'd talk.'

Maila had for days been lost in deep intrusive thoughts: his effort to sabotage the company might have stopped the novel fuel progressing into phase two. He didn't seem to realise or recall that Zoll 2 only occurred after he had tampered with it, and not before. Had he not done what he did, trying to sabotage the new hydrocarbon, there wouldn't have been anything like the vanishing effect. But he wasn't aware of all this. At least that's what he showed.

He could barely sleep at night, thinking the project had the vanishing capability all along until he intentionally messed it up. He wouldn't tell anyone about his behaviour, not even his girlfriend and other close friends. He would only think how good his adopted father had been to him; among other things giving him that sheltered job he wasn't even qualified for. And now to think he would have ruined his old man's investment made him shuddered in shame.

A week or so later, he decided to spill the secret to Marx Zytan himself, come what may.

'It's urgent and serious,' said the young man to his dad.

'Look here, as I said, this is not a good time.'

As he got up, put the papers away, took one last gulp of the drink, emptying the glass tumbler, then grabbed the car keys and heading for the door.

'It's about the new product, Dad.'

Marx paused at the doorway, turned around and asked with not much care in his voice:

'What about it?' Not expecting him to know anything beyond the ordinary about what's going on at the chemical plant anyway.

'I think I know what happened to Zoll, and please don't be mad with me.'

Maila pleaded.

And that caught his attention as if he had been jerked awake from an afternoon nap. He threw the car keys back on the dining table and sat on the arm of his favourite lounge chair, thinking his son was behind the failure to reproduce Zoll's second stage.

'What do you mean, Maila?' he quizzed angrily as he started feeling less nervous.

Whenever he calls him by his name instead of saying son, is the time he knows his old man is very annoyed.

He told all what he did after his office grade demotion. As soon as he mentioned peeing into the solution, Marx went off the rails.

He rushed and grabbed him by his shirt's collar. He looked rather awkward with his small body frame dwarfed by the lad's.

'You good-for-nothing son of a gun, I could have you hanged in the stables for this.' (Hanging someone in the stable literally means hanging someone in his disused horse stables, which is also a cemetery for some of his victims).

'Sorry, Dad. I only did it once. The day after I was demoted.'

Marx got confused. He slacked his hold on the lad, thinking the vanishing stage – Zoll 2 – only occurred a week after the lad's demotion, not before.

Questioning his son piece by piece, absorbing the whole event, he suddenly thought, maybe, just maybe, the peeing could have done the trick. And that could well be the reason, or at least one of the reasons why it could not be repeated on numerous attempts.

He let go of the lad, and even helped straighten the rumpled parts of his shirt he had been grappling.

'Sorry, Dad, I didn't mean to…'

Marx getting back to his chronic nervous state as he was beginning to calm down. He gently pressed his fore finger on Maila's lips, shutting him up, and said:

'SSShhhhhh. Sorry for what? Look here! Does anyone know anything about this?' he asked with a wide smirk on his face. Which was puzzling for the young man who was expecting some physical bashing, as he had had a few times in the past.

'No, Dad, no one.'

'OK, son, just you forget I asked that question. In fact, forget we had this conversation at all. Mention it to no one. You hear me? Don't tell anyone, got it?'

'Yes, Dad, but Dad why aren't…?'

Before he could finish asking the question, Marx gave him an intimidating stare that forced him to quickly say:

'OK, Dad. I'll tell not a soul.'

He reached for the keys as he headed out the door once again. Starting the car ignition, his heart and mind both racing in equal measure with wild imagination: Maila's peeing and mixing all those stuff with Zoll could have given it its vanishing power. Little wonder no one else could figure this out. It's one of those bloody hell freaks of an accident. Give me the betting odds, he smiled, then realised something. He switched off the engine and fell into loud deep thoughts:

'I have to make him still think he had done something wrong, and as his father I'd be protecting him. Or else he might feel too comfortable and let someone else in on our secret. He saw me smiled, damn! That was an unconscious mistake.'

In frustration, he smashed his palm on the steering wheel, mistakenly hooting the car horn. He quickly exited the vehicle and raced back into the house.

True to Marx's thoughts, Maila had seen his father's face lit up in excitement and was wondering why his expression had suddenly changed from an angry to a joyful countenance. I don't understand this at all. It's giving me the jitters. Still lost in his own thinking when his dad barged back in.

Once in the house, Marx Zytan woofed in pretence:

'DO YOU KNOW YOU COULD COST ME MY FORTUNE?' Keeping a poker face with such ease.

'I sat behind the wheel feeling powerless and couldn't even start the car, all because of this,' he lied.

'Sorry, Dad, I didn't mean to cause you any harm.'

Before Marx could respond, the young man's face lit up in a childish manner, saying:

'But Dad, I think my peeing into that Zoll solution could have given it its vanishing trick. Don't do you think?'

Marx felt as if a ton of bricks had just dropped on his small shoulders as the car keys fell off his hand subconsciously. Taking a seat at the dining table and looking away from his son helped absorb the shock. He knew the game is up and any bluffing right now could blow up his plans wide open.

He then managed turning his attention to his son who was sheepishly staring at him.

'Didn't you notice, Dad, the scientists couldn't reconstruct Zoll into the disappearing gel, no matter what they did to it?' Maila continued.

'No one knows I mixed it with urine, except you and me.'

The more the son spoke, the more he seemed to be having sway over his dad; the body language was the clue, and the young man seemed to have noticed it. It's OK whenever others like Bampor does this to him; outthink, outsmart him at times but a lad who only a few years ago was just a hopeless teenager who had failed all his exams, is far too humiliating. He then felt sorry for himself and almost wept in shame. But Marx hadn't shed a tear since as a child when he was once bitten by a stray dog. Maybe I'm just a misfit who got lucky making money eh. More like stealing people's money, he thought.

'Dad, please say something. Do you think what I'm saying doesn't make any sense at all?'

Anyhow, the older Zytan had to end this torment. He managed saying:

'Look here, son. Just write down everything you've just said. Or better still let me record it.'

Dashing off to his bedroom and returning with a tape recorder.

Maila feeling a bit better thinking they are in to something though still looking and sounding stupid:

'You going to the cops, Dad?' he asked knowing too well his father won't; Marx had never reported anything to the police in his entire life, and he knows the lad knew this quite well. Whether Maila was playing games or not, he wasn't so sure, but still he needed to be treated with care and respect, he then thought.

'Everything will be OK, son.' Quickly reassuring him.

Not wanting to be engaged in this discussion anymore, he went into the bedroom had a change of clothes. He then dropped the recorded tape into his jacket pocket, patted his son on the back, as he thought; what a man-child, and head off to his G.U.T.S even though it wasn't normal office hours.

The phone on Kai Londo's desk was ringing constantly with no one to pick it up at the V.I.M. company. The entire senior staff were engaged in an emergency meeting convened after Marx Zytan from rival firm G.U.T.S had walked into their premises uninvited and asked to speak with the managing director Mr Saztah Ajina. He shouldn't be seen approaching them, not even traced making any sort of contact. The reason why he neither called nor sent any mail. He just jumped on a commercial plane without both his cat and sword, and showed up in disguise at V.I.M.'s head office. Donning a blond hairpiece, strapping polyethylene pads around his thin body giving an impression of a chubby man and also wearing platform-soled shoes for extra height.

V.I.M. had purposefully head-hunted G.U.T.S's former employee Zapia in the hope that she could lead them to an information or two on not only Zoll but possibly other trade secrets as well. At first, they didn't believe her when she told them she had no knowledge on the chemical's recipe. All the bits of clues she had were of no significant use. V.I.M. bosses started regarding her as a strategic blunder which could one day backfire now that she knows what they are after. Fearing she could relay that with any other secrets she may have possibly encountered here, to other rivals like her former employers.

Marx had previously offered to sell Zoll 1's secret for ₩50 million to V.I.M. who having already secured it from their mole, turned down his offer and lied that their scientists are working on an improved version.

"What improved version, eh? Tell me what's faster than light speed?" he had bark-howled at them, thinking either they've already had it or have someone working on stealing it from G.U.T.S.

He was thinking; all that is irrelevant now that he has the formula and sample for Zoll 2 which he would sell to V.I.M., not for 50m wands, but doubling it to 100m. Who's the clever boy then, he thought, as he further reclined in the plane's seat. But wait a minute, he then paused for a moment, maybe I could even use a third party to sell it to G.U.T.S. themselves, since they also have no clue on how Zoll 2 is made.

He then horse-laughed out loudly, causing a commotion as some other passengers onboard turned around staring at him. He apologised and shut his eyes for the rest of the flight to Ob, Bria.

'There is a gentleman here who wants to see the MD, but he hasn't got an appointment. He says it's important and urgent,' the receptionist, Mahyeahny, said on the phone to Ontus, the chief security officer [cso].

'How the hell did he get through the main gates without an appointment code?' the security boss demanded, in a booming voice that gave her the frights.

'I don't know sir, but he has a pass alright.'

'Never mind the bloody-damn pass. Visitors has to have [he made a grammatical error] to have appointment codes as well,' he continued roaring over the internal telecom.

'I know visitors have to have (intentionally correcting her boss's grammar) appointment codes, but then again check with security, sir,' she answered with a hint of sarcasm to her voice.

Despite working with him for over a decade, he has always given me the creeps with that evil-looking scar on his forehead and an equally evil-sounding voice, she thought. Ontus has never liked her ever since she rebuffed his sexual advances several times over.

Once Marx Zytan entered the premises, three uniformed guards with weapons concealed not wanting to cause him any alarm, though still not trusted, ushered him to an unassuming building block quite different from the opulence of the others dwelling on the same grounds.

First guard walked in through the front door, then second guard ushered Marx in behind her first colleague and followed closely behind him, with the third guard coming in last. Not a word was exchanged between any of them with the exception of the initial greeting that was more like an identification process. Marx felt like a lamb being led to the slaughter. For a moment there he started doubting his reasoning for wanting to make more money, secretly selling his partnership's intellectual property, but simply gave it the brush off. Now is not the time for negatives, he thought.

Sitting at the head of a small mahogany conference table was managing director, Mr Saztah Ajina. 65, 7 feet 10 inches tall, green, big straight green-dyed hair, thick lips, facial features appearing to be larger than the average Brian man. Athletic-built: stout neck and broad shoulders that wouldn't look out of place in a shot put or hammer-throwing competition. Wearing dark green suit over a white shirt with matching green necktie.

On his right was Ms Nervna Patrazz, his personal female bodyguard and rumoured fiancé also 65. Green, six feet three inches tall, streamlined muscles but looking much older with rugged facial features: fiery red puffy eyes, button nose, almost lipless mouth and prick ears which seemed always alert. She appeared to be prickly too, toughened by hard life living in the streets as a youth. A black belt martial arts expert. She was wearing uniform-like long-sleeve green khaki jacket and trousers. Despite looking so fit Nervna consumes a lot of snuff. She'd store the dried tobacco powder inside the bottom corner of her mouth between the gum and the cheek, continuously enjoying the psychoactive highs draining through her bloodstream. She also has the nasty habit of spitting the spent glob tobacco into a pocket-sized container to be later disposed of. Walks with a heavy trod, most times seen in chunky ankle boots. Nervna was said to be a psychic. Rumour has it she once used her telekinesis powers (A psychic ability of person to influence a physical system without physical interaction) to stop Saztah's car rolling off a cliff. And that is how they first met. After breaking up with an ex-spouse, Saztah attempted suicide trying to drive off a steep cliff but the car's engine stalled at the last moment when Nervna who was out walking her leopards saw what was about to happen and stopped the incident. She then ran over to the grief-stricken Saztah and talked him out of the car.

Mr Zapir Bookizt, the timid-looking, bespectacled accountant, sat next to the MD's left. He looks well fed and a bit overweight. 6 feet tall .If not at work he'd be seen with his head buried in a book. An avid animal lover living in a three bedroom house, bequeathed to him by his late grandma, with 15 birds, 7 dogs, 4 cats, 5 snakes and a whole bunch of other creatures, including plants.

He was reported as saying all his income goes to caring for his natural stock, as he'd refer to them, and can't afford to have a partner and children. Marx knew him from his days keeping the books at a nightclub in Ob.

On Zapir's left was another strange-looking fella who some of the other V.I.M. staff at that meeting claimed to had never seen before. About 9 feet, an inch tall. Most of his face is obscured behind huge shady spectacles he claimed are medically-prescribed and he had to have them on at all times. His race is somehow undetermined but looked orange - probably mixed between yellow and red. He was wearing dark white business suit, cream-coloured shirt and brown hand-made bowtie. This guy oozes strangeness and nothing else is known about him. Not even his name.

There was another attendee who strangely enough was sitting at a corner, and the only one away from the conference table. He was Ontus Ajina, green, 80, 8 feet 1 inch tall, hooked nose, bulgy eyes with bushy eyebrow, pointed jawbones, hunched shoulders, all physical features that earned him the nickname "The Vulture". He hated it but won't complain; fearing that doing so would make it becoming an issue. So he simply ignored the name-calling. Ontus preferred to be called "The Eagle" which few people do. He is the cso. at V.I.M. He sat facing Marx from a distance with his right leg crossed over the left, dangling the right foot towards Marx's direction as if he was using it to regard him in a mocking or threatening way. He had moments earlier noticed Marx Zytan, his old nemesis, on the security cameras and had quickly got over the initial shock of knowing he is the uninvited guest of all people ,who had just marched onto their premises.

Two decades ago, both men had a run-in at the Dark Secrets night club on a late Glam bock Eve [Zist's equivalence of Christmas Eve]. Marx recognised the face, the scar and recalled the incident, though he can't recall the name. The tense atmosphere was making him feel a bit more comfortable. He just at that moment began to feel relaxed as he sensed trouble. Ontus's hostile behaviour had awakened the weird calmness monster in him; temporarily gone was his normal state of nervousness. Showing that much confidence, even in the enemy's lair, had Ontus himself very much impressed with him.

On that fateful evening at the nightclub they reportedly clashed over a young lady. Marx, who sometimes worked as a disc jockey at the nightclub whenever he went to visit in Ob, Bria, was flirting with this girl when Ontus, all dressed in white, tried to pull her away from him. They got into an argument and started fighting. Marx slashed the man in white across the forehead with a small blade that was concealed in his canvas shoes. The wounded man's white shirt was so bloody the police report got it wrong saying the victim was wearing a red and white top. Ontus had never forgotten the pain and stigma living with that permanent facial disfiguration he sees as an embarrassment.

'Good evening ladies and gentlemen. You all look fantastic and a solid, happy bunch today,' Marx said, showering unnecessary compliments on his hosts, which a few of their numbers regarded as excessive flattery.

This was a sign he was more in fear, rather than showing respect. Fear that was calming his nerves.

His hosts, a wide breath of characters, from saints to sinners, all replied in chorus, 'Good evening mister,' as if they had rehearsed it. No reciprocal use of the word gentleman. All stayed in their seats, no one got up to even offer a handshake or anything like that. It was at this stage Marx thought he had truly made a mistake walking into the lions' den.

The walls in the room are exposed red brickwork. All the furniture was draped in scarlet red linen with the exception of the black fixtures and fittings. This place looks more like an occult's dungeon to me, he reckoned to himself. The effort to continuously keep a smiley expression was beginning to hurt the tired muscles in his face. He yearned for a shot of omole if only to excite his nerves – he's not comfortable when he's calm. He wasn't offered any beverage. Moments later he started calming down and embarrassingly his nervousness returned. He wanted to feel angry so it would go away. He can hardly operate his mobile phone on which he had listed some of his business offers.

'Without any further ado, what can we do you for?' asked Saztah, with so much indifference to his voice notifying Marx he is rather useless to them. He took the seat pointed to him a distant two empty chairs afar from the others. He sat down thankful for taking the weight off his bony weak knees.

Zytan replied, with a face completely tired from those faking confidence smiles:

'I have ah, em,' he stuttered for a bit. 'I have a very good proposition to make.' His eyes darting around searching for any sign of interest from the lot. He didn't get any. All poker-faced, except for Ontus who was smiling and mopping his scar making a reminder of their last encounter. He can't be sweating in this cool air-conditioned room, Zytan thought, but he continued to deliberately brush his handkerchief across his forehead every time our eyes meet.

Marx went on to detail his deal and price for the recipe and specimen of Zoll 2, which got V.I.M. every much interested, having had their mole left G.U.T.S. with only Zoll 1 before its latter development was conceived. That first stage didn't have much in the way of a wider impact, for some reason they weren't achieving the same rate of success with the new fuel testing as had their rivals at G.U.T.S. And several other firms, even the smaller ones, were all working on Zoll 1. The novelty and uniqueness was gone; Marx had secretly sold it to all these other companies. Some of whom were beginning to think they could have been duped by him.

But they were wrong; he actually sold them the correct formula for Zoll 1, only that they haven't got someone with a razor-sharp mind like Prof. Nemad who could work out the ideal dosage and the correct timing aspects of getting the mixture right.

Not waiting to be asked why he was being treacherous to his partners at G.U.T.S. Marx felt compelled to give his reasons for selling their intellectual property secrets to a bitter rival.

'I am not just doing it for the money, but also to make Trillian pay for stealing my investment funds and business estate,' he lied, with yet another forced smile which he wasn't even sure was still showing on his face. Worn out by all his earlier efforts.

Not getting any response for his reason to sell, he went on to create further impressions all is not well with his partners; lying about his plans to disengage with G.U.T.S. and his hatred for Prof. Nemad, the chief scientist.

The only person who seemed to be showing any interest was a new member of V.I.M.'s staff, Ms Nogofia, 70, red, 6 feet 4 inches tall, ginger curly-haired, ex-model, ex-beach volleyball player, pencil-thin lips, almond-shaped eyes with natural long lashes, small pinched nose. A highly intelligent ex-spook but with an uncontrollable weakness for sex. She was sitting nearest to Marx , but with a couple of empty chairs away in between – she had wanted to sit next to him but Saztah ruled against it.

Marx's appearance reminded her of a former boss at her previous employment who committed suicide after she had dumped him. He was the only son and heir to the company's owner, and she had to leave the job as a result. Nogofia is an adrenaline junkie for taking all sorts of risks. Nothing intimidates her. She was willing to trust, or say, trial Marx Zytan's offer but then again she would try out anything in life at least once no matter what the danger, even though she had been briefed about him moments before this meeting.

'Let me get this straight,' said Saztah, with elbows on the table and head in his hands.

'You are selling us the Zoll recipe even though your investments are sunk costs in a project yet to take off the ground.

Wouldn't it be like you shooting yourself in the foot?'

Marx was caught off guard, not preparing for such a question.

Feeling increasingly uneasy, he replied:

'Great question! As I mentioned earlier, I'm settling scores with G.U.T.S.'

Saztah ogled him whilst breathing in and out loudly in a clear indication, I know you're lying, there is no score to be settled. And he quickly got the message.

He suddenly regretted telling the lie. Looking a bit shamefaced, he hurriedly flipped open a brown briefcase bailing out and strewing a couple of papers on the table top. But he just as quickly snapped back the lid shut after mistakenly exposing some fake passports and documents in the briefcase hold. This helped to divert attention from his lying blunder. He went on detailing what he'll do for V.I.M.

'I'd say with no small delight how I will help you close the technology gap on G.U.T.S. But I won't give you any of the documents proper as yet until the deal is struck. These are just the briefs,' using his fingers to spread out the documents towards the others.

His tired face now frozen stiff, made so by the permanently-forced smile, and no longer hurting.

'You're portraying yourself to us as being in a bind indebted to avenging alleged grievances against your partners but sorry, settling scores for what?

Tell us why you'd really be doing something like this which could hurt your own investment returns if it's not just about you wanting to make more money?' queried Zapir, who had been quiet so far. In awareness, he is not fully trusted on matters outside finance.

Marx then thought, this meeting is getting just too boring with too much repetition. Worse than the worst inquisition I've ever heard of.

The MD smiled, thinking, our accountant here could well become more useful than just keeping the books.

But such confidence thought on Zapir was only short-lived as he made his typical blunders when he continued to make demands, of Marx who had seemed to be lost answering his first question, by saying:

'So tell us? More so now that the U.N. body had reintroduced increased funding prospects to all participants on the mission to Earth projects.'

That last statement gave Marx a lifeline on which he used to reply to the same question they've asked him in different ways. So he quickly jumped onto the chance:

'I will benefit both ways really; with the United Nations paying my partners and yourself for the products, G.U.T.S. paying me returns on my investment, you paying me for Zoll 2, with both companies gaining as a result. Also the U.N. finally getting what it had previously failed to achieve, getting many firms, by extension many nations as possible working on the Zoom or Doom project. It's all that simple really. Technically by me dishing you our trade secrets, I am not only investing in you but helping the whole world of Zist as well. Everyone is a winner.'

He then paused for a few seconds and shrugged his shoulders, with the forced smile still evident. His outstretched arms resting on the table with hands clasped together over the documents.

Happy with himself, appearing to be ahead of the lot, he surveyed the room again. This time confidently with his nose up in the air sniffing for any response.

Getting no physical reaction but rightly sensing he had them cornered, he could have just ended his proposal there on a high but this is typical of Marx's greed for dominance. He went further, this time focusing more on Zapir, whom he thought was the weakest link.

'You're an old work colleague of mine.'

Throwing his chin at the accountant. 'Reason why I'm dangling these juicy options right in front of your team.'

Sensing victory, he pushed the papers which they've all been ignoring, further across the table. Some of them took it in turns briefly reading through documents this time (A clue he had his hosts finally cornered). Saztah with hands clasped together over his face, grimaced at Marx, but no one could see it.

He was thinking, my oh my, the same old Marx Zytan at his best again, displaying convincing words with such an ease that could sell sunlight to the Arabs.

'They are real deals, not baits. I'm a businessman like any other who'll try to squeeze…'

Saztah cut him off, saying:

'OK, we've had enough and the deal is done.'

The MD was disappointed in his accountant for throwing the trapped Marx a lifeline. He then gave Zapir a strong stare for all in the room to know it was a reprimand for asking a stupid question.

Marx started shaking more visibly in comfort having settled the trade. His hosts were so convinced they were willing to pay 50% more on his asking price. Without any further ado, they gave him a deposit of ₩75m, half of the total cost.

No sooner Zytan had got back into his hired vehicle in one piece, he threw himself backwards onto the headrest, blew out a short whistle in a sigh of relief and swore never to go back there, regardless of any further deal. He had felt thoroughly minced like having being placed through a wringer. To make sure that doesn't ever happen again he took out a gaslighter and burned the fake security pass. Suddenly his phone started ringing, on a call from a withheld number. He barked loudly: 'Who the fuck is this?'

And Ontus's familiar voice replied:

'How did you obtain…' But before the V.I.M. cso could finish asking the question, Marx knew he wanted to know how he obtained one of their security passes, and replied in a louder tone:

'I don't know who the fucking hell you are and the bloody damn why you're calling me. I hate disturbances from cold callers…'

Before he would continue the pretence, Ontus knew Marx was feinting innocence in case his people at G.U.T.S. were snooping on his conversation and could learn of the treacherous visit to V.I.M., so he quickly hung up.

****

Coincidentally, Zapia had a day off work on Marx's visit so she wasn't aware of it. Though by virtue of his stunning disguise, he was sure she won't have noticed him anyway and didn't see that as a problem.

In her first month at V.I.M., she overheard conversations about Brian spies working in Pris and Prof Nemad being mentioned as the main target for a destabilisation campaign against their rival's best and brightest.

She had also seen someone with similar appearance to the G.U.T.S.'s chief scientist at her new office. That someone, as it happened, had been away from V.I.M. and had also travelled overseas at the time of the sexual assaults back home.

There was also this talk about V.I.M.'s PM [Post Man] working in Pris whom she suspected could be the one impersonating Nemad and possibly be her sexual attacker. One thing she possesses in abundance is detective intelligence. Her foster parents would at times call her Sleuth Zapia or Zapia the Sleuth, and she loved it. She may not have brains sound enough for academia but was fairly good in solving mysteries. Especially those around criminality.

I have to let Nemad know about this, she thought, and then muttered a promise to herself while dressing up for work one Friday morning, saying:

'And that is the most pressing part of my thoughts that needed to be addressed no sooner I had the chance to do it.

'So Prof. Nemad mightn't have been the one who was molesting me in the office after all. You can see the innocence in his face when I cornered him in that printing room.'

From that moment onwards, she started neglecting her work, pretending to relapse into mental illness with the sole purpose that they 'ill sack her.

Resigning is too risky as they might even think of her as a spook even though they were the ones who headhunted her in the first place.

Her lucky break was realised after Marx betrayed G.U.T.S. She was then seen as useless and given the sack.

Getting fired from V.I.M. was the easier part but getting back into contact with her former employers at G.U.T.S. was much harder.

She had at one time sensed Marx was after her, seeking answers for his missing investment funds. But that didn't bother her, for she knew nothing about any funds missing.

The moment her plane landed at the Prisian city airport at 11:05 am the following Tuesday she tried contacting Prof. Nemad but her number was blocked. The weather condition was overcast and cool. Which was a relief from the almost every day hot temperatures in the summer.

As she boarded an air taxi heading home, the weather was getting a bit stormier with gale-force winds whistling around the aircraft/car hybrid. She had on autumnal clothes, well wrapped up against the elements and got home about 11:25 am.

Having learned that G.U.T.S.'s new Zoom or Doom joint project was faring far better than the erstwhile and much-troubled H2O-Planet Earth, she desperately wanted to be part of it.

'I hear the first mission is about to be launched,' speaking to a friend over the phone. Who replied:

'Yeah. Since the Government got involved things are moving pretty fast they say.'

But sadly, everyone of her attempts to reach other G.U.T.S. staff was unsuccessful until they received a hand-delivered letter she had sent to Mr Tallin. The letter reads of all her suspicions, and this attracted attention from the company's security staff.

Coincidentally, all this was happening at a time when judgement was being passed on Nemad's appeal. Which concluded:

"In the light of new evidence thrown before us by the defence, who is also now fully backed by the prosecution witness, the case against Prof. Nemad has been dismissed. Seldom has a defendant received such support from the prosecution itself..."

As a result both prof. Nemad Scyzpr and Zapia Zill were reinstated to their former positions in the company.

The big question on everyone's lips was:

'WHO WAS THE V.I.M. MOLE AT G.U.T.S. THAT STOLE ZOLL 1 AND COULD ALSO BE ZAPIA'S MOLESTER.'

And now that the Pris Government is working jointly with G.U.T.S., it became a matter of national security as well. So there were more resources available to smoke out the mole/s.

6

The TSG, bathed in the last available amount (Except for the tiny leftover lab samples) of the highly concentrated Zoll 2, suddenly become invisible for the trip to Earth. It took just five days flying from Zist to the I.S.S., onto which it secretly attached itself, waiting for the final journey.

On launch day, the crew detached the space ship from the ISS and then reattached it onto the Soyuz craft before they were hurled towards the Blue Planet. It was all timed with the arrival and departure of the Russian Soyuz craft. Before that first departure date, while still attached to the International Space Station, the researchers' preparation for life on the blue planet was to start experimenting with earthly stuff like the air, food, etc. Every now and then they would dispatch an invisible probe cutting a hole through the space station, and stealing food from its larder before resealing it again unnoticed.

The three-man crew were: team leader, Rallax Que, 75, blue, 8 feet 2 inches tall, bald, somewhat long face, hollowed cheeks, no eye brows, tiny eye lashes, prominent forehead and bigger than average ears. Almost every Zist scientist is automatically acknowledged as highly intelligent but this man is well above that. A single parent who lives with one of his two children.

His deputy, Zye Pee, brown, 70, 6 feet 5 inches, very symmetrical face with almost perfect features. To be simple, his facial description is cut short with just two words – extremely handsome. Very bright but could be lazy at times. Keen sportsman and known for his womanising ways.

The third member Xiz 56. The "baby" of the group. Blue, 7 feet 4 inches, tall, slim facial features and pointed ears, roman nose, straight jet-black hair. A tennis addict, nicknamed the Languages-Man-speaks 120 different ones, some more fluently than others. Also the taciturn introvert among the lot. He got to love the biscuits and salad after finding out about their low-calorie contents.

'These are some of the most organic food I've ever had. They look much the same our forebears used to have centuries back before we started creating almost all of ours in the lab,' munching away the grub as he spoke.

He didn't get any response from Que who was harbouring some concerns about the frequency of the raids into the I.S.S. He then continued to say:

'The Earth diet is really organic compared to our standards, though some of it had been processed in the labs as well. Though not as cultured as our ones. You know they still slaughter animals for food.'

He finally got a response from Pee who said: 'I have read some old books on some of our nation's culinary standards. Theirs on Earth, is quite similar to what we had hundreds of decades ago. Quite similar really, and even identical in some cases.'

The food dispute was one thing but when Pee got too accustomed doing regular peeping-Toms on the I.S.S.'s female astronauts whenever they were naked, to constantly relieve himself sexually, it then got too much, and Que, as team leader, imposed some restrictions.

A final decision was yet to be made as to which two nations' intelligence services Pee and Que would each has to join separately. Xie already had a defined task: to load up the cargo haul with ice and return to Pris.

'Do you guys think I'd bored going back home on my own,' he asked as if he wasn't so sure.

Pee replied: 'Well you had an option but you decided against it. I was wondering if that triple bonus had anything to do with it.'

Xie didn't like the answer but made no further comment.

Que went on to say: 'Actually as team leader I was going to be the one singlehandedly taking the vessel and cargo back, until you guys were given the options. But management wanted me be stay on Earth making the preparations for the masses to come.'

Xie responded: 'Yeah I did volunteer. Only that it just wasn't for the money.'

Pee conceded: 'I got it bro.' Regretting what he had said but didn't apologise or say about it. After a moment's silence, Que started a different conversation:

'Having learned Earth life forms resembled ours in so many ways, I was in great expectation both of us would at least speak similar languages, if not the same,' he said, while looking out of the windows.

No one replied to that. Pee instead started to marvel at Earth's atmosphere when they crossed the thin blue line:

'Little wonder they call it the Blue Planet. Everything thing here seems to be of that colour.'

Xie quipped: 'Much the same like ours really, the yellow planet, our seas, skies are all yellow. Even the largest animal ever known to them on Earth is called the Blue Whale, rather like our one the yellow Gigatrad. Though ours is a bit controversial.'

Que then continued: 'Later I also gathered our listening devices couldn't record proper sounds from the I.S.S. "Earth speaking" was of the infrasound quality.

One far too low for our hearing.'

'Yeah I remember the recordings were "fast-played" on ultrasound machines, speeding it up several times before the sounds made some language sense,' commented Xie. 'At the end, their languages were relatively easy to learn though, especially that Enlish one.'

Que tapped Xie on his shoulder as he hopped past him getting onto the controls, and said: 'You mean English.'

Xie wryed his nose at him and went: 'Yeah, whatever,' and further asked: 'What do we know about their intelligence services? We are yet to choose between them. Well, you two really to decide. I'm taking the load home.'

Que turned around towards and said:

'We already knew about the persistence of the American C.I.A., who would be daring enough to scale down the depths of an active volcano if there is information or someone in there they would like to contact. We've also learned of the British intelligence network's, MI5, MI6, and GCHQ, bravery modelled on the country's special forces motto of "Who Dares Wins".'

Pee then stated: 'Then there is the Israeli Mossad, whose far-reaching tentacles was said to rival the American's. All in addition to what we've already gained on the Russian, Chinese, French, German and even Iranian intelligence agencies.'

Xie suddenly quipped: 'Pee you almost spilled that Gbanbar drink [A super popular energy beverage] on me.'

Pee responded: 'Ah! Shut up ship mate. It floated away from you.'

'Yes, I know that. That's why I used the word "almost". Had it been at lower ground levels gravity would have let it spilled on me,' Xie explained.

Of which Pee said: 'Splitting hairs, splitting hairs.' And all three of them started singing along to a popular Zist song called "Splitting Hairs".

Que then set the vessel on cruise-control, though still attached to the Soyuz, and hopped back to the mid-section area of the craft: 'Guys, guys, back to the discussion on intelligence agency choices. We've looked at all these spy organisations on Earth. Technology-wise we know they are tens of decades, if not hundreds of decades lagging behind us. So we won't expect much of their cybersecurity resistance anyway. Pee made a suggestion saying:

But I think we should go for the CIA and the FSB. These two are still the biggest players in the game.'

'I am not so quite sure,' Que replied.

Pee then queried:

'You mean they are no longer of that status?'

Que hastily said:

'No, no I'm not saying that. What I was trying to say is, there are new players like China coming into the mix, which needs to be considered as well.'

Que, the slightly more intelligent one, continued to say:

'It's a good thing we have learned that Russian language which was dominantly spoken on the I.S.S., and also the second most popular one; American English. Notably we both speak Russian fluently and our English sound more Russian-accented. So it would be ideal to enter the Russian and Israeli spy networks. And now that that medication has finally changed our skin to becoming white, we'd blend in nicely.'

Pee then asked: 'OK, I can understand the need for getting to Russia, with their science and military historical achievements and all that. But why not match that with one of us joining the CIA as well?'

To which Que replied: 'Well, I can easily go to Israel and claim I come from Russia and have Jewish ancestries. And would just fit in, than me saying the same to the CIA who would question why I crossed over Israel and came all the way to the U.S.'

Pee looked enviously at Que, and as if trying to score some balance, he stated: 'OK, Que, I understand. Our Russian-English language variant would be the convincing tool. And getting into Mossad would more or less make it easier getting into the others. I get it.

Though with the possible exception of the German inner intelligence operations – the Core unit – which is not open to all German citizens.'

Pee's take on the German intelligence seemed to have upped his points a bit more, and it showed on the way Que looked at him with a smile on his face.

After an hour of discussion, punctuated by a 20 minute break, they finally decided to settle for the FSB and Mossad. Both men would at most times leave decision-making to the last minute whenever they are in disagreement. But while they were dithering over their choices of location, they were at the same time feeling reassured of future successes. All this discussion was done en-route to planet Earth, still attached to the Soyuz.

****

It was a sizzling hot day; most days on Zist in the last couple of hundred years are sizzling hot as its star continued to expand, Starday was Just coming from the golf course where he had been relaxing with some influential people at the lounge. The weather was too punishing to play the game. He arrived for his appointment with Marx at the Tunnel bar and restaurant in late afternoon but still a super-hot evening with temperatures bubbling around 65° centigrade, hotter than the hottest ever recorded on Earth. He was wearing a green polo neck shirt with the police insignia, so proud still showing off his profession even in semi-retirement and brown cotton shorts exposing two flimsy stubs for legs. He was also wearing golf shoes that had bits of molten tarmac stuck underneath due to the excessively hot daytime temperatures melting their roads.

While waiting for a taxi, he peeled open a toffee wrapper and slotted the sweet into his mouth. This would help to hold back his uncontrollable gob spilling habit.

Despite all his years working in the police force with his vast knowledge of underworld activities, he had never heard of this elusive place. No surprise, as this joint kept changing ownership and names every half year or so.

Following Mr Zytan's direction, he took a taxi cab driving him through the old mountain underpass tunnel, which is hardly used anymore since the construction of a new, above-ground, wider route to the main water front was opened to traffic a couple of years ago.

'Damn. Do people still use this road?' asked the driver, who didn't get any answer, as they went through the patchy carriageway leading to that lesser-known side of the beach frequented by naturists. The taxi drove down the slope towards the building sitting at the end of the road.

Though not too sure about this taciturn customer, the driver wanting to be more engaged, said:

'Back in those days, I used to drive by the other side of the beach. A bit up the hill over yonder to the dog-tooth mountains. There you will see nudists' backsides of all colour, shapes and sizes.' Smiling and looking at his rear-view mirror for any reaction from Starday. The ex-copper was lost in thoughts as to why Marx would have wanted to meet in such a place but he managed to catch the words: '…see nudists' backsides…' from the driver.

'Oh, you mean the naturists? I've seen and felt more backsides than the backseats of this cab, my friend. They just don't attract me that much anymore.' The cabbie burst out laughing, finally he's got his man, he thought, which encouraged him to continue the conversation.

'You a comedian, sir?'

Starday, reading the map on his phone ignored him and said, 'Stop here, here, just right here.' He paid the fare, got off and started walking, still stuck to his phone screen.

'Your change, sir,'

He still ignored the driver and continued walking towards his destination. The cabbie grimaced, saying to himself, 'Well, some talk, some don't,' as he drove back towards the tunnel.

Walking down the slope road, the building that houses the seafront Tunnel bar and restaurant looks like a bungalow but once you got there, it's a two-storey house.

'Everything here seems to be on a gradient of some kind.' Starday muttering under his breath, 'The beach, the roads. Why not just name it, Slope town or Slope village or something similar.' Trying to occupy his wandering thoughts as he approached the building's entrance. There wasn't any sign or anything to indicate this is the right place. He had just followed Marx's instructions to the letter.

He pressed the buzzer. Within a few seconds, a super-tall roundly lady, white, 6 feet five inches tall, good set of white teeth, with long, curly auburn-coloured hair, opened the front door. To just say she was beautiful would be a criminal understatement Her sweet-smelling perfume was the first thing that greeted him. She smiled at him as if he had won something. Not older than 55. She had finely-chiselled facial features that would make a shop mannequin sprung to life with envy. The elegant-looking lady was wearing a figure-hugging crimson red mini skirt, low-cut white blouse; also tight-fitting, held together by buttons which seemed to be under stress holding together her upper body. She had on crimson red open-toed shoes, completing an air-hostess appearance.

'The name's Anya. Anya Mahah,' she said in a beautiful brian accent and extending a handshake.

Starday, a good seven inches shorter, looked up at her face and said: 'Lucian Starday. I'm here on Marx Zytan's invite.'

'Oh, I know. I should have asked that first. Pardon my mistake,' Anya said in a voice that had suddenly changed from formal to casual.

Maybe she finds me attractive, he started kidding himself in thoughts. I better stop dreaming though.

She was towering over Starday's five-foot ten-inch frame, a midget for planet Zist standards. He had always fancied tall women but quite unlucky attracting any as such for a lover. Whether his height puts them off or his own complex turning them off is not really known. Dating agency after dating agency, he failed getting his ideal tall woman and had to settle for his wife who is just a bit taller, tall all the same, he reckoned, when they got married. Marx knows this and has set up this particular lady to meet him.

She led him inside through the main hall packed with dining customers. A live soprano on a side stage sounding more like a drowning cat as they exited the main area and walked past two toilet doors on the right and a waiting room on the left along a winding corridor. They then went further through a kitchen where he saw two cooks who seemed to have intentionally avoided any eye contacts with him. Anya was just walking ahead littering her trail with that sweet perfume, scent-marking every room and passage they have been through. He just followed, hooked onto her scent like a male deer sniffing the air in the rutting season. Each and every room has a speaker with the soprano's voice following them everywhere. Anya would every so often pull down her short skirt riding up her thighs as she walked leading towards the back garden. Everywhere seemed to be in shadows. He thought they were exiting the building when they entered another door on a giant mud-like mound attached sideways to the kitchen door exit. Starday started wondering where they were heading for. What a relief from that soprano with the cat-in-distress voice. Had it not been for Anya's attractiveness he wouldn't have gone this far through the hideout passages. Bowing their heads as they walked the through the mound's small door entrance which leads through to a smaller tunnel ending up in a smoke-filled backroom, so this is what they mean by the Tunnel bar, he thought, just seconds before he was about to ask her where she was taking him to. The smoke wasn't from cigarettes but from incense burning and scenting the air in a not-so-pleasant colourful fragrance.

The room was dimly lit but he managed to make out a lady sitting on a man's legs with her drawn-up frock covering his frontal parts. I don't want to think what they could be doing, he said to himself as Anya shuffled him past through two other tables then onto one reserved for two. Sitting him down facing the dating couple.

This is a bloody set up, he was again thinking when she asked if he's alright as she bent down low handing him the menu and an eyeful of her exposed breast in that low-cut blouse.

'Fine thanks,' was his swift replied, a bit annoyed.

Though he had been starving himself for this restaurant visit, the little trauma he had been put through so far in this joint had killed off that appetite.

Anya convinced him to have something after his initial decline .

'OK, just some snacks and a juice drink, no alcohol for me, thanks,' he said.

Marx must be up to his tricks again. I am too experienced for this sort of stuff, he muttered to himself after she left to get the order.

Moments later, she brought lobster and truffle pie for him and pizza-like pie for herself . They settled down to eat in armchairs, not dining ones, with a low table between them holding the food and drinks. Starday had a further eyeful from the front split of her skirt to the farthest parts of her inner legs, right up to her bits. All the time he refused showing any interest, knowing too well he can never pull such a lady and this is a fucking setup anyway, he thought.

'Marx tells me you're an intelligent man but unhappily married, is that true?' As she poured a soft drink for him and an alcoholic one for herself .

Starday had never been happy with any of his love relationships in his entire life.

He replied, trying to sound formal: 'I don't know why he said that to you but I am not in any way looking for any sort of relationship.'

'Ah, what a shame,' lowering her voice as if disappointed. 'For me, I only fancy intelligent men but have never dated any to my standards. With the exception of my ex-husband, who was just above average anyway,' she tweeted.

Starday still not too impressed and wise enough to a stage-managed process like this, asked:

'I'm here to meet him, Marx. Where is he as I have other businesses to attend to?' Sounding a bit impatient.

'He had asked me to keep you company as he was running a bit late and knows quite well you're a stickler for time. But if I must say your general disposition informs on that high-time preference characterisation, don't you think?'

Starday was about to say something when she cut him off and began describing his appearance and behaviour – not too faltering, not too critical either – using psychological terms accordingly. Starday, a psychology post-graduate who enjoys intellectual conversations, queried her analysis. She then went deeper into the subject matter taking him to depths he has never been before.

'I hold DSc. in psychology,' she tweeted, as she flicked a lock of her hair off her face.

'Oh, I'm off to get us more drinks, be back in a tick,' she chirped, with a smile as she got up to get the service.

'This time, please bring me some alcohol too. Omole perhaps, if you have it,' the ex-cop requested with a broad smile, who had moments before refused a strong drink.

She brought the omole mixed with milk while he was using his tongue to clean his teeth. She intentionally stared at his moving tongue and gave him a huge smile and Starday loved it.

Though still suspecting Marx could be up to something fishy and had to be careful, yet he had never before found himself in the private company of a woman this beautiful with a brain to match. Slowly feeling at ease letting his guard down, they started talking more. Telling him this joint was once owned by her criminal ex-husband and how stupid she had been for marrying her lecturer.

'I have a weakness for smart men you see. He was well aware of that and took advantage of me. The best I ever had was him and look how it ended up – being killed in a drugs-related gunfight.'

Starday has heard about her late husband and how unmatched he was for the foreign student he forcefully wed. It was making the headlines then. Her visa was expiring, she wanted to stay in the country.

Starday then watched more of her legs, this time deliberately staring at it for her to notice him doing just that.

She then excused herself to the bathroom for a couple of minutes, returned and sat again, this time the front split in her short red skirt was revealing what Starday rightly deciphered to be a scarlet G-string. On the left side, the panty slipped, airing bits of pubic sticking out. At that instant, Starday started feeling himself expanding in his trousers. So soon the bulge was there for her to notice.

'Could we go and wait in the bar instead,' she asked while staring at his bulge in pretence the situation is becoming awkward.

'Why? Aren't we comfortable here?' he asked solemnly as if he was begging for them to stay and very annoyed with himself for letting go so easily.

He tried suppressing his expansion by squeezing his legs together, only for the friction from his thigh on his private part to cause it to becoming harder.

She deliberately stared at his front again and said:

'This is not an ideal situation, we must leave, please. Only that I wouldn't want Marx to see us here in this secluded part of the building. When he told me you're clever and knowing my weakness for bright men I had longed for at least a kiss or a cuddle.

Anyway let's go.'

Starday bit his lips in regret for appearing too formal when they first met.

She stood up, poker-faced, waiting for him doing the same. But he can't just then. His erection is obvious and was causing an embarrassment.

'Sorry, we have to leave now,' forcing a pretentiously stern voice.

'I eh, I eh, would like a couple of minutes more just relaxing here for a bit if you don't mind,' scarcely recognising his own voice. There was some giggling from the couple in the dark corner.

She looked at those two in the dark corner and started walking out of the room. He had no choice but to follow, reluctantly, crestfallen and feeling defeated. No longer swinging her arse in his face as she did before when they were entering the room. For all his detective years setting up people in stuffs like honey-traps and the likes, Starday couldn't resist this obvious setup. He felt foolish and weak at the knees wanting this woman whom he thought is a once in a lifetime opportunity; her height, her brains, damn. Cursing his ever persistent bad luck failing to attract his ideal type of a woman. He then foolishly started longing to be honey-trapped again by this gorgeous lady in red and white.

They met Marx waiting in a corner in the bar.

He ignored their greetings, not even regarding Starday.

He then grabbed Anya by the wrist and led her a couple of yards away: 'What the hell you're doing flirting with my friend? The barman told me.' He yelled at her pretending to be angry, partially raising his voice loud enough for his guest to have heard.

'Once you've met with a stranger, who by chance also happens to be bright, you just can't keep your panties dry, can you?'

She fought back, feinting to wrestle her hand off his likewise feint grip.

'Let go of my hand, Marx, you're hurting me,' sneering at him. All in pretence.

Normally the ex-top cop would have seen through this sham but sadly, he was drugged with desire badly wanting to nail Anya. Though still a bit suspicious, Starday apologised to Marx denying any interest in the lady. He felt like saying these words about her gave him that freedom of fantasy associating them together.

For him, it's like having a wet daydream, a feeling he shamelessly enjoyed.

Marx told him about his change of plan and had forgiven his botched attempt on kidnapping Zapia:

'I am no longer interested in her. She is now back home, and there are bigger fishes to hook out of the river. Instead I want you to break into G.U.T.S. and steal a small dose of Zoll itself. No more blunders this time, Star and I mean it. This one is a bigger operation. I'll get the office layout plan for you to study.'

Marx knew no one can take any amount of Zoll out of the plant. The security is fool proof and password access is needed, not only to enter the premises but also that special walk-in cupboard containing the products. When Maila sabotaged Zoll; he didn't lift the bottle contain off the shelf, which would have alarmed everyone else, instead he poured stuff in it to destroy the contents.

Feeling angry but not showing any of it, Starday began thinking; this bastard, blinded by excessive greed, now wants to double-cross the Government and his group's investment, for his own selfish sake. What a sad stupid fool. I am not interested and have decided not to be involved.

He then told Marx:

'I no longer have the right sort of professional burglars who could break into such a highly-secured building. Sorry, Mr Zytan,' he lied.

Marx instantly knew he was lying and got very angry. He quickly stood up and started wearing his overcoat getting ready to leave. Adopting a cold stare towards him, he snorted: 'Look here, Starday, you probably didn't hear me properly the first time, so I'll give you another chance by repeating myself.'

He pushed his unfinished drink away across the table, picked up his car keys and roared:

'I get the sense you seem to be getting beyond your post lately by starting to defy me and mess up my work. So I'll quickly cut out the chase and get to the point. So listen and listen carefully as I won't be saying this again for the third time.

He then lifted his voice a bit. 'Whether by any fair means or foul, I need you to break into that bloody plant and get me the hydrocarbon itself. I'm not asking for much, just a tiny amount will do. I need it badly. You have no options. Just so you know.'

He said in an intimidating tone.

Starday getting a bit scared replied: 'Ah, no qualms Dr Zytan. Now that you've mentioned it again I think I can figure out how to do it myself. Yeah, sure, will get it done.' As he also stood up turning his back to retrieve his own coat hanging on the chair he was sitting on. Having his back turned away gave him an opportunity to scowled back bitterly without Marx seeing his expression, as he cursed under his breath.

'Sorry?' Zytan asked.

'Ah, nothing,' Starday replied. 'How I hate this bloody jacket my wife bought me for my birthday. I wore it once and no more. It's a bit too big you see, and she didn't like the fact that I don't wear it. And now she is holding my feet to the fire as a result. I'll get rid of it someday.'

Marx didn't reply, sensing that that "bloody jacket" could be a metaphor for him, which it was. They both bade the coldest of farewells and depart.

By that time, it was getting darker as the evening started rolling around twilight with the setting sun draped over the horizon where the ocean meets the sky. This stunning light effect was casting a huge shade over parts of the city's exclusive western district.

'How beautiful is nature, hey? Starday questioned himself as he was out walking in the streets hoping he would see that friendly taxi driver again. My new cabbie friend where are you?' he asked to himself as the cool wind kept fanning his face in the night time heat with the alcohol starting to have an effect. Still walking almost aimlessly down the road, he saw a cabbie emerged over the hill driving down his way. As the vehicle approached him, he recognised the advert and the number plate as the same one that brought him to the Tunnel bar. He hastily upped his pace covering more ground quickly towards the car, hailed it and got in. Unfortunately, it was another driver in the same cab, not the friendly one he was only snubbing sometime earlier.

Halfway through the journey, the TSG detached itself from the Soyuz vessel and landed on its own in the Arctic Circle where Pee and Que both geared up and started their separate journeys to Russia and Israel respectively. Whilst the third man, Xie, collected large chunks of ice blocks from the frozen Siberian tundra and loaded it into the vehicle's solid-fuel tanks, where it was processed into gas, and zoomed back to Zist. Using the magical superpower speed of Zoll 2 the return journey was completed in five days, in what would have been five years with Zoll 1. He would set the starship on auto pilot while he slept, watch sports, even those from planet Earth where he had favourite football teams; Nottingham Forest and the Arsenal.

Moments before landing, he noticed the very low load gauge readings. Not wanting to dampen the mission's spirit he forced himself into a state of suspended disbelief, at least for that moment, ignoring the cargo's meter.

Couple of days later, he disembarked in a national euphoria, welcomed by the presidential team, the media, the full publicity works. At the space port, Xie felt a little bit uneasy. Of all the 50 cubic tonnes of vaporised water, only a quarter of a tonne was left. Most of the gas had escaped through seams in the solid fuel tanks. The tanks' welding joints, built in Zist's heavily-reduced atmosphere, physically weakened when the spaceship entered Earth's oxygen-rich environment, and had been leaking throughout the return journey. Using solid fuel containers for a liquid cargo that was later converted into a gaseous state, was not a wise decision. The fuel tanks can be electronically interchanged between solid, liquid and gas containers' capability. Xie simply forgot, perhaps due to the excitement of this unprecedented journey, to do the adjustments. How much he had missed Que's guidance.

The 250 cubic metres of H2O left in the tanks was not enough to power 30 vehicles carrying 500 million Zistians on each craft, so adjustments were made to quickly build much bigger Star ships.

After the first trip made by the three-man crew. The second consists of a total of 15 TSG vehicles: 12 large passenger ones (Each, half the size of the African nation of the Democratic Republic of Congo) and three smaller ones (Each, half the size of France), which includes two excavators and a water cargo carrier. This time using only Zoll 1 – Zoll 2 no longer available – they took five years to reach Earth travelling at a million times faster than light. Each passenger flying ship carried a billion Zist citizens. The two excavators were load carriers for taking away the dug-up soil and emptying it into deeper space. The third, and last vessel, was a container that would load up with more ice blocks and return to the yellow planet in preparation for the third and probably last earthbound trip ferrying the remaining three billion Zistians. After the final trip, the load carriers would either be buried on Earth or placed somewhere in deep waters on the Pacific Ocean sea bed to act as shelters for marine life, or even laboratories for Zist researchers.

The fleet had dummied all of Earth's monitoring systems and entered its atmosphere unseen. Invisible lasers mounted on the front of the dozen vessels dug huge shafts and tunnels through Earth and set up subterranean settlements: first three flying boats went to the Sahara desert and interred themselves deep underneath the sands. The next three, under the anchored eastern half of the Antarctic (There was a bit of an incident when the Zist engineers thought the entire continent was land). Two other vessels did the same underneath the permafrost soils of the Russian Steppes. These spacecraft were all self-contained, air-conditioned [Now that Zistians had become biologically-accustomed to breathing oxygen] prefabricated countries with enough materials for living conditions: energy, agriculture etc. etc. Two other TSGs went to the Australian outback. The last two, one each to North America (Western United States of America), and the other in South America (Under the Amazon forest).

The Brazilian excavation was the most arduous task: the TSG had to move huge land masses to make room for the ship and replace the top soil with all its massive vegetation and waterways intact. They did it during the Rio Negro river flooding, using it as a cover. But that flood waters cover was a huge challenge, to stop the rivers and their tributaries from transcending below ground. It was tiring for the engineers. More so when they were only getting used to being exposed to all those amounts of oxygen, even though most of the work was done by super computers.

During the five-year trek to the Milky Way galaxy, Zistians had been breathing oxygen, in bits, seeping through their masks, as they get acclimatised to earthly conditions. Most of them weren't even aware they were travelling outside their planet. They were only told they'd be moving to a new location a bit further from their dying star. For some, the thought of moving home, not just on a planetary scale but a stellar and up to galactic proportions, would have been too much to comprehend. Therefore, the Zist UN body kept it secret for a while until the mission is complete. Whenever the flights encountered massive vibrations and loud noises from interactions with galactic cosmic radiation blasts, the controllers would falsely report them as just zist-tremors and zistquakes.

Pee and Que having already landed on that first trip had been super busy working their ways into Earth's societies, setting up the stage for the future. A future when the subterranean cities would resurface and establish their rights to live on Earth's landscapes, claiming they were lost civilisations that even predated Earth humans.

Before the bulk super-emergence of these aliens would happen, small amounts of Zistians would have already been slowly bubbling up from the underground living systems to the over ground, into some countries in the Americas. Asia, Africa Europe etc. as refugees. Those in America have been learning Spanish. Those in Africa learned English, French and Portuguese. In Australia, English. In Russia, the Russian language etc.

Que in Israel had good access to the developed western societies (And some developing ones also), acquiring more on intelligence, social, finance and technology etc. whilst Pee had the same in the eastern cultures, particularly in China, Japan and South Korea. As the Zistian pioneers, both men had forged historical documents claiming to have been found in several places all over Earth, portraying Zist's seven races as Earthians older than even the planet Earth's oldest civilisation of Suma. Ones that came just after Adam and Eve. Some of their evidence were even brazen enough to claim the Zist people pre-existed the first couple.

Arguments ensued among Earth historians; some reckoned the Zistians could be a long-lost civilisation part of the fabled Atlantis. Others were not so sure. Pee and Que had also set up new identities, initially for G.U.T.S. staff members and Pris government officials, and later for prominent Brians and the rest of Zist's citizens from other parts of that world, with Earth-like names and particulars.

Prof. Nemad Scyzpr was to be called John Smith; Zapia Zill, to Jana Ivanikova; before his death, Trillian Freeze, to Francois Pierrer. Pystrn Poiter, to Akim Mansaray; Marx Afaro Zytan, to Hans Schmidt; Maila Zytan, to Petro Sokolov; Bampor Ajina, to Maria Suarez; Fannie Zypisth, to Mei Xing etc etc.

Dr Rannas Annaz's comments about giving Prisians first-class travel priority was utterly dismissed. In fact, she was wrongly thought to be one of the three billion Zists who didn't make the first trip, having had to deal with perpetual matrimonial problems with her husband, Servo Annaz. Servo is green, 60, 11 feet 2 inches tall, bald, sunken eye sockets, raised forehead, raised cheek bones, pointed ears and yellow twisty-beard. Nicknamed "The Cosmic" [Meaning alien in Zist talk]. He is the one, some people say, responsible for her sometimes erratic behaviour. He was much of a wide-boy, wheeler-dealer shyster sort of a fellow, cheating on her constantly, stealing her money and at times getting physical. But she still stood by him. Even estranging from her own family in order to keep her husband. Servo once threatened Rannas's older brother, Mandrif, over the phone that he will come over to his house and slap his wife's bum and he, Mandrif, won't be able to do anything about it. Mandrif called his bluff challenging him to do that. Servo was actually on his way to his brother-in-law's house to carry out that uncouth threat, when Rannas Annaz called in the police who stopped him on his way.

There was another time he had a white T-shirt; printed in black on the front were the words: '**I love you more than Wifi.**' Whenever any of his numerous girlfriends would read it and say: 'So you love me more than **wifi**,' he would reply, 'No, read it again. It's "I love you more than **wifey**".' Whilst he would say to his wife, Dr Rannas Annaz, this is to prove I love you more than **wifi**, since you've complained I spend too much time on the internet.

Others on board the flight trip were Prof. Zytan and Zapia who have become a couple in the wake of their tribunal pyrrhic successes. An open verdict concluded someone did commit the crimes which they cannot place on the professor, nor totally acquit him of either. So the investigation continued on another route. The detective team then travelled to Bria to work on their findings after learning the PM had returned home to Bria.

The rest of the 210 countries that make up the Zist global population also had citizens on board that trip.

At the end of this story, the reader will be given answers to some nagging questions like: Is Trillian Freeze really dead? Where is Marx's missing money? Who the PM was and who impersonated Prof. Nemad in the office? Also why no one can remake Zoll 2; which the accidental inventor Maila Zytan himself can't?

A notable absentee was Marx Zytan, who had an urgent deal to settle in Bria before the departure date.

7

Marx was lured back to Bria to collect the rest of the money he was owed in settlement for selling the Zoll 2 secrets to V.I.M. The first deposit he had given to the TSG crew to be paid into his proposed new bank account on planet Earth under his new name and identity. V.I.M. boss Saztah was livid when he found the out Marx had not only given them the wrong formula for Zoll 2 but a fake sample as well.

Even back home in Pris, things are not looking so good for him. Starday had already betrayed his deceit to the State authorities who had an arrest warrant out for him. He had hopelessly relied on Maila to guess the solution correct, and when that failed he even urinated, "spend a penny", into the mixture himself to make Zoll 2. Blinded by greed, he didn't check the result and went straight on to sell it to bitter rival V.I.M. and pocketed the money.

He had arrived in Bria with his cat, which was kept in a separate place. They led him hands tied behind his back and blindfolded into a quiet room at rear end of the building. He felt the sudden change in room temperature, the staleness, which was quite different from the rest of the cool air-conditioning freshness that greeted him when he first entered at the reception. The tightly-tied blindfold was blocking parts of his nostrils as he started partially breathing through his mouth, tasting the stale air in the poorly ventilated room.

Once they took off the rag that was wrapped around his eyes, the bright lights almost blinded him. It was a fairly big hall with no ceiling. Two huge bright lamps hung from the corrugated metal sheets forming a high roof. The walls are exposed unpainted concrete blocks. One side of which has a large fading red smudge that runs from the wall onto the floor, in what appeared like a huge fading blood stain. There were more red smudges; either old blood stains or ones made to the effect to intimidate captives brought there. A chair was dragged with a screeching noise across the floor towards him. Every sound, even their footfalls, reverberates around the room, informing they are in an echo-chamber-like sort of a place.

This could only mean one thing, he thought, a silent execution. Choosing such a location to hold any noise inside, from going outside. He started calming down in fright as they sat him down strapped tight to a straight-back chair facing a huge mahogany desk. Leaning on the huge desk was Saztah.

He then thought, ah! No surprise here, it's Saztah, or should I say disaster. Who wasn't looking at him as he said:

'I didn't lie to you, man. Look man, I didn't know the Zoll 2 mixture was wrong. No one could get it right. I'm telling the truth man.'

Saztah replied: 'Don't man, man me. You bloody thief. How else did you know we were going to say the formula you sold us was fake if you didn't it was before trading it to our company?'

He replied: 'Oh, why then did you blindfold and handcuff me?'

'You knew all along that wasn't the right mixture but greed wouldn't let you control yourself,' the V.I.M. chief roared in fury.

Marx responded saying: 'I kept my side of the bargain and delivered the stuff, didn't I?'

'Oh yes, you did alright,' Saztah replied sarcastically. 'Only that your side of the deal came up short. You're not an honest broker. No wonder your first wife Hatzas left you, fucking loser,' he sneered at him.

'That bitch left me? If you must know it was me who dumped the bloody she-devil,' he replied in exasperation as he was feeling more and more relaxed.

Saztah quickly stood up and started circling around him, with the ear-splitting sound of his studded shoes stomping the bare concrete floor in a menacing way.

'Be careful what you say now, Marx. You don't know who is listening. You wouldn't want her to hear you say that.' Marx turned his head around searching the room to see who else was in there with them. Standing inside the door was Ontus with arms folded across his chest. He mopped that scare on his forehead when Marx Zytan looked at him.

'Why are we talking about my estranged wife anyway? Are you fucking her now or something?'

Saztah replied: 'Why ask such a silly question? You go fuck yourself.'

'Look, this is out of my hands,' Marx ranted. 'No one can remake the hydrocarbon's second stage. It was just one hell of a fluke it happened the first time. Just untie my hands and get me out of this hell of a hole.'

'This is the real Marx Zytan alright. Even when his life is at risk, he never backs down,' the V.I.M. boss said.

Marx who had hated Saztah from the moment they first met when he walked into their office in Bria unannounced to sell them G.U.T.S's trade secrets, is now beginning to respect his rival a bit more. But the feeling of admiration was only short-lived.

Saztah walked around the desk and pulled out from the bottom drawer a long object wrapped up in Bria's national flag and held it pointing upwards with one end resting on the floor. 'It's my favourite weapon and I going to finish you off with it once and for all.'

He started pleading for his life as Saztah advanced towards him with the object still in its wrapper. 'Please man don't kill me. I will give you whatever you want,' Marx pleaded.

'I told you to stop man, manning me. I am definitely not your man,' his captor snapped back at him.

With the sight of the weapon so close, though still concealed, Zytan felt like peeing himself. He looked across at Ontus standing by the door, as he once again dabbed that scar, and looked back at Saztah and continued appealing for his life.

'Look, Saztah, let's don't end it like this. This is only the second time we are meeting each other. Just let me go and I'll give you anywhere from five to ten billion wands, and I mean it. Even much more when I can raise it. Please don't shoot me.'

'I might just uphold your plea not to shoot you but your offer to trust you with money is completely a different matter?' Saztah bowed his head and burst out laughing in filthy fits, with one hand holding onto the object and the other rubbing his forehead in the sticky atmosphere in the room. He raised his head again, still laughing, looking at Ontus who joined him in the laughter. Their laughing was chillingly echoing around, continuously in a super scary and sinister way in the almost empty room, as one is ending the laughter, the other begins, in a chain process. It's an old tactic Marx had used before on some of his victims. Now he's getting a feel of his own treatment. He glanced once more at Onus who then swiped his forehead again, and this got him irritated. He turned his attention to Saztah and sneered:

'Will you just tell him to stop doing that. Every time I look at him he mops his brow at me.'

'Oh that is between you two. When you cut him mercilessly in that nightclub, he was only looking out for his underage baby sister, who ended up being your wife.'

Almost shouting in anger Marx asked: 'What the hell are you on about? Your guard here wasn't in any way related to Hatzas!' With a quiz look in his face.

'That's where you are wrong. There are heaps of things you don't know about sweetheart. He is my older brother.' Marx got really confused. 'What the fuck you're talking about?'

Saztah gently laid down the object, approached him and bent down to his ear, close enough for him to smell his stale tobacco breath, whispering:

'I am Hatzas (nee Ajina) Zytan your estranged wife. Saztah is just a name, spelled in reverse. Which I took on after my gender transformation, yet to do the operational bit though. Reason why when you asked me if I'm fucking your wife? I said to you, "You go fuck yourself," because I don't fuck myself Marx. And as my ex-husband you should know that.'

Walking back to the desk, he continued: 'You made me a misandrist (A hater of males) until I met with Ontus here again, after almost two decades of alienated affection caused by your action. He bitterly disapproved of our marriage. Seeing his scar reminded me of the sacrifice he made for me, and that helped to heal me from my men-hating.'

Marx wasn't impressed, thinking it was part of an intimidation tactic to destabilise him, though at the back of his mind he started giving the situation some serious thoughts, as he continued listening:

'I then bought Voyage Amalgamate International [V.A.I] and brought him along after you and I broke up. I changed the name to Voyage International Management [V.I.M]. The name-change wasn't because G.U.T.S were mocking it. No, none of that; it was more to do with you already knowing that brand. I then set up a trap getting you to come back here wanting to sell us Zoll. I know you are a very, very greedy bastard, Marx, and you'd come.

'Though I must admit I thought you'd at least sell us the real stuff.'

Zytan's complexion changed from lime green to emerald, now beginning to believe the story. His mouth halfway opened gaping at his now estranged wife who moments earlier was just a business rival in a male suit he had only met once before.

'I even got one of my guards to sell you a V.I.M. office pass and fake Bria passport, since you destroyed the diplomatic one given to you by our Government.

Are you still working for them?'

There was a pause, he couldn't answer – his brain was blank, so she continued: 'I sent the disguise too which you used to get here from Pris. Didn't you notice everything was so easy for you to acquire, Marx? You damn fool, your greed always come in the way. Ontus didn't know about it all because he hates you and might have disapproved. I only let him in on the secret late last night and he's happy to face you here on his home turf. Well, our home turf once again, Marx.'

Marx finally believed it all, having known her for such a long time he can tell by her facial countenance whenever she was dead serious. She then went on to give details of their marriage on matters only the two of them would know so intimately. It was at this stage Marx's head slumped in front of his chest, fainting in utter shock.

He came around few minutes later looking as if he had aged several years in an instant. The lower part of his face sagged after the denture holding it up had dropped out of his mouth when he lost consciousness.

'Ah! Welcome back, she mocked, wrying her nose in the air. 'By the way tonight will be the night the curse of the Zytanas – bearing so much trouble to the clan – is at long last brought to a close,' as she slowly picked up the long object again and in a slow deliberate fashion, started unwrapping it.

He didn't hear her properly, so he asked: 'Zyta who?' But she ignored him and carried on speaking: 'I know quite well for that to happen, a wife of anyone of the Zytan males will have to kill her spouse and then destroyed the blade. The curse can't be eliminated otherwise.'

He wanted to ask another question if only to make sure he had really heard what he just heard but words couldn't come out of his mouth. She continued:

'Legend has it the handle is made from the human skull fragments of the bitterest enemy of the great Banday tribal chief, Abona the second, your great, great, grandfather,' she said as she finally revealed the whole sword.

The shocking sight of the weapon involuntarily forced spittle and phlegm up Marx's throat choking him, as he began coughing and trying to yell at the same time:

'That is couoo ououuuugh my missing coouuugh oou ssword. My long stolen couuuuu couuugh Zytana. You damn thief. All this time…' But he couldn't complete the sentence. The coughing was forcing his head down which he was struggling to keep up looking at Hatzas.

With some effort, he managed to sit up straight. There was obvious horror, anger and relief to his voice. Horror at the sight of being threatened with a sword; anger thinking his ex-partner knew where it was all this time; relief the "Beautiful Zytana" is still in existence.

'All this time what? Eh? You had me shackled up with you in a Faustian pact using the mythical Zytanas as the lock and key but no sooner I got control of it,'– as she cast her eyes at the sword and ran her fingers downwards on it–'I broke out of that mould you forced me into, a life of servitude to you since I was a teen, Marx. Tonight you'd be falling on your own sword. Maybe not quite literally, but who knows eh, you might still do.'

Oddly enough, Marx started fancying her again. Seeing her weaving power over him for the first time ever in a role reversal.

'When I first saw you disc-jockeying at the Dark Secrets nightclub I was barely 13 years old.' She continued, 'Your lyrics and word-power mesmerised me. I then walked up to your booth, gave you a peck on the cheek, though you went for my mouth. We couldn't hear each other properly over the loud music so I used my lipstick to scribble down my phone number for you on a piece of tissue. You said you love my slim-fitted open-back mini dress. And you were also about to take me home that same night when Ontus here tried to stop it, warning you I'm way underage. But you wouldn't listen, would you? You two then got into a fight and you viciously slashed him across the face, Marx.'

Half-turning around to face Ontus she asked: 'That same day was Dad's birthday, wasn't it?'

'Yes, Dad and I have the same birthday,' her brother replied as he shifted his standing posture. She went: 'Oh yes, oh yes. Sorry, I forgot you two have the same birthday. Coincidentally which is the same day as today.'

Ontus cleared his throat then unfolded and fold his arms again across his chest and said: 'What are the chances.'

'Just imagine savagely cutting the birthday boy on his celebratory night out. You like cutting people, don't you, Marx. Even that spooky skull in your bedroom has cut marks across its brow that makes it look like it's frowning. Was it someone you cut so deep it left scars on the bone? What about that other time when that gentleman down the fish market asked if you not eating fish has anything to do with your surname meaning swordfish. You took one of the knives on the counter and chopped off his left ear. I can still to this day see his severed ear doing a chicken-dance on the fish stall. Oh Marx! You've left a lasting ill-famed impression here in Bria. Society still casts judgement on your violent behaviour even after all these years. And it was badly affecting me until I dropped your surname and transitioned, trying to live my life true to myself.' She then looked at the sword and hissed menacingly, 'How I have been longing for this day when you'd be at my mercy, Marx.'

Giggling for a bit, she continued, 'Actually a clairvoyant once told me it will happen someday. Though I didn't expect it to be this soon. When I'll avenge all your evil deeds to the universe.'

Putting up a brave face, he decided his best hope of survival was to talk her around. Something he had done successfully many times in the past. So he quipped, more in hope than expectation:

'Some psychologists say much of our sadness is derived from holding too much onto the unpleasant past and those yet to come. Let bygones be bygones.'

She paused for a moment and went:

'Hmmm, sounds familiar eh. That sweet-syrup salivating tongue wringing its way into vulnerable women's hearts.'

He couldn't bring himself looking at Ontus again for he knew what would happen. But moments later he wilted, turning to take another look when he saw him yet again wiping his face with a tissue, and giving him a wry nose also.

'Your brother here is still doing this wiping thing. Provoking me,' he bellowed.

'That's between you two. He is well aware it brings you out in cold sweat every time he does that. Probably his way of reminding you of past grievances. He was only protecting his baby sister, Marx. Haven't you got siblings too? Oh I forgot you even tried to kill your younger brother to save yourself from the Zytanas curse a lifeless thing you love and worth more than even humans.' Hatzas moaned.

Marx made attempts getting up from the chair but only managed falling flat on his side onto the cold concrete floor, still tied to the seat. Ontus sat him up again by raising the chair, and avoid having to touch him.

'Let's tell the story behind your Zytanas, Marx.'

'ZYTANA! Not Zytanas,' he snapped at her.

She stared at him and continued speaking, ignoring the correction:

'No one in your clan knew where this "sacred" (She raised both hands open in the air folding the fore and middle fingers indicating a quotation) sabre came from. Absolutely no one. Though there are about half-a-dozen or so legendary tales on its origins. One of that says your great, great grandfather, Chief Abona the second followed instructions he got in a dream and received it from birds that feed on human carcasses on high mountain tops.'

She hunched herself and grimaced towards him, expressing doubts about the story, and then continued: 'Your own grandfather, the great Abona the fourth, passed on the custom to your father who hated the Banday culture and its strict demands so much he sold the Zytanas, sorry Zytana, to a private collector whom you later bought it off to save the family face. Your dad then renounced his hereditary and became a Bria intelligence officer. He was meant to be a sleeping double-agent-plus sent to Pris with the aim of you having a child that would one day become a 3G spy. Sadly, your dad went there and became too fondly of Pris and completely abandoned the plot. Bria intelligence then liquidated him for treachery and tried training you instead. Unfortunately, you were simply not intelligent enough to become a spy. You were fancifully expecting the daft as a brush Maila to become the 3G man, (Or he bearing 4G or 5G children who would then become spies) which all along was our spooks' original plan. But alas, like father like son, he wasn't smart enough and failed the intelligence tests. You then rescued him out of his life in the criminal underworld, in Pris, and brought him to G.U.T.S.'

Once she completed that part of the story, he suddenly became angry as to how she got to know all this: 'Look I don't need you giving me any bloody public lectures on my family history. Just let me get out of here and I will pay something towards my freedom.'

'What family history? The one you've picked apart? Oh you're going to pay alright, this time with your life that is,' she groaned chillingly. Hearing the death threat scared him to bits; he was now as steady as a rock. He'd prefer she continued with the clan story instead of threatening his life, so he remarked: 'I was loyal to my home country.'

'Oh yes, you were I must admit.' As she dragged the sword across the floor making loud scratching noises and leaving marks behind. 'Unlike your turncoat father who not only sold his family silver but his country's as well.'

'"Home is where the heart is," something you were reported to have said at one time to our PM spy in another country. I don't know which one.'

Marx won't discuss anything to do with spying so he changed the subject to continue with the lie that Maila is adopted and not his biological child.

'Don't give me that bullshit, my darling, Marx. Continue with the pretence if you want to. I just gave you a shot to make amends, lauding your patriotism but you threw it back in my face with your classical deceit. You should know better than most how I hate liars. And it's for that matter I will tell the whole story which is being recorded. Sorry, I forgot to mention that earlier.'

Marx was pressing to see Ontus's reaction so far but he doesn't want to be reminded of that creepy scar anymore.

As his estranged wife went to sit back at the desk and continue her story. Surprisingly for her, Marx was still showing interest in listening. (Which was good for him, since there were parts he didn't have much knowledge of before now):

'Bampor is our daughter whom you drugged and impregnated to give birth to Maila. The young man is your son and grandson all in one, typical Marx Zytan fashion of chaos. My stepson and grandson also in one. Reason why you continued lying he is adopted. The sadder bit is Bampor doesn't even know that was the baby she gave birth to at the tender angelic age of eleven and had to give him away to an orphanage. Maila probably got his height from grandma. Poor Bampor. We, I mean you and me, changed her surname to my maiden one of Ajina, to hide the family disgrace. Isn't that so, Marx? No wonder she is a bit like you, so exploitative. I also understand whenever she asked you to make love to her, thinking you are only a family friend who had adopted her, you go cold with torment, not guilt. But I wonder why. Because you simply have a heart of a cold stone and don't feel guilty of anything whatsoever.

'Sad but true, Marx. You're the common denominator to all your family troubles. Things you brought down upon yourself, from you wanting to kill your own brother to save your skin, you also fucking his wife, impregnating our daughter, raping me, stabbing my brother, and now betraying your own colleagues, just to mention a few of your evilness.'

Ontus gave a loud sigh. Marx can no longer hold back not looking at him. He glanced over his shoulder towards him and to his surprise Ontus didn't wipe his face. He turned back to his estranged wife who continued the story, 'Ooooh, Marx, you see how you have a lot to answer for. Enslaved to selfishness which has always brought misery not only upon yourself, but your family as a whole. So as me still being your wife, slaying you now would be a huge favour to us all, unburdening the next generation of the Zytan curse. Just as I mentioned earlier about you wanting to slay your younger brother in order to end the Zytana curse. An ancestral oath that can only be erased once a wife of a Zytan family member will kill her husband and destroyed the weapon stained with his blood. Sad, Marx, sad. You were not only screwing your younger brother, Tambay's wife but also paid her to kill him with the sword and hand it over back to you. When she refused you killed her in a setup road accident. I have had enough of you Marx and now it's time for you to say farewell.'

Ontus cleared his throat loudly in anticipation of what is about to happen.

Hatzas got up from behind the desk and lift up the sword facing Marx.

'He who lives by the sword…' But before she could complete saying the last four words, he joined her, saying it: 'Dies by the sword.'

'He that is down needs fear no fall,' he continued, reading figurative expressions, mixing them with music lyrics and airing his talent for word-power. All those memories of them together started streaming back to her head; recalling how he had seduced and deflowered her when working as a disc-jockey the same night her brother was taken to the hospital.

Now looking at him helplessly strapped to a seat at her mercy, she was beginning to feel sorry for him, and this Marx was quick to have noticed also. So as a last ditch attempt at saving himself he went deeper into the lyrics. Looking away from her, avoiding eye contact, the colourful words were airing off his lips making music to her ears. She slowly lay down the sword back on the floor and wanting him to look at her, beginning to fancy him again. Begging inside herself for him to do her like he used to, basically wanting to be fucked by him at that same moment. She turned around to her brother and asked him to give them a moment. All that childhood rape was still having psychological effects on her mind, still trapped in his love cobweb of deceit.

Ontus was quick to notice this. He bit the tip of his forefinger expressing disbelief, released the digit and snapped furiously, 'What the freaking hell for? Why should I leave the bloody room?'

'Just want to say a few final words, that's all's,' she whispered in a dropped-down voice weakened by desire. Lying to save whatever was left of their relationship so she can have him again, even if it's just for that one last moment.'

Her brother was having none of this and reminded himself of the night he was stabbed.

Had she walked away when I was holding her hand and asked her to, I would have been in a better position to defend myself, he kept thinking. He also remembered that meeting when Marx walked into their office and convinced her to pay him ₩150m for Zoll 2. Which was a fraud.

'I've had enough of this evil monster,' he roared, as he picked up the sword, grabbed his sister by the arm and forcibly ushered her out of the room, ignoring her crying pleas Once by the door she stopped, and said: 'Look Onts, let me just say some final words. Please it's important.' So he let her speak. Sobbing and sniffing, snort running down her nose:

Sniff, sniff. 'By the way.' Sniff. 'That guy you saw at the meeting in dark glasses,'–sniff, sniff, mopping mucus from her nostrils as she speaks–'the one wearing off-white suit and brown bowtie who wouldn't speak to anyone, is our son, Laxin-Togo. I only found out I was pregnant weeks after we separated. Though 3Q is claiming him as his (Marx didn't hear her last sentence about his old nemesis, 3Q who is serving triple life sentences).'

Marx sprung to life and said: 'Really? I want to meet with my son, eh, our son. What's his name again?'

Hatzas responded: 'Laxin-Togo! Trying to sound all affectionate now are we. When did you start caring, Marx?' She hissed.

'Oh, he thinks that would now save his skin.' Ontus laughed. 'No chance, pal. That young man hated your guts and only kept the disguise as a condition of him being in the same room as you. Otherwise my nephew risked killing you then,' Ontus added and finally pushed his sister out of the room.

He then faced Marx and said: 'We gonna have some real fun, chum. Just you and me, eh? Old friends, after all these years.'

As he took off his jacket threw it on the floor and rolled up his sleeves, revealing well muscled heavily-tattooed arms.

'You may have noticed I'm enjoying this. Having you under the cosh is something I have long been dreaming of since that fateful night up to this day.'

He then paused for some response from his captive, which he didn't get, so he continued the taunting:

'My hatred for you ranges from the deep personal; after you scarred me for life, to the familial, after what you did to my baby sister. Now stand up!' he ordered. Still Marx didn't respond. Just staring pokerfaced at him with deep hatredness.

One so deep he can hardly breathe properly. But his silence was just beginning to unnerve Ontus, who in a desperate bid to assume control barked out another order, in a louder tone: 'GET THE FUCK UP!' But still no response. 'I SAY STAND THE HELL UP BEFORE I SLASH YOUR FUCKING HEAD OFF,' trying to sound with much menace as possible. Still Marx refused to budge. And this got him very angry. They were just staring at each other with such grudge, it was Ontus who was trembling with nerves, whilst Marx was almost as cool as a cucumber.

Then for a moment there the room went eerily quiet, a complete stillness to it as the two men continued gazing at each other in pure nastiness and hatred, not saying a word. Ontus who was bisexual, even felt like giving him a sadistic kiss in the mouth but then controlled himself, thinking that would be inappropriate after what he did to his baby sister. Then the Manx cat began scratching at the door. Both men ignored it.

'I'm going to literally put you to the sword.' After having forced himself to overcome his masochistic thoughts.

'I, like my sister, have been longing for this man-to-man face-up, and luckily that itch is now finally being scratched good and proper.' Gnashing his teeth and moving very slowly towards him.

Marx wasn't responding to the threats, no longer even looking at Ontus. A confidence display making Ontus more and more nervous, now shaking like a leaf thinking his nemesis might have something up his sleeve. So he suddenly decided to end it all before anything else might happen.

He lifted the sword with hands almost paralysed with fear. The dazzling blade's reflected light from the hanging lamps, momentarily blinded Marx, as Ontus in one fell swoop slashed into his abdomen with such a force to disembowelled him instantly and unintentionally cut off the rope tying him to the chair. Zytan whined slightly but still stayed calm almost feeling no pain. Just his guts had popped, hanging out but with no blood. But seeing his own intestines frightened him a bit. He had wrongly thought for his sister's sake Ontus won't kill him. Cut him maybe but not to kill him. As he stood up, that was when he started feeling intense abdominal pain as more of his guts seeped out. The huge blade came swinging at him again at the same time he was crouching to sit down due to his weakened legs The sword swished past over his head by a couple of inches, missing him. The force swung Ontus off his feet, losing his balance as he almost fell to the floor.

Regaining his stance, he grinned at him with his huge gap-toothed:

'Ah lucky bastard. But I hated wasting time, so there will be no torturing.'

Marx thought about begging for his life but the words simply couldn't come out of his mouth, not to this man standing in front of him of all people, he thought. Ontus then plunged the blade once again, this time deeper into Marx's torso making a thud sound followed by muffling noises where the steel blade's force was being absorbed by his rival's internal organs. Ontus deliberately twisted the weapon around inside the stomach for maximum damage before retrieving the bloodied weapon. Marx squealed like a pig and started grunting in pain. Ontus then sneered: 'Now that I know you won't survive this I'll call my sister and get her to finish the job. If not the Zytana curse will continue to haunt the family (Saying 'the family' avoiding to say 'your family' that might sound as if he is helping him in particular), threatening Maila and future generations and I won't let that happen.'

Hatzas was in the other room crying bitterly when her brother went and brought her back into the room. She was followed in by the Manx.

She first thought about refusing to kill her estranged husband, but for Maila and others in the future she had to.

The cat seeing her owner lying on the floor in distress, a stranger standing over him with a bloodied weapon in hand, sprang in rage at Ontus scratching open the old forehead scar. Ontus felt the pain and blood running down his face dripping onto his white shirt, reminding him of that Glambock eve (Christmas eve) fight with Marx when his white shirt was blood soaked, lashed out at the cat, slicing it deep in the neck. Hatzas winched in horror, pulling herself away from the splattering gore. The badly wounded animal dropped onto the floor as Ontus yielded another blow at it but the sword missed its target as sparks flew from the metal smashing into the concrete floor. There, the cat was purring, slowing dying alongside her master when Ontus gave it another severe blow, cutting off its head completely on the blood-spattered floor.

'Come on and get this done quickly before he dies,' he ordered his sister. 'Even in death these two are giving me the creeps,' pointing the weapon at Marx and the manx.

Looking at her brother's forehead still dripping blood, she held her mouth in both her hands and chuckled: 'Talking about opening old wounds.'

He got angry at what he sees as her insensitivity to his pains, 20 years ago and then now again: 'So you think this is funny, don't you?'

She replied: 'Noooo Onts [Onts is his pet name].' She then appeared to have choked, making a gulping sound, but managed to ask: 'What makes you say that?'

'Since the start of it all it's been fun and games for you, isn't it?' Swiping his left hand through his dyed jet-black hair while leering into her face. But he can now see the remorse in her eyes. 'Now take this bloody sword and finish him off before it's too late to kill off the curse.'

Slowly, she took the weapon off him and quickly plunged it across her ex-partner's throat almost killing him. Despite three deadly stabbings, the almost immortal Marx was still not dead. Blood spouting viciously from his severed jugular vein, spraying out of the deep wound in his throat. With one eye opened looking at her, he uttered some spluttering sounds as if he was trying to say something but the effort was too much for him. With one last brave attempt, he flung his left hand at the Zytana, clinging on to it as if he wanted to snatch the blade away from his estranged wife and take it along with him. He was getting weaker with every effort made, as his struggles to do something was only making matters worse. The eye rolled over and closed. He was gone. Hatzas burst out crying inconsolably holding both hands over her face. The legendary Marx Afaro Zytan is gone forever. Famous for being infamous. Gone without his billions and the cherished dream to continue life on planet Earth. Fellow Earthians should be thanking their stars.

****

Before his death, Marx had accused Starday of reporting him to the Prisian police. This, in addition to that botched raid on Zapia, had the rogue billionaire seething in anger and wowing for revenge. He had three of his men kidnap the ex-police chief and took him to a disused garage at his holiday mansion in the Prisian suburbs. It was raining cats and dogs that morning, blurring the vehicle's windows as they drove him to the hideaway location. Though he wasn't blindfolded, Starday had difficulties making out the journey. For them to allow him seeing where they were heading warns him of something, he thought. And that something could be his death as he won't live to tell the tale. He sensed they were travelling to the north western Prisia suburbs after they drove through the famous Seven Sisters undulating A33 motorway. Feeling the tumbling effects on his stomach nerves like a roller coaster ride, he used this experience as a navigational tool correctly mapping out where they were driving to Marx Zytan's hide-away villa.

They had captured him on a corner street when he was out walking his dog. He saw a man lying looking helpless on the pavement making grunting noises, and appearing to be in some sort of agony. His policing instincts kicked in and went to help. No sooner he made an approach, two other men came running towards them asking what's wrong with their mate. Starday was just about to explain when they bundled him into a waiting car, leaving his barking dog behind. 'You have a lot to answer for,' Marx chided, as his men stood up the ex-police chief, stripped to the waist, in front of a chair that had a poisonous snake, on a leash, tied onto its legs. The reptile had two menacing fangs sticking out of its mouth as it hisses around. Suddenly, Marx's cat jumped out of his hand onto the serpent and the two animals started play fighting. You can see the joy on their faces that they like each other.

Starday already trembling in fear was startled, almost paralysed in shock not believing his eyes. He had never before seen a snake put on reins, neither had he seen one play-fighting with a cat. These two types of animal are known to hate each other vehemently. Marx Zytan is well known to be evil and weird, but this takes a beating, he thought. Marx saw his old friend was in great fear and cautioned him: 'If you don't alarm it, it won't harm either. It's blind you see, reason for the leash. And it hates to be disturbed with noises as it can't see what's going on around it. You'd be sitting just above its head. All you have to do is just stay calm. And all I want from you is quietness.' Marx deliberately picking his words, sounding different to Starday's ears.

'As you can see this is a very peaceful neighbourhood and I want it to stay that way. And as for these two liking each other,'–pointing his sword at the two animals who had just stopped playing and had their heads hung adoringly towards their master–'they grew up together. The only thing he can see is her glow. Otherwise the serpent is completely blind,' he said, smiling and trembling more visibly as he was in a joyous mood.

The former police chief inspector had witness a couple of his colleagues killed by serpent bites on two different occasions. They had gone in to rescue the animals from an unlicensed dealer who then deliberately released the reptiles onto harming the police officers.

'I, I, I don't understand. Why, why dooo I have to siiit there?' Starday stuttered in a trembling voice.

'I'll show you why. Just look, listen and learn,' Marx replied as he then hollered out loudly, 'BLAHHHH, BLAHH, BLAHHHHH'. The reptile got agitated and started meandering around biting several parts of the chair's legs.

'You see what I mean?' Marx said. 'So just sit and stay calm and make no noise. No sound, and everything will be fine.' The men slowly dragged the ex-police boss and again slowly and deliberately strapped him to the chair.

'You see how the boys are handling the situation with care and respect for the animal? You just do the same.'

Marx started pacing around his seated old friend, dragging his sword along across the floor making scratching noises. He then began to air long-held grievances against his captive, some of which the former cop himself wasn't even aware of.

He chuckled towards him. 'I'm going to take you to the deepest end of the pool and drown you. And afterwards hung you out to dry.' Laughing hysterically.

It was a cool mid-morning, the heavy rain had ceased, but Starday found himself soaked in sweat like he had just come out of a steam bath.

'We have always been cool with one and another, aren't we?' the ex-police chief pleaded, drooling saliva from his mouth in large enough quantities that would make a buffalo's salivating habit look like nothing in comparison.

'I really don't know where all this hatred from you is coming from Marx,' As he sat trembling and rattling the chair. 'I warned you not to alarm the rattle snake,' Marx chided, just stopping behind him.

Starday made an effort to turn around facing him but he physically can't, realising the chair he had been tied onto is cemented into the concrete floor.

'What about that time I begged you to delete those evidence against my friend before he was convicted and sent to a life imprisonment, eh?' Marx asked, narrowing his eyes towards him.

The ex-cop's eyes popped out wide in shock and disbelief as if his throat was being squeezed:

'But Marx you have to realise I have done that sort of work for you three times before, and that channelled was blocked afterwards. Mind you I only managed to escape prosecution by the skin of my teeth after getting caught the last time. I just wasn't able to do it again. Please be reasonable man.'

Marx and reasonable are two words that never goes together.

Then suddenly there was a huge whacking sound as a raw, wet and hard leather strip was lashed out on Starday's bare back with the force of an execution's blow. He wanted to scream in pain but bit his tongue instead, suppressing any sound. His face twisted in torture holding back the pressure to cry.

Marx moved a bit closer towards him: 'Well done. You're tougher than you look.'

He then with a heavier force whacked the wet leather strip again on Starday's upper back, closer to the neck. This time he couldn't resist screaming as he screeched out loud relieving the pain. The rattle snake got agitated once again and started biting violently at the chair. Starday closed his eyes expecting the worse, all he could hear was the fangs gnashing and gnawing against the woodwork.

Marx's thugs couldn't believe their eyes. First time ever someone in that chair never got bitten after the snake was alarmed. They were staring at their captive in awe when Marx lifted his sword and started stabbing him in the chest. The ex-copper didn't even make any sound and just died on the spot almost peacefully.

This is the reason why Marx Zytan and Lucian Starday never made the trip to planet Earth.

8

Earth's new inhabitants had settled in their new subterranean homes, still living on the 12 TSG flying boats dubbed "Noah's Arks of the Seven Races" (Another evidence of their knowledge of Earth's literature).

A late decision was made not to bury the two empty TSG excavators. One was placed in the deepest place on Earth, the Challenger Deep in the Mariana Trench in the Pacific Ocean. Whilst the other was laid in the Puerto Rico Trench on the Atlantic Ocean sea bed. They both serve as reefs and habitat for marine creatures and also laboratories for Zistian scientists. These are some of the points on Earth no human has even been. (The aliens got there before us. Little wonder earth scientists say we have more knowledge of outer space [the cosmos], than we do of inner space [the deep seas]).

The last and 15th vessel started loading blocks of ice into the gas-fuel containers [Avoiding the last mistake] for the five-year return journey home to Zist.

Xie, known for his famous blunder, wasn't in charge this time; he's now part of those living underground on Earth.

Two new pilots took on the task. They were, Braz Coldoz, male, green, 59, 7 feet 7 inches tall. Lean-faced, sharply-pointed nose, almost lipless mouth, high cheekbones and round eyes. Green wavy hair. Reputed to be highly intelligent but a bit too playful as well. Co-pilot Thoruxe Daprah, female, black, 49, 6 feet 5 inches tall. Round face, Nubian nose, firm round lips, dimpled cheeks and huge round eyes. Black hair in braids. She has won several beauty pageants at university. Also highly intelligent but tend to be over-cautious at times. Coldoz and Daprah's characterisation tend to balance each other out. Probably one of the reasons they were paired together, not to mention intelligence.

They were just about to complete filling up the containers with ice floes from Siberia when Coldoz said:

'Let's go over to Alaska and get some more.'

Daprah was not so sure, she replied:

'What's the point? Why not just finish here and return home.'

Coldoz smiled at her and said: 'Wouldn't you want to tell the remaining folks back home that you got American ice too. Tell me, would you want to miss out on that?'

She tried arguing ice is ice and better for them to leave immediately. He simply ignored her pleas and swung the flying ship heading west.

Once over North America she recommended: 'OK, just here in eastern Canada will do. Alaska is just a bit too further away.'

'Oh come on you spoil sport,' her crew mate said, childishly grinning.

'You just sit back and enjoy the ride. I simply want American ice. I've read about them from information we got from the I.S.S.' As he accelerated the vehicle further west over to Alaska.

They were about to land when he said: 'Oh! Oh! I think we've left some of the electronic digging gear back in Russia. They are very expensive and would be very difficult to replace.'

'That was because you were busy arguing about making the wholly unnecessary trip to the United States,' Daprah replied, leering at her companion.

They turned the starship eastbound again. Throughout the return trip to the Russian wilderness they didn't speak, she was really annoyed. When they got there, she was waiting in the vehicle whilst he disembarked to retrieve the items very close to the foothills of the ice mountains.

Suddenly, a giant ice sheet the size of a small country dislodged, due to vibrations caused by the TSG's rushed landing gear, and crashed into Coldoz, trapping him underneath it. Dapram jumped out of the vessel to help rescue him but it was too late he had been crushed and shredded into tiny pieces being transported underneath, alongside ground debris moraines by the glacial mass. Then the moving ice giant crushed into the ship's rear end. She rushed and jumped back in trying to rescue it. The vehicle soared into the air, its alarm system persistently blaring warnings, 'Too low terrain, too low terrain…' She skilfully managed getting it higher to about 35000 feet, trying to launch back into space but too much physical damaged had been done to the craft. The TSG started descending, veering south eastwards. Further southeast descent careering out of control and plunging into the South China sea.

Before it crashed, Zye Pee and Rallax Que received S.O.S . calls from the ship but were helpless to do anything successful about it. They tried using electronic web magnets from their cosmic sub-stations dotted around the universe, to capture and haul it back in for repairs, while simultaneously trying remote-controlled remedial work themselves, all to no avail. The digital nanoelectronic computers weren't responding properly. Even the gossamer materials, that should be self-repairing after damage, on the fuselage, were damaged beyond repair and had lost its aerodynamic capabilities.

For some bizarre reason, the crash's shockwaves restarted some of Earth's monitoring systems, that were only a couple of hours earlier electronically, blinded by Zist's crew, bringing them back to life.

The ISS, in collaboration with the Russians, Americans and Chinese, alerted the world a giant UFO, the size of a very large country, had crashed into the South China Sea. The TSG split into multiple parts, closely missing the Beijing-controlled Spratly Islands by less than two nautical miles. The crash almost sunk American aircraft carrier the USS Bara Ohama, drowning two of its crew. The ensuing flood waters destroyed Chinese military personnel equipment and infrastructure on the Paracel Islands.

'Surround the vessel's main hull and seize it,' bellowed the United States Navy Strike Group commander from the bridge of his destroyer to other American patrol vessels. At the time, British and Australian ships plying the area were all rushing to the scene just a few nautical miles away from the Philippines.

'Quite some fancy spaceship, sir,' quipped an admiring Marine Captain to his commander on the radio.

'This is no time for alien admiration, McCarthy, get going.'

'With all respect, sir!' he replied as they tethered giant steel cables around parts of the damaged TSG and started towing it to waters away from the Spratley Islands.

Beijing cried foul. 'You can't do that in our territorial waters.'

Chinese ambassador to Washington venting his fury at the State Department. Beijing sent a flotilla of naval vessels blocking the American moves. Chinese aircraft carrier, Liaoning, armed to the teeth with its new hypersonic missiles, moved into position around the accident area.

Moscow for the first time publicly backed China's territorial claims after calling for a negotiated settlement.

With Coldoz killed, Daprah, still trapped inside the damaged starship, was listening to the arguments. Had she not been in a serious situation she would have laughed out loudly at the outdated communications system these people are using earth-side. First she thought of blasting them out of the water with her own handheld high-powered rifles which were fast as light speed and capable of destroying an entire aircraft carrier in a single blast but decided against. Something the playful and adventurous Coldoz would have done, perhaps.

Some countries were sending interest units and agents, all flocking to the South China sea that was fastly becoming overcrowded with all sorts of aircraft and naval vessels streaming around. Some with military and intelligence interests, others, just simple curiosity to witness for themselves extra-terrestrial life forms and technology. Rumours have it the alien pilots have been captured and taken to the American base in Guam. Others say they are held on one of the Sprately islands by the Chinese military.

****

The agent, a C.I.A. operative tasked with retrieving some of the missing TSG parts, was of west African origin. He was 37, black, 6'2", round/straight nose and round mouth, blue-brown eyes, round forehead and handsome. Athletic physique, broad shoulder, bald and sometimes bespectacled. Dual citizenship of Sierra Leone and United Kingdom .

He was just stripping off his clothes alongside his date, Bich, who was already curled up naked in his bed with her limbs brought up close to her body, inviting him to warm her up, when the bleep on his phone broke the sexual tension building up in the room. He lives in a one-bedroom bachelor pad with his cat. The message reads: 'Up and leave right away for [location given in secret code]. You can't delay, you know the situation.'

In their espionage world, "you know the situation" means "no delay, no alternative".

'Look, sorry we have to leave now,' he said to the lady from Hanoi he had known from their university days.

'What?' she asked in slight annoyance.

'I have an urgent assignment and got to be somewhere within 20 minutes. 'It's urgent,' he replied, almost snarling at her.

'OK then, let's just do a quickie. We've built too much into this, even before the meal,' she begged unashamedly.

Almost losing his patience, he grabbed her arm, gently but firm, and ordered they leave now. She is 5'6" tall, small, cute and perfect facial symmetry and straight dark hair pinned back in two plait snoods. She was wearing a short black dress and matching boots when the agent picked her up earlier from the train station.

As he was driving her back to the station, they hardly spoke when his mobile phone bleeped again, with a message saying the deal is off today and back at same time tomorrow. He turned sideways facing her, not even knowing how to say it.

Spilling out the sentence in the most tender way he could muster:

'The assignment is off for today we can go back to mine now.'

She really liked him and they have never been this close before and was really yearning for his company. But that sudden stop earlier and his almost forceful insistence they call it off, was still hurting. Taking a moment to answer, she replied:

'I don't know.' Scrunching her shoulders up by her ears. 'Maybe next time eh, Mr Busy.'

Now he started wanting her more than before. Apologising and saying all nice things to her, before recalling her favourite food. He, in a childlike excitement to nice her up:

'Oh! What about having some Chai Voi fish (A classy and expensive Vietnamese dish)?'

'We only had a meal about half-an-hour ago,' she replied with a grimace.

He was still trying to make it up to her and said:

'OK, just any soup?'

Seeing all his effort to apologise, she finally agreed.

Less than five minutes driving through a Sunday afternoon with little or no traffic, they got to a Vietnamese restaurant in Shoreditch, Hackney borough in east London.

'Phat phuc,' a lady behind the counter greeted them on arrival.

The agent not knowing the meaning, thinking they sound something odd for a restaurant, asked:

'Sorry?'

Then the counter lady repeated: 'Phat phuc,' just before Bich explained it means welcome in Budha.

Once they sat down, the agent having not much appetite, they just had dinner together just over an hour ago, asked for the main house soup, to which a waitress replied: 'Pho.'

Yet again he felt confused with the words. It was only when he went through the menu and saw the English translation that he then felt comfortable, and they had a fantastic meal. All that supposedly lost appetite resurfaced with the smell and taste of the delicious south east Asian cuisine.

The Agent showing appreciation for the food, quipped: 'I rather feel so moreish and could do with another helping.' She liked his appreciation of the food and did tiny giggles in return.

During her second glass of wine, he had noticed Bich getting a little bit frisky.

In trying to get her drinking less, he said:

'I can't drink more than a glass tonight as I'd be driving us home. I think it would be nice if you would hopefully do the same.'

No sooner he had said that, he regretted, thinking he could have put it in a better way.

You can see the instant annoyance in her eyes:

'Look here my friend!' she hissed, slamming the glass back on the table that she had held halfway towards her mouth without drinking from it.

'I am a 35 year matured woman with a university degree and a good job also. I don't take social advice from old school friends. Least of all those rumoured to have dated half the students in his class.'

She then picked up the drink again and drained it down her throat in one gulp.

'OK, OK, fine with me,' he replied with a smile, raising both hands in the air, jokingly signalling surrender. 'I only want things to be OK. I don't know much about your alcohol tolerance,' he said calmly.

'Keep digging, keep digging,' was all she replied.

They were just about to finish their meal when a young afro-caribbean man about 5'10" tall, wearing blue denim trousers, a brown bomber jacket over a black jersey with hoodie pulled over his head, came running through the restaurant door. He had fine symmetrical facial features – rather good-looking – with round lips and a Nubian nose. He looked scared and was breathing heavily. Probably in his late teens but looked no older than 21/22. Chasing after him was a gang of three armed young men all but one in hoods. The first chaser was quite tall, dark skin, lanky-built at about 6'4", fairly straight nose and round lips, almond-shaped eyes, and prominent cheeks, dressed in dark clothing. The second, about 5'11" tall, came in just behind the first, was similarly dressed in dark clothes but was mostly covered up. The hood and mask concealing much of his face. It's the third man, Asian-looking, and appeared to be the youngest and smallest among the lot. At 5'7" tall, round nose small eyes, small mouth. With a face looking like butter won't melt in his mouth. He was wearing a brown sweater and grey corduroy trousers. He seemed hesitant but very alert, just standing by the doorway with eyes darting in and out of the building, acting like the gang's sentry or something. He had no hood.

The front two were wielding machetes and cursing. The third at the door had a large kitchen knife held by his side as if he was hiding it. Their target crouched cowering behind a table with fear in his eyes, but that didn't stop the first machete man going in for the kill.

In a flash, he swung the weapon at the victim, catching him in the hand he had raised defending himself. Suddenly, a white flesh cut became visible on the injured man's left hand between the thumb and fore finger seconds before blood started streaming out.

The second attacker was jostling behind the first, was rather out of a hitting range with the tables and chairs in between, looking for an angle and opportunity to strike at their victim. The sentry, not part of the attack, was still at the door acting as the lookout.

The machete man was about to attack again, this time standing above the victim who had fallen to the ground screaming in pain, when the agent leapt off his chair in a flash, caught hold of the attacker's hand, twisted it out of position, disarming and sending him sprawling onto the floor. The attacker got up in a flash and very irate. Confronting the agent, he snarled:

'Who the fuck are you, pagan?' Before throwing a straight right hand fist, his fingers encrusted in spike knuckle dusters. The agent caught the attacker's arm and twisted it behind his back in martial arts' Kimora style.

'Ahhhhhhhh! Let go of my hand you bloody pagan, you're hurting me!' wailing in pain.

His mate, the second attacker, stabbed at the agent, who dodged the strike and threw a left kick at his neck. He dropped to the ground fainting instantly. The agent was still holding the first attacker's arm who continued crying in agony in the twisted position.

He then sneered at him: 'It was meant to hurt you, punk. I gonna give you one chance to get out of this. The choice is yours to take.'

'Aaaha! You fuuuucker. Could get you done for this. I swear aahhhaaahhh. OK, OKKKKKKK, I'm done. Pleeeease let go.' Having seized their weapons, the agent pushed the first attacker away as he crashed into a nearby table.

'Leave now!' The agent barked at the lad who quickly picked up his wallet and was having trouble searching the floor with his weaker left hand for some of his other personal belongings that had fallen out. His right hand was temporarily disabled. He seemed desperate, probably not wanting to leave anything behind that could identify his person. He stood up looking frightened and ran for the exit door with his sore right arm dangling at his side still hurting from that Kimora hold. Meanwhile, the second attacker seemed to have recovered, he hastily got off the floor and both men scrammed out of the door, the sentry had already fled the scene, leaving their victim who was taken to the backroom for first aid treatment whilst the police and ambulance services were called.

The Agent's companion wasn't too pleased with his adventures: 'You risk getting seriously hurt by these boys. They are ruthless.'

'Don't worry, I can take care of myself,' he replied calmly as if he didn't find the incident that dangerous at all.

'But you also risk placing my life in danger,' she whinged, looking him straight in the eye. They argued a bit about the situation and was just about time to leave when he said:

'Come on Bich, let's go,' as he stood up wearing his jacket.

A couple of diners who had taken fright behind the bar and had admired his courage and skills were now looking at him in dismay when he called her out to leave. They mistakenly thought he had called her a bitch, sounding like her real Vietnamese name, Bich, which means Jade in English.

She grabbed her coat and swilled back the rest of the red wine in her glass. Her third that night and purred: 'Come on, Tiger, let's go.' They went back to his place in north London.

He was in his kitchen putting some plates away in the dishwasher when he asked: 'Would you like some snack? I'm making myself smoked salmon and cream cheese in a toasted roll to soak up the alcohol. I need a clear head for tomorrow morning.'

'No thanks, I have no place for any food right now. Man you eat like a wolf.'

Before he could answer, she joined him in the kitchen.

Staring down the wine rack she retrieved a bottle, waved it in his face and asked: 'How about having some of this?' Slanting her head sideways, grinning with perfect tiny white teeth towards him.

'Em! Em! That's a fortified wine…' was his reply in a stern but gentle voice.

'Oh, how I love Sherry,' ignoring him and started prising open the bottle.

At first, he thought about physically stopping her but after her insistence earlier, he instead produced another bottle with minimal alcoholic content. She ignored him and still continued to undo the cork stopper and then poured herself a generous amount in a wine glass.

'Look I have to be honest with you. I think you're drinking too much,' he moaned with a stony face.

Feeling very much tipsy she didn't hear him properly. 'What was that you said? Something about being honest. Yes I'm an honest person. Are you? Constantly giggling as she speaks.

It sort of put him off romance for a bit. Not that he doesn't fancy her anymore but rather she is drunk, and having a sexual encounter with a woman in that state is not appealing. More so for the first time. Not least the risk of regret by her and all that could come with it. He stared at her in the eye for a few seconds she looked a couple of years older in that instant.

'Look, love, I'm tired at this moment. That fight earlier is still making me nervous,' he lied.

'Let's sleep it off and talk in the morning. Alright?'

Looking at him in annoyance:

'What's wrong with you, eh?' Bich demanded.

'First, it was an urgent call from a friend, now the fight in the restaurant.'

He didn't say anything and just lifted her off the floor and took her to his bedroom. Her countenance changed from anger to joy in expectation they were in for some action at last. But yet she felt disappointed again after he explained the situation of him having to sleep on his sofa and she in the bed.

'The bathroom is over there if you need it.' He pointed out and left the bedroom as she began to argue again.

She woke up the next morning feeling all shy with regret, asked what happened the night before. Saying she can only recall him refusing to sleep with her in the same bed and nothing more.

He explained some parts of the incident, skipping the embarrassing bits.

They then had breakfast together and made love later, which she reckoned was one of the best she had ever had. He later dropped her off at the Liverpool Street station.

Later that Sunday afternoon, to kill off time waiting for orders from his handlers, he went to his local watering hole for a few drinks and possibly watch a weekend Premier League football match. He then retired home late from the bar that evening and went to bed feeling a bit battered and bruised with still no message received.

In the following Monday morning, the late autumn sun's glare was weak gleaming through his bedroom window but still strong enough to have him dazed as he pulled back the curtains. Having a sore head from the night before might have something to do with it. He then drew the curtains again, retired back to his bed, staring at the ceiling in an effort to go mindless and relax.

But he just can't, and started thinking of that previous Sunday evening's event at the bar:

There was a brawl that had him sucked in reluctantly. He had tried to help save a young woman, 5'8" tall, short crop brown hair, very clear skin, good complexion with no makeup, pretty features; button-like nose, huge bright brown eyes. Barbies seem to be blonde but if there is a brunette one, this could be it.

She was wearing a black mini skirt and white crop top exposing her belly area.

The young lady was being slapped around by a much older man between 45–60, 5'9", round lopsided tired face, with rather asymmetric features. Slightly-built with protruding stomach, brown receding hair. Looking a bit worse for wear and apparently tipsy. He had on blue jeans, black canvas shoes and a white t-shirt. A bit heavily jewelled.

'Leave me 'lone you old creep,' she wailed in an east London accent. 'I'm not going home with you,' fending him off as he grabbed for her arms.

No one in the bar half-full of customers showed any interest to help out or at least do something about the situation. Even the bartender showed no interest. The barman was once an unsuccessful professional boxer who was advised to give up the sport on doctor's order. The broken nose bridge, lopsided lips, puffy-faced with a weak flabby chin showing the tell-tale signs of having been knocked around a few times. He had bushy eye brows, stoutly built, about 5'6" tall, narrow slopey shoulders and short portly hairy arms. He was wearing a black and red stripped polo shirt. An E-cigarette lazily perched between his lips as he kept on drying and polishing his drinking glasses and humming a tune to himself, as if nothing untoward was going on in his bar.

The Agent took the last gulp from his drink, slammed the empty glass on the table hard enough to command some attention as a few heads turned looking his way, when he called out loudly to the old man:

'Let her go, you heard her say so.'

The old man turned around, gave a snobbery stare at this stranger and continued attacking the girl. The Agent took about four quick strides before reaching the fighting pair and jerked the old man off who then fell to the ground crashing the nearby table with drinks spilling onto the floor. He kicked at the agent's calf so hard he almost lost his balance. But for his Brazilian Jiu-Jitsu black belt training, he could have fallen backwards.

'How did you get here punk? By a boat or a plane,' the old man cursed at the agent, in a cockney accent. 'Me and my boys will help you pack your stuff in no time.'

He then folded his hands into fists to draw in a fight.

'Come on! Oh! You've lost the bottle?' As he waved his fists around and began to circle the agent, who was still ignoring him.

All of a sudden a man sprang out of a dark corner in the room. He had similar resemblance; heart-shaped lips, arched nose and round eyes with long lashes and brown thick volume hair, much like the young woman's. He wouldn't look out of place on the catwalk. Nor resemble a typical bar brawler or any of that sort for that matter. But then again you never know.

Without saying anything, he rushed and threw a big overhead swinging right punch at the agent, he missed and got sucked in the rib with a counter-blow that sent him reeling back into the shadows. A second man, whom the agent didn't know was behind him, attacked from his back, cursing:

'If you want a damn fight with my family then you'd have it, you punk.' He grabbed the agent and threw him backwards slamming him to the floor. Impressed with himself the second man, who much resembled the first man in facial features, rushed in at the agent who quickly rolled himself back up on his feet and sent a slapping kick to the inside of the young man's right thigh that almost sent him down. The man became angrier; he also quickly got up and threw a snapping right hand blow followed in quick successions by a left hook, both missed the agent returned the compliment with a flying kick catching him on the left side of his neck that sent down like a tonne of bricks. As he got up, the agent rushed at him locking his head in a giloutine choke, just restraining him and not squeezing. Surprisingly the first attacker was just standing there, probably scared, letting his younger companion do all the fighting until there was this sudden heavy blow to the back of the agent's head as he went down on one knee. The older man who had been physically abusing the young lady had smashed him with a stool and ran hiding himself in the toilet. And there seating on another stool just a couple of yards away was the young lady the agent was trying to save, holding her hands covering her mouth, giggling in fun at the fights. Before the young men could gather themselves a couple of strangers burst through the doors scanning the room as if they had been alerted to the fight.

The bigger bloke with a perfect physique, looking ex-armed forces personnel or something: the military moustache, strawberry-blond crew-cut hair, broad shoulders and disciplined stony face with a roman nose and thin lips. He wearing green combat fatigues (The storyteller thinks he could be ex-military because if he was still in the forces he won't have been called in to settle a bar fight. Then again he could just be a civilian military fan). The other was wearing a tight-fitting white T-shirt with bulging muscles and stonewashed blue jeans. He looked a bit more rough and tough like a combat sports prize fighter or something. He had a broken nose, cauliflower ears and blood-shot eyes completing the very rugged-scary looks. Built like a bison with huge muscular shoulders and powerful upper body complemented by a narrow waist and somewhat shorter legs. The floor boards seemed to quake underneath his feet as he walked. They bundled the fighting lot with such ease; old man, the young girl and the two other young men out of the bar, ignoring the agent as if he hadn't been part of the brawl. He later had his head treated by the barman who told him:

'That was the MaCain family. When they fight, which they quite often do, no one gets involved, because at most times they'd all end up against you even if you were only trying to help one of them. Barred from almost every bar in town. I have twice before kicked them out and ordered them not to come back. It is the bar owner who keeps overturning the ban. Word has it he is plugging the young lady. What can I do eh? She is old enough.'

The Agent just muttered, 'If he is their father, they probably got their good looks from their mother.'

On his way exiting the bar, a drunken man staggeredly walked up to him and slurred:

'Thank yoooouu for taking care of the McCains. This is the first time someone has ever stood up to them lot. They are always pushing their weight around these parts of town and everyone seems to be afraid of them.'

The agent shrugged his broad shoulders and grimaced at the man. They then shook hands and he left the bar returning to his hotel.

Still resting in bed while recalling this incident, the agent drifted off into a light sleep for a couple of hours. He woke up in a fright half-hour before midday thinking he might have missed the call. He hadn't. He then had a shower, completely avoiding the breakfast his neighbour sent him that morning. One more meal from her will kill me in an instant with food poisoning, he thought.

Having been holed up in his flat awaiting instructions from his handlers was tiring stuff, and he felt hungry. On his way to a local cafe a young man in a hoodie unexpectedly pulled out in front of him with a gun in hand. He is in his late teens or early 20s. About 5 foot 10 inches tall, curly dark hair, huge eyes and fairly-straight hooked nose: 'Han over ya fucking walleh [wallet] now or else I'll pin a fucking 'ole in between ya fucking eyes,' he ordered, trying to sound menacing in street talk which wasn't even convincing.

The agent took out his wallet and gave it with no hesitation. The mugger snatched it with his left hand in such a speed a lizard will to catch a fly. But he was struggling to open it with one hand, his left, whilst his right hand was still holding the pistol trained on the agent. He then managed to partially get a couple of his fingers inside it, and with excitement started scooping out banknotes and credit cards, some of which fell to the ground.

'Wow wha' dah hell. Look wha' we've goh here,' he grinned showing teeth in braces. To better access the contents, he secured the gun under his left armpit becoming a bit complacent, to enable him using both hands emptying the wallet. Doing so just give the agent an opportunity with the threat of the pointing gun compromised. He then took one quick aim and slammed a straight right fist into the mugger's face. Alas, the blow half-hit and half-missed him as he was quick to duck. Though not so quick with him being partially caught. The glancing blow bounced off the top of his head but was still strong enough to reeled him backwards, dropping the wallet and gun to the ground. He ignored the contents and threw a big overhead right aiming for the Agent's head and missed. The Agent gave his own back with a uppercut which the mugger dodged beautifully this time. He then warned himself this kid is no walk in the park, he seems to be a very alert fighter. It was just as well as he threw a flying knee at the agent who caught hold of the leg and spin himself and the young man to the ground, still holding onto his leg and twisting it in a knee bar.

'Ah, aaaahhhh please, sir, leh go. OK, sir, OK ya won ya woaaaahhhh!' he was pleading when suddenly as luck would have it a police vehicle just pulled up beside the fighting pair. Two uniformed officers disembarked and were approaching them. As soon as he saw the cops coming the thief started shouting louder: 'Help! Help he's mugging me.'

'Oh, Rajesh. You again, what's going on here?' demanded the leading police sergeant who seemed to know the mugger. The youth started explaining, almost shouting, with tears running down his face, pointing his finger:

'De geezer's trying to mug me. He twisted and locked up me ahrm, den me leg and stole me walleh.'

The agent was surprised yet calm as to how the lad was able to act so convincingly.

As he tried to explain his own side of the story, the mugger kept on interrupting. Probably not wanting the truth be told, until the copper threatened him with arrest if he didn't shut up.

The other copper picked up the purse, asked:

'Whose wallet is it then?'

They both men answered, 'Mine officer,' almost simultaneously.

When the youngster noticed the officer checking the contents, he quickly said: 'He threw me stuff out and replaced it with his,' while pointing at the agent, who just can't help smiling at the time.

Before handing over the wallet to the agent the police corporal showed its contents to the sergeant.

They then handcuffed the youth and read him his rights regarding the arrest.

As he was being taken him away, the agent quipped:

'If you're this good at acting, with those convincing tears and all that, I'll be happy to pay your way through drama school. It might be a better investment for you than mugging people in the streets.'

The hoodie didn't reply, he just turned around and looked at the agent in disgust and spat towards the ground.

The agent gave up the idea of going to a restaurant, instead preferring to cook himself a meal for a change. He went hunting and gathering for food ingredients at the local supermarket.

His mobile phone went off with a bleep, message informing him in code language: 'The target is leaving Freetown, Sierra Leone, West Africa, which is the agent's native country, in the next couple of days and he has to act fast.'

Off onto his mission the next day, he jumped on a plane at Gatwick airport in southeast London at about 07:30 am on a Tuesday morning flight, and landed six hours later at the Lungi international airport just before 2 pm in the afternoon. The airport sits on a small island about twelve and half miles from the capital, Freetown. Word is around this is one of only two international airports built on a natural island, Manilla in the Philippines is the other. Though this hasn't been verified.

He carried his Sierra Leonean passport through immigration, wanting to look as normal as possible.

From the airport a cabbie drove him through a narrow lane to the ferry terminal. Either side of the road was covered with trees and bushes in beautiful dark greenery. Feeling rather nostalgic, having not visited his homeland for years, he hung his head outside the car window for a short moment, feeling the cool wind rushing against his face and absorbing the scenic view.

He then boarded a ferry for the mainland. The boat seats a total of 50 passengers with a small V.I.P. separation for about 15.

It was somewhat a calm journey as they slowly skim across the waters that were crystal-clear enough to see shoals of fish darting around.

Sailing closer towards the coast, parts of city swept into view with people teeming everywhere, mostly the locals. Many of whom were petty traders peddling stuff they sold in small containers carried on their heads or in their arms.

He took another taxi heading for a pre-booked hotel around the Lumley beach area where he hooked up for the night to study the target's details.

The target was supposedly an old school friend of his whom he hadn't seen for over three decades.

Feeling dead tired, he overslept a bit ignoring the blaring alarm clock the next morning. The snooze timer jostled him awake for the second time.

By mid-morning, he had a bit to eat, far less than his usual breakfast, and readied the necessary tools for the day's mission that was to take place that same Tuesday night.

He liked making early preparations, with checks and double checks all in place, leaving little or no room for errors.

After spending most of the day indoors, reading the local newspapers, watching TV and a little bit more resting, he managed forcing himself going out for a walk about 5 pm. He went to a cat sanctuary, tip the caretaker a couple of pounds and borrowed a sphinx cat which he then returned an hour later and went for a stroll. But it was too brisk a walk and got back at the hotel in no time. On the second outing, he took a much longer stroll down the beautiful coastline where the sun was just setting over the horizon in a huge orange-like glow. Once there, he kicked off his shoes and started walking on the water's edge where the waves smashes onto the beach, reacquainting himself with the familiarised squishing sounds of the wet sands squeezing in between his toes. He then went further knee deep into the sea, letting his open hands paddles through the cool white foams of the wave breakers. The temperature was getting cooler about 06:30 pm that evening.

Retreating to the sands, he walked past a long line of fishermen pulling out slime-covered green nets out of the sea. Most of these men were muscle-bound. Probably made so by all the regular tugging and hauling of huge fishing chains-laden with assorted marine life out of the waters.

The agent then settled in a small makeshift bar tending a cool poyo, a natural white wine freshly sapped from palm trees, when he noticed a lady customer sitting opposite him with another female, staring at him fixedly. He simply ignored her and finished his drink. No sooner he was leaving she smiled at him and he returned the compliment.

Returning to the hotel about 07:35 pm, he saw a very attractive and classy-looking lady at the lobby giving instructions to three other hotel staff members She could be the manager or something, he thought. She greeted him and looked away, just as she saw him looking at her, and continued her briefing. It's nice to see attractive people every now and then, he thought as he raced to his room.

The rest of the evening was long and boring, with the hours seeming to be dragging for much longer. 'Maybe I could do with some company,' he said to himself, 'that would help to kill time.'

Off he went, down the stairs again back to the lobby. Not really seeking to get that attractive manager but it would be nice just to talk with her. Just a brief chat if possible, he kept dreaming. (The Agent at times does this sort of fantasy thing to ease off tension when facing with an imminent daunting task. It's like a relaxer for him) Alas, she was no longer there. The bar was half-full but he ignored it and reached for the telephone in pretence to give reason coming down to the reception.

Soon it was 9:15 pm, time for action. He hurried out of the hotel, and in the next few minutes found himself scurrying around for a taxi but none was available. Badly pressing for time, he hurriedly flagged down one of those three-wheeled motor vehicles instead. Ones they called Kehkeh, and headed for neighbouring Aberdeen village. Far slower than a taxi it was still better than just standing there wasting precious time. On their way along the beach road, the agent was once again enjoying the scenery with the sharp smell of sea salt heavy in the air. A scent he didn't remember sensing on his earlier stroll, maybe it's to do with the wind, he thought. He just let his idle mind go wandering through the rest of the journey. Recalling the days when as kids he and his friends used to play football on the beach. More fishermen were seen in small boats which they call canoes, paddling out far at sea. He completed the very slow journey feeling satisfied as if he had already got what he came for.

The target's small-sized flamboyant aquamarine-coloured boat, named the Flamingo, a little over 33 feet long, was anchored about 30 metres off the marina at Aberdeen village.

The once impoverished West African nation had just moved into the big time with new oil finds which was attracting investors of all sorts.

The target's wealth 'Suddenly coming out of nothing' to quote a close friend of his, was a big surprise to many. Especially when considering his dull, and sometimes lazy demeanour. One of his several nicknames in school was "The mouse"; timid and quiet in equal measure as the creature.

When not anchored offshore, his boat would be seen moored in the standard eastern bay area where it would overshadow other smaller vessels. One time the target was away on business, and had returned to find his beloved Flamingo in the exclusive western bay area basked in the shades of bigger and more beautiful yachts.

He was so furious he sacked his operations manager, complaining of being denied sunlight by the other boats. That can hardly be the case since the sun is mostly overhead during the day, shining light on all the vessels regardless of size.

He was to later ordered the boat be recoloured from white to blueish-green.

The target was reported to be a fishing magnate with boats trawling the waters of all of the world's seven seas, stretching across all the oceans from the Arctic to the Antarctic.

Donning his new wetsuit, the agent slightly slackened the purse around his waist which got a bit too tight as he sat down in the rented canoe beside his grapnel rope. The purse contains a waterproof pistol, a large folding serrated Rambo blade, two energy drinks, biscuits, some medication and a small wad of cash. He had hired the small fishing boat with two oarsmen on board, who were to row him across to the Flamingo yatch. The two men had quite similar facial features and appeared to him like a father and son team. Paying them three times their daily wages for just half-an-hour's work.

In order to arrive in silence and unnoticed, halfway through the journey the canoe men were to turn-off their outboard motor and paddle the rest of the journey across in silence, getting rid of the noise coming from the engine.

The men were also expected to do the same when returning to the coast, but without the agent.

On that cool Tuesday night at just past 10 pm, they set sail under the cover of darkness. The mild local temperature was surprising to the agent who was expecting warm weather conditions, which is typical even at that time of the day in Sierra Leone's hot wet equatorial climate. He had forgotten about the West African coast's cool harmattan period greeting the country around that time of the year from December to January.

The younger of the two oarsmen, thinking the agent was a pirate, recommended: 'Maybe it would be better to sail off a couple of hours later. Say like after midnight or something, when the coast would be clearer of people.'

The agent with a wry smile on his face gently placed his hand on the youth's shoulder, responding: 'Any time of the day would do my friend, thanks.'

Whilst the older man was staring at his younger companion as if he shouldn't have made that suggestion.

The agent has been well informed on the Target's daily routine: midweek periods on a Tuesday, Wednesday and Thursday he is a lark, retiring to bed quite early at around 8:30 pm–9 pm, and waking up early about six hours the next day. These were the times he has solely for himself and would hardly entertain anyone. Reason why the agent decided to make his move at this time in the hope of catching him alone.

Coming from afar, almost a mile away from the marina floodlights, the yacht was a bit harder to detect in the dark with its colours blending in with the turquoise coastal waters. What little light you get from the distant flood lamps is of no significant help.

The canoe approached the yacht on its starboard side, deliberately avoiding portside where a couple of people were seen standing by the railings.

The Agent unfurled his rope and threw it up at the ship's upper railings.

The hook missed and plunged into the sea in a splash. He tried again.

This time the older oarsmen grabbed the sides of the little canoe to steady it as it swayed sideways in reaction to the agent's second and stronger attempt, drawing in water from the sea.

Yet again the grappling hook missed the upper part of the railing, but on its way down caught the lower part and stayed in place.

He then tested the rope's strength by pulling on it a bit tightly. Satisfied, he bided his fishermen friends farewell and pulled more of the rope towards himself, using it as a leverage as he jumped off the canoe and landed both feet onto the ship's hull.

'Should we wait for you sir?' the older oarsman asked as The Agent started the climb.

'No thanks. I will be fine. Just make sure not to turn on your outboard engine until you're far away from here.'

He doesn't know how long it will take him to complete the task and the canoe could possibly be spotted returning and hanging around waiting for him; these are risks not worth taking, he had thought.

The younger oarsman then yelled out: 'But how are you returning ba…?' before he could finish his sentence, the older oarsman stamped on the lad's feet to shut him up and threw a hand over his mouth suppressing any sound.

The agent turned halfway around saw the lad now sitting down nursing his sore foot, and just waved them off as he started ascending towards the top of the vessel. With both hands secured around the rope, the right hand an inch further up from his left hand with his feet resting side by side on the ship's hull.

He then moved his right hand one place up the rope, followed by the left.

Then pressed his weight into his feet and released the pressure by hopping upwards on the side of the ship. Repeating the same hands and feet movements up the rope each time progressing nearer towards the top.

More than halfway up, for some reason unknown to him, he felt a bit uneasy, but continued with the mount until he had reached the top.

He then swung his right foot onto the lower railing to get some of his body weight into it when suddenly the rope snapped, dropping him in a huge splash into the sea.

'Did you hear that? What's that noise?' one of the guards manning the left side of the yacht asked.

The other replied: 'Probably some basking shark or porpoise. This time of the year is the mating season for most of these marine animals, and fighting among the males for breeding rights is very common.' Though he was more attentive to watching pornography images on his mobile phone than to pay much attention to anything else.

Falling into the sea reminded the agent of the times when he was a kid and his voluptuous Auntie Neneh would give him those huge, sweaty, suffocating bear hugs. Well I could do with that now, instead of this, he thought. Feeling wet and hopeless he started cursing to himself: 'I'll get him for this. Let's see if I don't. The first time I saw it I had suspicions Adam didn't buy me a new rope as he had promised. Bloody petty crook he is. With so many things on my mind, you can see how I easily forgot to do a final check.

'I definitely didn't test the rope's strength well enough when I was leaving the canoe. This could cost me my life,' as he tried to get used to the unexpected situation. 'OK. No time for regrets I have to go back to work.'

Sensing something in the water moving around his feet, he got alert and reached for his purse. The shock of it all – it was no longer tied around his waist. It's gone. He dived into the sea in a futile attempt to search for it but all that was there was pitch darkness. It must have fallen off during my big fall from the top of the ship. Damned! He remembered loosening the purse to ease the tightening strain around his hips when he first sat down in the canoe, but he forgot to retighten it after he had stood up to disembark.

He became almost breathless in annoyance. The saltwater kept getting into his eyes. And for the very first time felt lonely, naked and marooned at sea.

I now have two options, he thought, swim back to the beach and save myself from this nearly impossible task, or continue with the mission of getting inside the boat and confronting the target?

It was no brainer for him choosing the latter option.

He again cursed himself for not securing the satchel strong enough round his waist to survive any rough handling, especially when facing an arduous task like this.

The purse only had half-an-inch-wide belt and a smaller buckle holding it in place, little wonder it got detached.

How am I to climb onto the boat without so much as a rope or anything else for that matter.

During his military training days as a marine cadet, climbing up ships at sea was a routine enough practice. Only that they had ropes, chains etc. used in the exercises. The only times they didn't use any was when they were provided with gripper gloves.

The waves were a bit gentle but still strong enough to push him around.

Worried he could get drifted away, he held on to the side of the vessel that appears like a huge house slanting over him.

His grip on the hard and rough barnacles at the side of the ship was rubbing his hands raw as the waves swayed him sideways, upwards and downwards.

'This could be what they mean by saying, "blistering barnacles"' he muttered softly to himself.

The climbing and falling off the ship had sapped most of his energy and spirit but he just stayed there for a couple of minutes resting, regaining his strength and thinking what to do next. His hands that were moments earlier feeling like hell – burning red – holding on to the barnacles for dear life, had suddenly become deadened and numbed, no longer feeling any pain. First he thought about swimming around the boat to the portside where he could climb up the anchor chain. That's too risky. The guards had it covered apparently. Having no other alternative and with dogged determination, which even surprised himself, he started spider climbing up the hulk. The barnacles that were few minutes ago giving him rough sore hands were providing the initial foot-hold aiding his ascent. But the grip was weakening as he steadfastly inched upwards, and was about to involuntarily let go when he saw a porthole and reached for it. He climbed onto the circular window on the starboard side using it as a foothold, then stretched his hands onto the lower railing and heaved himself up onto the wet upper deck. The sea was beginning to get a bit rough on that cloudy night with high waves smashing up to the gunwale at the top edge of the hull. Good thing I'm still not out there, he thought.

The lighting was poor but he can still make out the two uniformed personnel who could be the target's bodyguards: one African, the other, Asian. The younger-looking one was relaxing on one of the deck chairs still flicking through his mobile phone. He had a rifle laid across his lap and an Alsatian dog lying on the deck next to him. The dog's head resting on his feet. Hard to guess his height when he was lounging but he seemed about medium built, flat face, round nose and wide mouth, was all The Agent could make of him in the dim lights. Probably in his mid-twenties to early thirties. He also appeared a bit paunchy around the waist.

The other, looks a bit older, was standing by the rails carrying a rifle strapped around his body. He was also much taller with streamlined Bruce Lee-like features and physique.

The Agent had to get past these two robots, and whoever else is on board if he were to search the ship for his target. Under the shadows of the dimly-lit deck he half-walked and half-crawled towards them, thinking how much he had missed his lost purse containing the gun and Rambo knife. An armless man against two gun-toting guards and a German shepherd is as fair as challenging a one-legged man to an arse kicking contest, he thought. As he advanced towards them a creaking floorboard under his feet alerted of his presence, giving away his position to the guards who suddenly became alert. The lightning-quick dog with ears pricked stood up and sprang towards the agent as the standing guard swung the rifle strap off his shoulder and took aim.

The second guard shouted: 'Don't shoot, don't shoot. You risk hitting Bozzo.' And slapped the rifle off his companion's hand, hard enough for the gun to slid off across the slippery deck and dashed into the sea. Apparently, Bozzo was the dog's name.

Reversing backwards with his wide alert eyes still trained on the fastly advancing dog, the agent tripped, perhaps on the same creaking floorboard, and fell on his back. The dog with its hind legs stretched out, front paws in the air over him and ready to pounce, he simultaneously kicked both of his feet into the canine's soft underbelly and flung it in the air over his head with all the strength he could muster. Suddenly there was another splashing sound in the sea, much louder than the first, the dog had crashed into the drink.

The Agent was halfway up on his feet when to his surprise the second guard rushed past - ignoring him- towards to railing. He leant over the deck rails crying out: 'Bozzo, Bozzo.' The anxiety in his voice informed of his concern for the dog. The Agent was looking at the fella still carrying his rifle foolishly and bravely jumped into the sea going after his dog. The second guard took advantage of his distraction and lunged towards him with a huge knife. Swish, swash, swish the blade whistled cutting into the still night time air narrowly missing the gent who was ducking and diving away from it. By the fourth or fifth strike attempt he caught hold of the guard's right hand in wrist-control with his own right hand, then manoeuvred the guard's back against the front of his own chest positioning his left hand under the guard's chin in a rear-naked choke. Both men's right hands were still struggling for the weapon and the guard using his own left hand to ease off The Agent throttling him.

The guard stated choking and coughing. Suddenly The Agent felt him go a bit limp. He could be fainting, he thought, his body slackened as it felt as if he was about to drop down on the deck. But it was a trick by the guard, he viciously stamped on the agent's toes with some brute force from his heavy military-styled boots, making the agent winced in pain. The guard then dropped the knife, shifted his weight around and twisted his neck out of the agent's grip. But he still had the weapon under his right foot, pressing against it, securing it to the deck. Smiling sinisterly at The Agent he went to pick up the blade. The Agent then thought for him to have been able to twist his head out of that strangle hold warned this guy could be a trained fighter. He kicked away the knife before the guard could grab it. The weapon went skidding away along the deck and slammed onto the railing with a clanging sound. Unlike the gun and the dog, it stayed on the deck, stopped by the rails.

The Agent threw himself at the guard, half mounting him in order to ground and pound him onto the deck, but he got trapped in his opponents' long, strong orangutan-like arms wrapped around his body in a vice like grip restricting his breathing efforts. After a bit of struggle, he managed to loosen the grip as they both scrambled back onto their feet. Learning from his mistake, he didn't just thrust himself at the guard, instead he grabbed him in an arm's spin and rotated him over his own body as he landed on top the guard in a full mount this time. And started raining blows on the guard's head and neck, mauling him like a wild tiger. Pounding after pounding with his fists raining blows, hit after hit, saw both the guard's eyes cut wide open, blood pouring out masking his face in red gore. The agent wouldn't stop until he noticed the guard had passed out.

At that moment the second guard was in the water with his dog calling out for help. The agent ignored his cries and made his way down a small flight of stairs onto the lower deck quarters to continue the search for the target. Down there, it seemed no expenses was spared. The lushness of the bottom floor belied the somewhat plain upper parts of the ship. Almost everything is made of oak.

The Agent opened a door in the oak panelled Aft cabin leading to its rear sleeping quarters. A moderately décor room with uniforms like the ones the guards were wearing hung on its walls. This must be their sleeping chamber, he thought. Spacious enough for two beds separated by an aisle leading to yet another door – a much bigger and solid-looking one made of cast iron, looking more like a strong room. The look of the door seemed ill-fitted to the wall around it, as if it was an additional security enhancement replacing an original door.

He gently turned the brass handle and entered a lavish bedroom stinking of stale food and beer. A tray half-full of leftovers from what looked like a clumsily eaten meal with bits of rice, fish head, chicken bones, and half-drunk drink in a glass, rest on a footstool by a chest of drawers. Opposite is a cedar-lined wardrobe. From floor to ceiling the room is covered in highly ornamental plywood.

Lying on his stomach on a hand-sprung mattress draped in red linen in a huge four-poster bed which occupied most of the room, was a stout hairy man in red silk boxer shorts with a football club's logo embroidered in it. In what could possibly be his favourite team. It immediately dawned on the agent this could be the target. What had helped with that instant identification was the word "Chubs" etched on a gold colour bracelet resting on a deeply tufted ornamental table top.

Without turning around the fat man in the bed bellowed: 'What is it you want Foday , I don't remember calling for you?'

'It's only me your old school pal, Akim,' the agent replied. Guessing this must be John Seasay a.k.a. Chubby, who is the target – a Sierra Leonean. At least it looks like him from the back; the small turtle-like head perched on a thick stiff neck a bison would envy. His broad back widest at the shoulders tapering downwards past a paunchy belly sticking out at the sides, onto a narrow waist with tiny legs and large feet attached. An odd combination of body parts giving him an awkward figure. At school, some kids used to call him frog-shaped, others named him the platypus.

This guy lying in the bed as far as the agent knows, was as bright as a full solar eclipse. How he made it into the big time is a mystery to most people.

John Seasay [Surname changed from Sesay to Seasay – in self-styled reference to being a "Man of the Seas who says what he means"]. Dark skin, fleshy face with small button-like eyes, small lips, small mouth. In fact, all his facial features were small-sized bits, except for the nose, imposed on a big head. He is about 5 feet 7 inches tall, stocky-built and obese. The orphaned chubby wasn't the smartest kid in school. Dropped out at the primary level and couldn't make it either on vocational training courses. He started dealing in petty crimes aged only 12 while living out in the streets until his older sister introduced him to her old college friend, Koke, a half-Chinese half-Mongolian wheeler dealer businessman.

Chubby started working for him as an apprentice sales man, selling counterfeit and stolen goods until he fastly graduated into the fisheries sector. For some reason, most likely for his sister's sake, Koke kept promoting him in quick successions, flying through the ranks until he was made operations manager in his Freetown office in Sierra Leone, covering the entire West African sub-region. Suddenly, Chubby moved into the big time. He was reported to be running dozens of fishing fleet dotted all over the globe.

To cut a long story short it was only when planet Zist's fallen TSG flying boat disintegrated over the South China Sea, amid rumours a couple of his fishing boats had hauled parts up out of the waters, that John Sesay, a.k.a. Chubby, overnight became a centre of attention in the eyes of the world's intelligence agencies. Most of whom were interested in the search for the missing parts for which Washington and Beijing had accused each other of stashing away in secret, for possible use in the technology race between the two rival nations.

John had it written into every contract he would sign with his fishing crew that every stuff – marine life, treasuries, etc. etc., picked up by his vessels belongs to him as owner of the fleet. He only added this clause to their employment contract after a former captain of one of his boats won a high court case to keep valuable artefact trawled from the Indian Ocean. The captain took his fortune into early retirement. Chubby then swore to never let this happen again.

He quickly spun around, got up, sitting on the bed nervously twitching.

This is the final giveaway informing he is really Chubby, The Target.

You can see the fear on his face.

'Who are you and what do you want?' he asked. Either not recognising his old school mate or maybe just pretending not to.

'I said it's only me, Akim, your old class mate,' the agent replied, as he was smiling at the fat man to reassure him of no harm. 'I'm here on a quick business and nothing more. I haven't got much time.'

Chubby was having none of it, and sneered through gritted teeth: 'Get the flipping hell out of here before I have you thrown out.

'And If I must remind you we are out here at sea,' he snarled, trying to sound more menacing than he really was.

'Don't you remember me pal?' the agent insisted. Chubby paused for a moment probably recognising his old school friend but still playing innocent and managed to say: 'Look, I don't know who you are and I want you out of here.'

Could he have possibly forgotten an old friend who had rescued him from bullies on numerous occasions in their primary school days.

Suddenly, the surprise had gone off his face. His voice sounding more or less normal again but probably still playing the ignorance game.

Reaching his right hand across his body, he grasped the left side of his chest, whingeing:

'You're giving me palpitations. I have long been having trouble with my heart.

Where is my damn medication?' Still clutching his chest as he slid his left hand under the bed's pillow.

'Just don't try it with me,' Akim warned with a cunning smile on his face as he raced towards the bed grabbing the Chubby's left wrist.

Knowing he has no chance in hell to physically defend himself he wailed in pain, 'Let go of my hand, you're hurting me.' Akim tugged and pushed him away stumbling across the room ending up on the floor.

Underneath the pillow was a loaded silver-coloured colt semi-automatic pistol which the agent retrieved, and started toying with it between his fingers as he spoke.

'Look what we've got here. Is it loaded?' grinning at Chubby who didn't answer. 'Man look, this is not really you, is it? OK now tell me who is putting you up to all this, Koke Altan, isn't it?'

'Where is the cargo haul your men fished out of the South China sea about a fortnight ago?' As he spoke sitting on the bed looking at his old class mate still sprawled on the floor like a sick walrus and was beginning to shake like a leaf. And this is the Chubby he knew. But he didn't answer the question.

'As I mentioned earlier, I have no time to waste, just hand me the parts to that crashed alien warship and I am as good as gone.'

He still didn't say anything, just staring at the tipped over tray on the floor with splattered bits all around it as if he was regretting the wasting of the food.

'Eye witnesses accounts say two of your trawlers sailed south from the Paracels and picked up debris from the waters. Your men were also seen unloading huge chunks of cargo resembling parts of an aeroplane into the Malaysian Port of Penang.'

'I know nothing of what you're saying,' he groaned, tightening his lips and still looking away from Akim but finally answering the question.

'My boats were not involved by any means.'

'Well if you knew nothing of the incident why did those same boats take the unusual routine going the other way to avoid the Port of Malacca?'

He then raised his head making eye-to-eye contact again.

'That damn place is not the same since the Chinese took over. And we no longer want anything to do with it. Look here, just leave me alone. We are having enough trouble as it is with Washington and Beijing bothering us.'

'Who's we? Who's us?' the agent asked with a puzzled face.

Suddenly, the door forcefully swung open. With one lightning-quick movement, Akim grabbed Chubby, raised him back to his feet and stood behind him with the gun barrel held to the back of his neck using him as a shield. Standing by the door were the two armed guards; one with a dog, both drenched and dripping water making a small puddle on the carpet, and the other's face reddened with blood smudges standing in front with deep hatred and anger in his badly swollen eyes.

Both had their weapons pointed at the agent.

'He pusssshed me into the water,' the wet guard snarled baring his teeth even scarier than his dog did earlier.

The poor hound looked timid, his ears dropped, shivering with cold and fright.

'That's bull's turd,' the agent snarled back, annoyed the guard is lying through his teeth. He went on to briefly retell the incident.

Chubby took one look at the other guard and asked: 'Is that so, Foday?' Who then turned around to his mate and said, 'Sorry, Bozzo, the pirate is telling the truth.'

'So he named the dog after himself,' the agent quipped out loudly.

The guards edged a bit forward as if waiting for orders from Chubby to attack.

'Be careful now gentlemen, don't get too excited and hurt me. Not a good idea. I still have Tabitha with instructions that my friends skin it alive if anything bad happened to me on this mission.'

The agent lied as he burst into fits of laughter.

'Oh I like that, "skin it alive". That would be easy since it has no fur. And don't forget,' he then whispered into Chubby's ear. 'As they say, there are many ways to skin a cat.'

Saying that struck a nerve. You can see that in Chubby wrinkling his nose.

Tabitha is his favourite pet that had been reported missing a week ago. And it was on that happen chance incident, the agent had decided to make this trip after the C.I.A. had asked for his help in tracing the much sought-after TSG parts. Mentioning the missing animal activated, Chubby with enough strength for him to be able to pull himself away from Akim, rushed to his men and turned around to face the agent.

He lives by that Sphinx cat. 'It's my life,' he is reported to have mentioned on several occasions.

'You have no bloody clue where Tabitha is and only trying to save your own skin now that you've found yourself dug deep in a hole.'

He suddenly looked bigger, swollen with anger, as he moved a bit closer to Akim as if he was about to hit him.

The cat story had livened him up a bit.

'And is that a statement or a question,' Akim asked, his gun still pointed at Chubby.

The guards also inched forward behind their boss who half turned around and pushed their weapons away as if to protect the agent. Chubby started querying about his missing feline friend.

The Agent had pictures of an identical hairless cat complete with Tabitha's distinctive signature markings which he had tattooed on it, photographed and saved on his yahoo email inbox.

'To make matters short, let's access my email on your computer or mobile phone.'

'I lost my phone falling off your boat.' The guards regarded each other as if trying to recall that incident – the splashing noise they had thought was from basking sharks.

'There is your life.' Showing photos of literally the copycat with the agent smiling for the camera.

A recorded message about his proposition played alongside it. He had only days before seen reward offers made on posters and other media outlets on the missing cat and had acted on instinct.

Chubby scanned the images in deep sadness with teary eyes.

He is well fond of his adopted Sphinx cat which he got from an ancient monastery in Thailand.

He believe she brings him luck but on condition that if she ever goes missing for more than seven days, strange and bad things will happen to him.

A couple of times Tabitha had gone away from home for over a week or so, they thought she had been lost, serious and grave consequences did occur in her owner's life and he suffered as a result.

It got so worrying for him he once started planning getting rid of the animal, or even return it to the temple.

But the Monks wouldn't have it back, telling him 'Gifts are not meant to be returned. But if you had paid for it, then that would have been a different matter. But you didn't pay for it, so now it's permanently yours, for good or for bad.'

Something he has been stuck with ever since and at times very frightened of.

Chubby finds himself lumbered with this superstition. In spite of all its anxieties, he still reckoned having the cat is for the better, bringing him luck and fortune, as long as it is OK.

Whether reaching that conclusion is a way of reassuring himself, no one knows.

He started telling the story of the TSG catch:

'My workers hauled out of the sea parts of the said spacecraft, and of course duty bound, they handed it all to me. I then offered some to various organisations in the shadows (A term for the criminal underworld) but not to the intelligence agencies like the C.I.A., M.S.S, F.S.B, MI5 or Mossad. A couple of the underground dealers double-crossed me, never paying a cent. I then offered what I had left to science and history museums, all of which declined having anything to do with them due to the conflict between the Americans and the Chinese. Not being able to sell them for any serious cash, the rest was dumped into the sea. And that is a regret.'

He then paused for a moment, going quiet for a bit. He picked up a wine bottle cork off the floor and started playing with it. No one said anything, waiting for him to continue and the agent gave him time to gather himself. The sudden stillness in the room was somewhat eerie. All you can hear is the waves smashing against the boat. Few seconds later, he continued through with what seemed like the whole story. From time to time, Akim would ask him to skip some bits. He can see what Chubby was telling him is the truth, with probably a couple of little lies which he dismissed as insignificant.

'Then why didn't you sell it to the likes of the spying agencies.' He paused in hesitation for a couple of seconds and said: 'Rather for the same reasons, the museums would not have them.' This time Akim could tell he is lying completely. He had not only paused to think but also looked away and his explanation didn't make much sense.

'I have to leave now. Sorry about the way I barged into your premises.' Akim said, 'You had ignored all my efforts to see you and coming over to the boat is the only option I had left. So long pal.'

He was still covering the three men and the trembling dog with Chubby's borrowed handgun. To buy himself a safe exit, he mentioned he is the only person who can release the cat.

As he was making his way out of the room onto the deck, Chubby anxiously raised his voice saying: 'Wait, wait, I've a scow, flat-bottomed sailing dinghy, that will take you back safely to the coast. The tide's in by this time of the night and it could be dangerous out there.'

Akim turned around smiling:

'I'll be alright, thanks. I know it's about your cat's safety rather than mine's. Don't worry, it's in good hands. I'll post you your gun back later,' he concluded and jumped back into the sea.

'Me having any one of the guards together in that scow would probably result in a fight having one of us drowning the other,' he muttered under his breath.

He was swimming halfway across to the coast when he heard this splurge sound behind him like a pebble being thrown into a pond. Then there was another, this time a few inches in front of him. Instinctively, he looked back and saw what he made out in silhouette shapes, two men grappling over a rifle.

Could this be Bozzo taking pot shots at me and the other guard, Foday, trying to stop him, he was thinking. A third shot whizzed past his right ear as he ducked below the water surface. Bozzo still trying to settle scores probably for me bathing his dog, or Foday, for me mashing up his face; it could be either. He then held his breath and dived under and started pulling himself faster across nearing towards the coastline.

This confirmed his suspicions all along. Chubby has no actual power or any significant control beyond acting as a stooge. He was just being used by someone else. For if he had had some proper level of authority or any at all for that matter, firstly, Bozzo would not have jumped into the water to save his dog, instead he would be trying to stop the intruder. Secondly, the guard, more likely to be Bozzo again, would not have been firing at him after he had left the boat. The fact that his companion was trying to stop him also showed he perhaps wasn't acting on their master's order. The agent also recalled how Chubby had physically pushed away the guards' gun from threatening him, as if they would not follow his verbal command.

9

He got back late to the hotel about 11:45 pm still drapped in his wet suit. As the receptionist greeted him, he asked: 'Is Adam around?'

'No sir. I haven't seen him all day,' she replied.

'OK thanks. It's about that grapnel rope he bought for me at the street market. Anyway later.'

He was then heading for his room when the receptionist asked:

'How was the late night scuba diving, sir. Any good?'

He just smiled, waved her attention away and ran up the stairs to his room, avoid using the elevator.

This time using his mobile phone he called the station master, Helen Regan, in Washington DC:

'Hello! Who is this?' barked Colonel McBride, her semi-retired deputy. A short thickset man who used to box in the army. He has brown sandy hair and a bicycle-handlebar moustache. Round face and similarly round facial features, nose, eyes and mouth and fair skin.

'It's me Akim. Is Ms Regan in there?' the agent asked.

'Aheey, Aakim [McBride dragging the name in excitement] how's the going buddy?'

'Helen has just gone off to the ladies to powder her nose. How can I help you?' the colonel asked.

'Fine, thanks chief. I've just got back from visiting the target here in Freetown. Apparently, he had some of the stuff but lost them all.' Akim can hear the colonel's heavy breathing down the line:

'What do you mean he lost them all?'

The agent went on to narrate the whole mission with little interruption.

McBride apparently feeling disappointed, growled:

'You went all that distance and came up with nothing. It was rather like a "Busman's holiday" for you, wasn't it?'

This deputy station master has an abrasive reputation, some say hardened from his days in the jungle fighting the communist Viet Cong.

'Not exactly, chief,' Akim replied. 'It was rather hard out there and I did my best for the land.'

'Did you search the Platypus's strong room? For all we know the missing TSG pilot might be hidden there somewhere. They found just a handful of male body parts in the waters. Word is around the Russians have the rest of his remains and could also be holding the co-pilot.'

Before Akim could answer, someone in the background was telling McBride U.S. intelligence only found out about the missing alien last night, so the agent wouldn't know anything about it beforehand.

This kind of shut the colonel up whom some colleagues had wrongly concluded as racist and sexist. He came from a long line of Irish democrats who believe in labour and expectation. And he's always wanting good results.

The agent was thinking, no wonder Chubby's cabin door looked like that of a safe or a strong room, one that had replaced the original. For all we know the fallen pilot could have been bound and gagged lying underneath the bed or somewhere on that boat.

'OK, Akim, well done, kid. I'm not surprised we got that information late. Apparently, our Taiwanese mole in Hong Kong is more of a badger, unnecessarily building a data dam and only feeding a trickle down our communications network as and when he sees it fit. He wasn't hired to do that.' He then cleared his throat, 'Mmh Mmh,' and continued.

'He should just let everything come through whenever he gets the information. That's his job. Anyway, when are you coming over, buddy?'

Akim replied: 'In a fortnight, Col. First, I'd be making a call to London, fix one or two loose ends and then Washington. I would be happy to pay the Platypus another trip to search for the missing alien.'

'We'll discuss that later, Col,' McBride said. 'Bye for now.' And they both hung up.

The agent was then thinking how much fun it would be going back to Freetown. Not only meeting with his old chum Chubby again but also with Bozzo, and he wasn't thinking of the guard. Then suddenly his rang phone;

'Helen Regan here.'

Helen, 43, just under six feet tall, far taller than the average woman. An ex-olympic gold medal winner and captain of the female national volleyball team.

She went straight into the navy after studying at Yale University. Auburn-coloured hair, most times in beehive style. Crystal-clear complexion. Slightly round face with a dimpled smile the envy of most. Beautiful ocean eyes and cow like eye lashes. She has twice won "Rear of the Year" awards from a popular fashion writers' guild but she turned them down, saying there's more to her than having admirable buttocks. The third time she accepted it, only for charity and raised millions of dollars for good causes. 'How's it going, Akim? Just returning your call. I couldn't answer it from that unsecured line.'

He replied: 'Fine thanks. The deputy tells me you were…'

'It doesn't matter what he says, off to the ladies, having a lunch break, off on vacation. On flight to Mars. I just couldn't take that open call.'

The agent smiled and quipped: 'Ah I got it. Since 9/11 we've upped our game. It's an ever-evolving race ma'am.'

'You got it. Reason why you work for us, Akim.'

'I tell you everyone hold their weight in our department,' she said with a chuckle.

After a few more informal chats, they went into talking serious business.

He briefly explained his adventure, not wanting to repeat himself after speaking with Colonel McBride. Saying as he was concluding his story:

'I'd be heading back to Freetown to help search for the missing pilot. Probably hidden somewhere on the west African coast where those fishing fleet are registered.'

'That one is being taken care of. It's female,' she said.

Akim then asked: 'You mean the missing pilot?'

'Yes, we learned that by her voice pattern from a conversation she had with what appeared to be two other of her people back where she came from. The line is so clear it's as if they were all in the same area. We had lots of technical difficulties before deciphering the female tone but we still don't understand the language. They speak on the ultrasound spectrum.'

'Forget about Freetown for now. I need you to go to Ho Chi Minh city, Vietnam. Our men picked up some parts, wings and tails, of the fallen space vehicle close to that port. But what we really want are the main cockpit and possibly the blackbox/es too.'

'Why Vietnam if I may ask, ma'am?'

To which she replied:

'We have managed to secure some hydrophone recordings from our mole based in Taipei, Taiwan. Detailing the acoustic gravity waves caused by the sudden water pressures caused by the spaceship's impact. This has led us to the coastal waters of the Vietnamese capital.'

'Good! Then we are in luck,' the agent quipping with excitement.

'Not so fast buddy,' she cut in.

'There are holes in the data showing half-an-hour void in the recording. Meaning it has been cut off and/or doctored, missing out on 30 minutes of the event when the UFO, if I may still call it that, crashed. That is where you come in to search and close that information gap.'

Akim slightly raising his voice:

'Wow!' Rubbing his right hand on his thigh in glee. 'First, Freetown, and now Ho Chi Minh city.'

Helen then quickly said: 'You shouldn't have wasted time in west Africa anyway. Your old chum Chubby is powerless, he's just a front.'

'I thought so too,' he responded.

'OK, Akim, you're off first thing in the morning. Good luck.'

And was about to bid him farewell when he said:

'Oh ma'am. I have some coded information I copied and sent from Chubby's phone when I accessed those cat photos. Here:

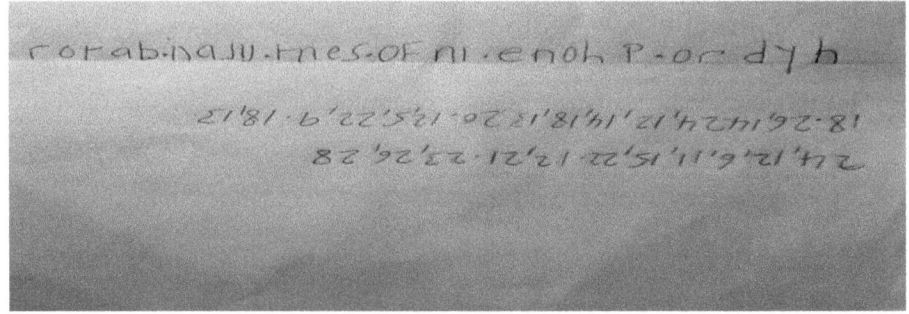

'I'll send you my own interpretation of the message (A copy at the end of this story) on the secured email address The top one is quite easy to decipher, hope it matches yours. If not, please let me know anything I could have missed. Also if you have any question please let me know as well. Thanks.'

'Oh Akim, you're a star. Quite unexpected this. I can't wait to see you back in Washington. We'd go to your favourite restaurant just a stone's throw in New York.'

He replied: 'Thanks once again. Anytime.' And they both hung up.

That's it. I have to find Koke Altan or even his dad, Altan snr. They are the owners of the company and could probably know more about the missing hydrophone recordings.

He went back to his room completely worn out. The time was late, about 1:30 am. He fixed himself a light meal, had a shower and later crashed into bed.

****

Intelligence officer, Altan (Snr.), was accompanying a trade mission from Ulan Bator to Shanghai when he escaped his encourage to seek asylum in China as a double-agent [DA]. At first Beijing was a bit lost as to why a very senior-ranked spymaster, almost in retirement, would do such a thing. Friendly and unfriendly countries alike engage on espionage activities against each other but nothing as such was expected between these two nations.

Their centuries-old peaceful coexistence was beginning to change when the double agent, an ethnic Bayad from Erenhot, a southern town in Mongolia bordering China, spilled the beans to Beijing on a new wave of nationalists uprising in his home nation. According to the Mongolian spook, the rebels were planning to undermine China and force her to hand over the upper part of its territory, Inner Mongolia, back to its neighbour in the north, Mongolia (Proper).

All this had started about five decades before the TSG crash. The supposed double-agent married a Han Chinese and was living in the Quandong region. Yet he was actually a double-agent-plus working for the General Intelligence Agency of Mongolia [The G.I.A.], who staged a couple of fake assassination attempts on him to increase his worth in Beijing's eyes. He would at often times feed information, some fictitious, some a bit factual, on the Mongolian nationalists to the Chinese intelligence. The fictitious bits were setting trip wires against Chinese interests in Inner Mongolia and using all sorts of subversiveness diverting Beijing's attention from the actual strength of the rebellion. The half-truths were used to impress his host nation, keeping them sweet. His son, Koke Altan (Jnr.), [Koke is pronounced Koh-keh] an international businessman, showed little or no interest following his father's footsteps, nonetheless, this was a pretence and part of the senior Altan's plans. Koke then had a son, Abaqa. Abaqa showed up as a fervent Chinese national with strong anti-Mongolian separatist tendencies. He refused to learn the Mongolian language, and joined the People's Liberation Army Navy (P.L.A.N.) as a high-ranking intelligence officer [He had a plan alright]. This is when the little-known G.I.A. spy network's long-term plans started bearing fruits. For Abaqa matured into a third-generation [3G] mole spying for Ulan Bator. This stage had been the strategic plan all along when Altan, the grandfather was sent off as a fake double-agent with the sole intention of raising a 3G spy grandchild. At first, deceitfully playing off his son, Koke, as a Erenhot (A cross border trade hub between Mongolia and China) business man not interested in espionage, whilst secretly training him as such. As part of the setup, the young Abaqa had a physical fight with his dad and granddad, getting the police involved, and moved out of the family home. He would only visit his grandmother when the grandpa is out for a walk or something. Giving a pretence they can't stand each other's presence.

This gives the lad time to collect and pass information hidden somewhere around the house. His granny as a Han Chinese was kept in the dark on the entire operations. In fact, she was also secretly spying for Beijing and the senior Altan pretended as if he didn't know, this gives him another route to misled his host nation. It was Koke who owned the fishing business, Altan Fisheries ltd with Chubby acting as a front in the west African region. They became friends through Chubby's older sister, Jariatu, whom had met the Mongolian at the Paris College of Arts. Koke nicknamed her, Khar goo saikhan, meaning black beauty in his native tongue. They dated for a couple of years and later just stayed as friends after she politely declined his marriage offer.

Akim knows quite well Chubby is big fool, a very stupid one at that. He just can't see him being of any success in his own right, but was ideal as a cover. Once, he recalled having a three-way conversation with Koke, and Chubby at a local Freetown restaurant:

Koke started it saying: 'When I was over in America my cousin took me to the Super Bowl.'

'Oh yeah?' said Chubby. 'So what did you have for a meal then?'

'Who said anything about eating?' Koke replied, before reminding himself Chubby is as thick as two concrete slabs placed together. He was just about to explain to him what the Super Bowl was when Akim cut into the conversation saying:

'Leave it out Coke [Koke's nickname], we are going to be here all day.'

Chubby got a little annoyed. Turning to face Akim, he sneered:

'What's your problem Akim? Coke here said he went to some fancy restaurant in the States and I was only curious about what food and drinks he had.'

There was a moment's silence, you can see the irritation on Chubby's face.

Akim told him to forget about the conversation, and exchanged glances with Koke.

Previously, Koke's fishing fleet and private yachts were registered in Monrovia, the capital city of the West African state of Liberia; a former American colony. Liberia, alongside Panana, is one of the world's biggest shipping flags of convenience. The CIA had strong presence in Monrovia, so Koke and his father, Altan Snr wanting to avoid American scrutiny, relocated to neighbouring Freetown in Sierra Leone. And this is where Chubby comes in.

This is what Akim, the fly-by-the-seat-of-his-pants CIA free-agent found in his investigations into seeking the missing TSG parts. He also found out secrets he passed on to MI5: Beijing had military installations buried in submerged islands tunnelling to those visible above water. Some have silos housing hypersonic missiles. The last time he also discovered secret tunnels running at wider angles through the Bering straits, not at the narrowest points between America and Russia that would be prone to suspicions.

Que and Pee relayed the TSG cargo crash details back to Pris, of which every detail was kept under wraps for a couple of days before the news became public. This was to avoid setting panic among the remaining three billion Zistians who would be worried about they own chances of reaching the safe haven of planet Earth. In just six months after the first TSG, crew only, landing, Que was already sitting deep in the Israeli spy networks. His colleagues were very impressed with his apparent superior intelligence in most areas of their work. But they were also perplexed at his lack of knowledge, or rather his laziness, to work out simple mathematical calculations without the need for using instruments like calculators. The technical upgrade he did to Mossad's infrastructure was literally out of his world, connecting and mining energy from distant stars. It was only the lack of the ideal equipment available anywhere on Earth that was holding back some of his exceedingly brilliant work. Some sharp Jewish minds could not keep up with him either. There have been instances in which he was intentionally working on outdated Zist technologies [Super-G series, thousands of years ahead of the likes of Earth's 5, 6, or 7 Gs]. Strenuously tailoring to what is available at hand.

Some Israeli spooks were in awe. They alerted their western allies about some of the "suprastate-of-the-art" advanced technologies their kindred had brought in from Russia.

'Have you seen some of the works Que is doing on our communications system?' The Mossad chief, Levi Sharon, quipped to his second deputy, Anna Sokolova.

Who replied: 'Yes I have actually. The other day I ran into the Shin Bet's, the Israeli internal security, personal characterisation analyst and he tells me either the Russians are sitting on a secret super-sophisticated information technology or this Que guy is just a freak of nature. He then continued to say how they've checked his background and is well documented in Moscow. But there are a few clouded areas: he shared personal identities with about 250 other Russian citizens, half of whom had died previously under unexplained circumstances. A few of which were my blood relatives.'

'Anyway so long as he is helping us we are happy so far and have our ears to the ground,' quipped Levi, to which Anna asked:

'You mean to say he's being watched?'

Her boss just replied: 'Chat later,' and was smiling with shoulders hunched and tiptoeing out of the room when Anna quipped again; 'By the way, Que claimed not to have shown any of his work to Moscow's intelligence services. Saying he had been saving it for the day he'd coming to Israel.'

Levi Sharon turned around holding the door halfway opened and touched his nose whilst still smiling at her. He then exited the door as quiet as a mouse, closing it behind him as if it was made of a wet cardboard.

Que's countryman Pee, operating in Russia, had similar problems. He wasn't having much luck with trust issues as some of colleagues were wary of his history. Israel badly wanted people, even accepting non-Jewish ones but Russia has no such a problem. And one more thing about the FBS, you can't just be accepted as smart or stupid or loyal or disloyal; on first, second or even third impressions. There is always a cynic tendency the observed could be acting. Reason why it is very difficult to fool the Russian intelligence.

Pee and Que, the two alien geniuses, by earth standards, had already started recruiting their own country folks from their subterranean settlements. Gradually resurfacing them into various organisations, not just into the intelligence agencies like the C.I.A., MI5 etc., but almost every fabric of society. Most of them though were struggling to adapt. Zist is of the highest civilisation category three [C3], experienced so far in the known universe, with ambitions to reach C4 status. Earth is merely category one [C1].

Rumours have it there is an "unheard of" category 5 civilisation, one that can harness and control the energy of the known universe. Such a civilisation, in theory, has the capability of travelling through wormholes and even small Black holes and making a return from where they had started.

Before he met with his death, Trillian Freeze once said that:

'We at G.U.T. S. have the guts and will power to be the first civilisation not only to reach Cat. 4 status but also possibly the final and last theoretical Category 5. One in which the inhabitants would be able to time travel both forwards and backwards via normal Black holes generally dotted around galaxies. And even the gigantic ones also, the super massive Blackholes found in the centre of galaxies.' He had at one time given Nemad a dressing down after the science man questioned the physical possibility of travelling through super massive blackholes. Who knows, maybe his prophesy would one day be realised.

Pee was on a nightout dating an Earthian for the first time when his mobile phone, the buckle on his belt actually, started ringing. His female companion can't hear it. The ring tone is ultrasound.

'Sorry, I need the bathroom for a bit,' he told the lady as he left for a while. In the bathroom, he set up the communication-link on his buckle to "Thinking Converstion Mode". Chatting by thinking and not speaking; a technology out of this world literally.

He came back and continued the evening with his date while simultaneously having Que and Xie who were in different locations on Earth joined in an intergalactic conference call with the new Pris Government and its new chief scientific adviser, Pulfrig Manz, nicknamed the bull-frog. Green, 75 (Who is still in Pris). He actually looked like one: flat narrow head, round face with dark freckles, toad-like hooded eyes and wide cheeks and wide mouth. He is 5 feet 10 inches, wide belly and small waist and thin legs and even sounded like a frog in his croaky voice. He'd rather not be called Pulfrig the frog but would only stay quiet about it. Thinking if he made a fuss, then the joke on him would become more of a fun thing for some.

He was narrating the latest events back on Zist, saying:

'Starday was reportedly slain by Marx, who himself was by killed his estranged wife and guess who that was?'

Que replied: 'V.I.M. director Saztah, a.k.a. disaster, as we used to call him. She had a sex change.'

Pulfrig replied: 'Brilliant, you got it all in one.'

He started giving them details of who is new and about the fresh plans to travel to another galaxy nearer to home and not the distant Milky Way. And we've also discovered shortcuts; Active Galactic Nucleis [AGNs], which are actually doorways to wormholes.

Before Que could start asking questions about the change of plan, Pulfrig yelled in excitement:

'And I have the final investigation report on those five questions that were nagging us.'

'Spill it out,' yelled Xie, in expectation, and Pulfrig started with it:

1. 'Trillian Freeze actually died in that road crash, not killed by foreign spies as rumoured.
2. There was no PM. It was just a propaganda decoy from V.I.M to hide the actual spy, who was Marx A. Zytan himself. He was the one working for the Brian intelligence, not Trillian as first thought. Though born here in Pris, he was still a citizen of that country. He also sold Zoll's recipe not only to our Government but to Bria's, as well as others. Which enabled us sending that probe to Earth's ISS. It took five damn years to reach there and another five relaying the data back to us. All this happened exactly ten years after Zoll 1 was discovered. So while G.U.T.S. were shelving their project, the Government was hard at work with theirs. Dr Annaz almost gave away the Govt.'s secrets at that second joint convention by revealing too much of its programme. So while our people were putting G.U.T.S on the defensive, accusing them of keeping secrets, it was the Govt. who were guilty as such. We were even surprised a massive trans-stellar company like G.U.T.S. didn't have enough of a good spy network. We were only covering our information source, Marx Zytan, by saying, 'A once-abandoned ancient Prisian Government probe' did the job. That was just fake news; a complete goat's turd not even fit to be a plant manure, as the media didn't know we had the powers of Zoll fuel. So Zytan worked for V.I.M.; indirectly for Bria and also worked for the Pris Government, all against his own partners at G.U.T.S.. That man was something else.

3. Zoll 2 couldn't be replicated in the lab because Maila had used a rat poison container which he took to the toilet to pee in it. He didn't want to be seen carrying any of the lab equipment, which would have looked suspicious. No surprise here, that idiot didn't realise that the poison mixed with those contaminants transformed Zoll 1 to become Zoll 2 (the invisible state).
4. No one actually impersonated Prof. Nemad. He did all those acts himself unaware of his own actions while heavily sedated. Reason why his fingerprints did convict him. That blood on the carpet was that of a patient the laboratory was studying. Maila was the V.I.M. mole working as a 3G spook for Bria's spy network, passing on Zoll 1's formula to them. He fried Nemad's brain with a delayed-action comatose drug and also doctored his CCTV recordings. His mechanical left hand was causing him to drop things uncontrollably; reason why they called them "butter-fingers" or "butterly feathers", or whatever. I can't remember. V.I.M. honoured their promise and gave him a better hand. He was also trained to play stupid so no one would pay him much attention to him, and it worked. Marx who was supposed to be the 2G spy was completely unaware of it all. The only part not fully understood is why Nemad, who is no longer interested in sexual relationships, would sexually attack Zapia even in a drugged-state.
5. Marx's funds were not missing as he claimed. Half of it was paid towards the project costs and the other half, as you may already know, was paid into his proposed new identity of Hans Schmidt (At a german bank in Munich) his earth-adopted name. Unfortunately for him, the Britain-based interpreter translated everything on the documents from German to English, including individuals' names. The money that was meant to be paid to Hans Schmidt (Marx Zytan's) went to John Smith (Prof. Nemad Scyzpr), the English version at a London bank.

'But how do you know all this? We made the payments here on that first trip and didn't know anything about it,' Que questioned, with some concern in his voice.

To which Pulfrig replied: 'Well, let's just say, there are bosses, and there are also BOSSES. The latter must always be in control.'

They ended the conversation with Xie being in a very suspicious state of mind. Slightly lowering his head, rubbing his right eyebrow with two fingers, he said:

'Maybe sending us out of Zist is our United Nations Organisation's way of population control of some kind. Why are they no longer interested in coming here?'

Pee, whilst at the same time separately chatting with his date, replied, by thoughts, to Xie's comment: 'But there is a genuine reality of our star being blown up rather like its neighbours had already in other stellar systems. You and I know that quite well.'

His date, a Siberian born women's national volleyball vice captain, he went for the tallest one he can find, at six feet nine inches, had no idea what he was doing. She was just enjoying her time with this gentle giant as she calls him.

Que crossed and then recrossed his legs and responded: 'That may be factual but what I am no longer certain about is the timing.' He was looking uneasy as he shifted his sitting posture once again.

'All that emergency talk of having only five hundred years left before our banana yellow colour planet became fire yellow in heat and burned up to cinders is becoming a doubt to me.

First of all they made an error of commission saying five hundred years, when it was actually five hundred thousand years. They simply lopped off hundreds of thousands of years to make things look bad and urgent. I know in astrological terms half-a-million years is like an emergency but one still long enough to do something about it. 500,000 years is nothing to sniff at.

But we'll see. I still have contacts over there and will find out more. TRUST ME GUYS, WE'LL FIND OUT MORE.

At least we all have our families and loved ones here with us. Including our rivals and favourite sports team. We are all here; friends, enemies all here.

We would just continue with life as best as we know it. We will also see who is better off; them still there and us here on Earth. AND AS I'VE MENTIONED, WE WILL FIND OUT MORE.'

'You guys are scaring me,' cautioned Xie, looking from Que to Pee, and back to Que.

He was in a way ignored, as had happened on numerous times in the past. Pee quipped:

'Then again it could be our Government's ploy not to trick us into coming here but rather to trick those left behind consoling them after that TSG crash. Knowing no other such vehicle is available, at least for now, and no Zoll means no intergalactic transfer for them. Don't forget, most, if not all, of the decision-makers, are already here on Earth with us.'

Que quickly responded:

'Good thoughts, Pee. But still there was too much of a rush to carry out the transfer. We could have been a little more patient in our searches for a closer solar system. One with a satellite even younger and promising than Earth. Which as we all know is also in a decline, by some considerable measures; its environmental degradation, resource depletion, succumbing to climate change, to name a few. I really harbour some doubts about the timing of this project. It could have waited a bit longer. Half a million years before our star will die is a long time indeed. Though one could also argue the heat was getting too much and hence the need for the hastened move.'

The debate then continued late into the night.

Pee was beginning to think it's unfair on his date what he is doing, not giving her all of him when she appears to be paying all her attention to him.

He didn't open himself to be seen in the conference call so his folks didn't know he's out with someone. They thought he was only having some temporary technical issues with his cameras. They can only hear his voice.

'What about the missing pilot? That was that elegant looking Daprah wasn't it. I know it's somewhat an overused characterisation but I won't be ashamed to say that lady has everything from beauty to brains and beyond. How the authorities allowed that man-child to lead her on such an important trip is beyond me,' Xie commented, while holding a fist over his mouth suppressing a yawn.

'We're in secret communication with her. I can't say much at this stage,' Que replied.

Pee sniffed, and then quipped: 'Trust Coldoz to run such an important mission.

The lad is too childish.'

'Bloody brilliant too. But oh ya if only he could had grown up a bit too,' Que replied.

'He was crushed. Some of his remains should be out there in northern Siberia. Or probably in a Moscow morgue somewhere. Though no report on him has been made so far. Either because they haven't found him or they are clever enough not to communicate about it in the open. That is Pee's patch anyway,' Que remarked, as he turned sideways towards their colleague's blank screen at a St Petersburg cafe. 'He should know more about it.'

For a moment there, Pee had neglected the conference as his date stretched herself towards him for a kiss.

'What was that again?' he asked but no one answered. He could have rewound the bit he had missed but also risk missing the other current running parts, more so after having asked a question.

This is another Zist custom; to be attentive at all times when you're doing something important like meetings etc.

Instead, Xie quipped, 'Earth nations with their constant rivalries, eh, poor guy.' This was the giveaway that notified Pee what he could have possibly missed; Coldoz's demise.

'Thank God, ours was not so bad eh,' Xie added.

Suddenly, Pee's video link started showing his images and they saw him touched his nose, he had only just switched it on after his date had left indicating he can't say anything in the open about Coldoz's corpse.

His colleagues knew straightaway he must have been with someone moments earlier. Pee and his weakness for sex. A complete addict. And they all knew and accepted that but not at the detriment of the job. Their communication system can't be spied on by Earthians, why was he touching his nose signalling secrecy? He had simply got distracted and lost tract of himself. It was at that stage, in annoyance, Que deferred the meeting and Pee knew he had been caught.

****

Before the passengers-trip was launched, there were send-off parties held all over Zist, in fitting celebration and prayers for the missions' success. Those living on the same streets had theirs on the public highway but also have options to go to others like your work place, relatives, membership clubs, or wherever they'd prefer. G.U.T.S. held theirs on their industrial premises. Despite Zist's soaring daytime temperatures, their nights are really cold. Marx wasn't there, there were all sorts of rumour on his absence. Some say he had been arrested, others say he had been killed by gang members.

Dr Rannas Annaz was wearing a smoke-grey coloured ankle-skimming pea coat over a stone-grey coloured sequin gown with a matching mock altate handbag [Altate is a rare lizard-like reptile on Zist]. She coloured her hair dark-white grey and looked exceedingly glamorous. For one moment, there her ex-lover Dr Poiter almost forgot the reason they broke up, what he saw as her constant bad behaviour, and felt like holding her hands. She noticed the feeling in his eyes and started blushing as if she's no longer interested. They had been talking after he had given her a hand-tied bouquet of flowers but apparently, she was dragging her heels wanting for him to make more of an effort.

'You look wonderful tonight,' he tells her.

'Oh thank you. You look just as wonderful too,' she replied glowing in delight with that beautiful smile and brilliant white teeth.

'You missed a bit,' pointing his fore finger to part of her bottom lip on which she was applying a moisturising balm.

'Oh thanks,' she replied shrugging her shoulders feeling him that close after such a very long time.

'I'm just protecting your lips from the very dry wind.'

'Oh, OK. Thanks.' She giggled. He paused in silence, not saying a word, just intentionally gazing into her ocean eyes and cocking his eyebrows at her, in reflection to her continuous smiling at him. Normally, she'd find eye-cocking from many of her admirers tacky but not the man-of-her-dreams.

After all their recent public spats, they both still fancy each other.

She almost thrust herself forward towards him but stopped short when somebody close by loudly cleared his throat, 'Ahem! Ahem!' They both ignored the source of the noise.

'Ah sorry, I almost tripped on my long coat.' She laughed.

'I'll always be there to catch you if you fall,' was his witty reply.

Resisting the temptation was getting too much for both of them as they yield, forcing themselves to abandon their past differences and fell into each other's arms and kissed passionately. Holding each other so close and thinking of all the good times they have been missing together, more than the good times they had had together.

(The very next day she seen wearing a grey T-shirt with the words: ***Zoom or doom with no room left for the groom*** written in black on the front. Some people were saying it was a reference to both her rekindled relationship with Dr Poiter [Who coined the project's title Zoom or Doom, and also to her ex-partner as the "groom"]. Getting back at her soon-to-be ex-husband, Servo Annaz, for all the years of humiliating her. It was his silly habit wearing all those funny messages on his T-shirts like "Love you more than wifi," and the lot, that had really got to her.). She had one T-shirt made with the saying "Love you more than hobby" but decided against.

At the same party, Bampor Ajina was wearing an open-front glittering turquoise jellyfish embroidered gown over a sapphire blue dress, neglecting her trademark matching of all in green for a change. Her facial makeup, plastered with thick eyeshadow and aided by the blue-coloured street lighting cast a flattering glow over her natural sad eyes. Disguising her most "unpleasant look" as she would sometimes refer to that part of her face.

Zapia Zill was wearing low-cut crimson satin side split mini dress revealing so much of her cleavage and thighs. Carrying a jam-red and black handbag complete with scarlet stiletto shoes. She had her hair in beehive style and looking glamorous . An envious onlooker quipped:

'That short time living in Bria must have changed her personality, and wardrobe to go with it. Quite unlike her, the dress, showing so much skin. And also the high shoes for that matter. She looked like a high-maintenance hooker if you ask me.'

Fannie Zypisth was donned in all metallic that evening. And in contrasting colours too; a metallic silver gown draped over a metallic gold thread dress. Carrying a steel colour knitted hand bag and chrome knee-high boots. She appeared too robotic. Not just with the clothing but her way of walking too in those killer-heel long boots. This only helped to unwittingly compromise her natural beauty, making her a bit unattractive. The bouffant wig arched on her head was of no help either. It all made her seemed much older and looking worse for wear.

Dr Annaz took one look at her and smiled in her heart. She still hadn't forgiven her for getting drunk and pinching Dr Poiter's bottom when they were altogether at an office do.

As for the men at the global sending-off party, most were just being their usual selves; casual suits and nothing extravagant comparatively, with just a few exceptions.

The food, some of which quite similar to what we have here on Earth, was literally out of this world. Variable options on offer for all carnivores, herbivores and omnivores.

Prof. Zytan went for the stoned meat variety: poultry, beef, mutton, venison etc [Cooked in heated stones, reputed to giving the food that extra tender texture that needs less chewing effort] seasoned with kelp and sea-bed mud, giving the meat that smoky flavour. And many more.

Dr Annaz, a herbivore, went for the vegetarian offer. Some of which were sourced from hydroponic plants and a few others grown from outer space and dubbed "food seasoned by the stars". She and Prof. Nemad, with the help of Dr Poiter, made peace and became friends.

Once settled on Earth, well, in Earth, as the Zistians's case would be, they discovered huge aquifers in many places like underneath the Saharan desert and the desert areas of Western United States.

One evening, some of them were having a social gathering, chatting about the recent events when Poiter said to Nemad: 'You remember that Omole drink you offered me back at your house which I turned down? Well, my friend, now is the time for that.'

Nemad got up and embraced his colleague in a bear hug. He seemed like a new person; gone were his taciturn behaviour and even transformation of his dress sense, no longer in baggy clothing, now more of tailor-made variety.

And celebrate they did. The psychological effects of the earth-move, what with the cooler climate and all that, had changed most of their behavioural patterns for the better. Dr Annaz who was divorcing her useless husband, Servo, didn't miss the trip as first thought. She had to sneak in with him on the tenth ship, and immediately started divorce proceedings on reconciliation with Poiter. Prof. Nemad gave a resounding public speech starting off saying:

'The public-spirited courage of our daring crew in helping us carry out our scientific aspirations has made this dream to save ourselves possible. We've had an experience almost as rich as life itself.'

And who of all people was cheering him the loudest? – was Dr Annaz.

He had also made peace with Zapia and are engaged to be married. He wanted to return the money mistakenly paid into his new name but the Zist global community forced him to have it all, saying he deserved it after the troubles he had been put through. He gave some to charity and moved in with his daughter and fiancé.

On finding out who her real parents were, Bampor changed her surname from Ajina to her favourite colour, Green. She started a mother-son relationship with Maila, and reconciled with her own mother, Hatzas. Maila changed his surname from Zytan to his grandma's Ajina and still waiting for his request to meet and apologise to Prof Nemad in person. Every one of them dropped the Zytan family name.

Nevertheless, there are still some questions to be answered:

- But what would Zapia do when told it was Nemad himself who had committed all those crimes, though in a drugged state. Will she call off the wedding?
- Has Pee got it right over Que for the first time, ever, about the government's plot?
- Where are the missing TSG parts? And also the lost pilot Vice Captain Dapram, who we know is still alive and has been in constant communications with Pee and Que since the crash, where is she?

What would happen if any of Earth's own intelligence agency found out about the secret invasion. Will there be war. Zist's own intelligence knew quite well the divisions on planet Earth with its various military alliances and the distraction of a virus attack, and took advantage of that time coming to Earth. Now that American leader Donald Trump had been voted out of office, would this be an opportunity for some of Earth's nations working together again and focusing on an alien threat? Threat that is not just coming from an object like an asteroid but from living organisms as well. The planet was just about defeating a biological invader; the coronavirus when another, taking advantage of the distraction, settles in unseen, in the form of extra-terrestrial Zist people. Who daring enough to start planning to divide Earth between themselves and us. They want to occupy the whole of the northern hemisphere, saying their population more than doubles ours and so need the bigger space. Leaving us Earthians in the southern hemisphere. This could be war. Time for the U.S. Russia, China and the rest of NATO to join forces?

- Would destroying the sword, stained with Marx's blood, still be able to end the Zytanas curse now that it also has the Manx cat's blood stains also. Would there be any contamination by the feline's blood?
- 3Q was Marx's bitterest rival who was framed for murder by Lucian Starday on Marx Zytan's order, and given three life sentences for crimes he didn't commit. Now he's free and out to step into the footstep of his nemesis. With the death of two of his most hated enemies, Marx and

Starday, he is out to dominate again, not just over the Zist people but the hosts, Earthians, as well. For whom he has little or no regard; seeing us as far less intelligent and lacking sophistication. Though now on a different terrain five million light years away, the game is the same. Watch out for the new villain, 3Q, in phase two of Zoom or Doom. He confuses people with his aliases, is it: 3Q, Trick You, Three Queue, Tick Que, Tree Q, Tick You, Third Quarter, and several more codified titles sounding more or less the same to camouflage his presence. On phase 2 of Zoom or Doom 3Q faces a new deadly rival in ex-mafioso boss Albertini dei Costi Irrecuperabili [Albert of Sunk Costs], a.k.a ACI. This is the man expelled by the mob because he was too ruthless and violent and refused taking part in some of the Mafia's charity work which he says is for wimps.

- ACI buys or/and borrows government business deals, particularly enormous infrastructure projects, sometimes forcefully, off contractors and run huge costs overruns at the State's expense. Later, he would either return the contract to the seller or complete the job himself. Either way he pockets the increased expenditure costs. Reasons why his Italian name translate as Albert of Sunk Costs.

When ACI and 3Q crossed paths on Earth there are more than fireworks and the usual murders associated with crime bosses. Here, entire families are captured and made to work as slaves to pay off debts and contribute body parts for sale in the shadowy human organ trade.

All the answers are in Phase 2 of Zoom or Doom

G.U.T.S.'s investigation team's final report given by Pulfrig got it wrong saying there was no V.I.M. Post Man [PM] spying on their premises. There was actually a PM in Prisia who was secretly working with Maila's assistance for Bria's intelligence.

This was the code note Akim the agent copied from Chubby's mobile phone.

The first line reads backwards from right to left: ***hydro phone info sent ulan bator***. (C.I.A. boss Helen Regan had sent Akim to Hanoi, Vietnam but it seems he would have to visit Ulan Bator also to help span the missing 30-minute information gap on the hydrophones).

The second line is a bit more complicated. Figures were used to represent the letters of the alphabet. The 26 alphabet letters are written and counted backwards from Z to A to enhance encryption. Meaning Z is number 1.Y, 2. X, 3. W, 4. V, 5. U, 6. T, 7. S, 8. R, 9. Q, 10. P, 11. O, 12. N, 13. M, 14. L, 15. K, 16.J, 17. I, 18. H, 19. G, 20. F, 21. E, 22. D, 23. C, 24. B, 25. A, 26.

Normal reading should be: 18. 26, 14. 24, 12, 14, 18, 13, 20. 12, 5, 22, 9. 18, 13. 24, 12, 6, 11, 15, 22. 12, 21. 23, 26, 2, 8.

I.A, M.C, O, M, I, N, G.O, V, E, R.I, N.C, O, U, P, L, E.O, F.D.A.Y.S.

The figures were then not only joined to make it complicating but also written in reverse, and in upside down mode. A letter is separated by a comma and a word separated by a dot.

Ingram Content Group UK Ltd.
Milton Keynes UK
UKHW020638220623
423865UK00007B/379